In the face of a massive earthquake and tsunami in the Pacific Northwest, a respected geologist must make two gut-wrenching decisions: one could cost him his reputation; the other, his life.

———

IS THE NORTHWEST overdue for a huge quake and tsunami, or will the region remain safe for hundreds of years yet to come? No one knows . . . *or does someone?*

Dr. Rob Elwood, a geologist whose specialty is earthquakes and tsunamis, is having nightmares of "the big one," which are way too real to disregard. His friend, a counselor and retired reverend, does not think he is nuts. Just the contrary, he believes them to be premonitions to be taken seriously. No one else does, however, even after a press conference.

Some live to regret it, most don't.

In addition, we have a remorseful, retired fighter pilot who is attempting a twenty-five-year-late apology and Neahkahnie Johnny who has been in search of a legendary treasure chest, buried since the late 1600s, most of his life.

All are about to *live* Rob's nightmare.

Cascadia

by

Buzz Bernard

Bell Bridge Books

Bell Bridge Books
PO BOX 300921
Memphis, TN 38130
Print ISBN: 978-1-61194-679-6

Bell Bridge Books is an Imprint of BelleBooks, Inc.

We at BelleBooks enjoy hearing from readers.
Visit our websites
BelleBooks.com
BellBridgeBooks.com
ImaJinnBooks.com

10 9 8 7 6 5 4 3 2 1

Cover design: Deborah Smith
Interior design: Hank Smith
Photo/Art credits:
Tsunami waves (manipulated) © Ig0rzh | Dreamstime.com

:Lcxd:01:

Dedication

In memory of Hal Bernard, my father, who loved to fish the beautiful rivers and streams of Northwest Oregon.

Prologue

Thunderbird and Whale

Clatsop Indian Village
The Oregon Coast Near Present-Day Seaside
January 26, 1700

THE YOUNG BOY, unable to sleep, opened one eye and surveyed the interior of the cedar-plank lodge. Embers in a fire pit near the center of the lodge cast a weak, flickering glow throughout its interior. Smoke spiraled lazily upward through a slit in the roof. Shadows danced on the walls. Cured salmon hung, like slumbering bats, from overhead racks.

A strange amalgam of sounds permeated the building: snores, wheezes, a soft belch here and there, the occasional sharp "blurp" of someone passing gas.

Other than these reverberations of life, the night seemed strangely silent. The endless dampness and incessant winds typical of the dark season along the coast had relented, at least briefly. But the boy, like all residents of the tiny village—four lodges perched above the banks of a short river rich in salmon and steelhead—knew the rains and gales would return. They always did. Thus, this period of relative dryness and calm offered a great reason for celebration.

That evening, the inhabitants of the community had dined on a special meal of elk and salmon, and berries and roots. Even now, the aromas of the feast lingered in the still air of the lodge.

After eating, the men had sat around the fire talking and smoking, sharing stories of adventures past, while the women and children busied themselves with chores: tidying up the lodge, cleaning utensils, and shaking out the sleeping mats to rid them of as many of the ever-present fleas as they could.

The pests could not be totally exterminated, however, and the boy scratched absentmindedly at a rash of bites on his hip. He sat up on the raised sleeping platform and gazed at the area around him. Next to him, his mother and sister slept. On the other side of the room, his father and grandfather slumbered, undoubtedly exhausted after their hunt for elk earlier in the day. They had brought down a large one.

They'd mentioned to the boy upon returning from their pursuit that they'd had to thrash their way deeper than usual into the dense forests of the coastal mountains. For a reason that mystified them, the elk had moved to higher ground. This, they explained, was strange behavior for the season, when *moolack* usually remained close to the shores of the ocean where they didn't have to wade through the deep, wet snows that often coated the mountains.

The boy settled back onto his mat and closed his eyes, hoping sleep would overtake him. It didn't. Outside, the *kamuks*, dogs, had raised a clamor, barking and baying, presumably at an unwelcome visitor—a bear, a mountain lion, a wolf—that had wandered too close to the village.

Normally, the ruckus would quiet after the intruder had fled, but not tonight. It continued, eventually morphing into whines and plaintive howls.

The boy arose from his mat and noted that several others had stirred. His father arose, too, picked up a spear, and, wearing nothing but his breechcloth, crept toward the doorway, motioning for the boy to stay put.

His father reached the door, then disappeared down a short ladder leading to the ground. Outside, the barks and yowls continued. The man returned shortly, clambering back into the warmth of the lodge and shaking his head—*nothing out there.*

At that instant, the ground beneath the lodge shuddered, then quieted, only to be followed by a second, more intense shake, then a third, even harder. Moments later, the earth heaved upward, a violent motion that tossed the boy and his father off balance, sending them sprawling onto the sand floor near the fire pit. As abruptly as the earth had risen, it sank, the boards of the sleeping platforms cracking like ice in a sudden winter thaw. Scattered screams and yells filled the semi-darkness as the remainder of the structure's inhabitants jerked awake.

The boy attempted to stand, but another upward surge of the earth knocked him down once more. One wall of the lodge sagged, then, with an explosive crack, split. Two heavy logs, the overhead beams of the structure, plunged to the floor. Cries of pain and pleas for help followed, permeating the devastated interior of the lodge.

Again the ground subsided, only to be followed by yet another swell. The boy staggered to his feet and stumbled toward the exit, or at least the place where the exit had been. Nothing more than split and rent wood now marked its presence. He turned to look for his father and grandfather.

Through a gaping hole in the roof, light from a waxing moon illuminated in feeble light a horrific carnage within the lodge. Friends and relatives lay maimed, many motionless. The boy spotted his father and grandfather attempting to pull people from beneath the massive timbers that had fallen from the roof. He staggered toward them as the earth continued to roll in jolting surges. It felt no different than riding a large dugout in heavy seas. The sickness that sometimes afflicted him on the ocean attacked him now. He bent over and regurgitated his evening meal.

The violent shaking continued, unrelenting in its ferocity, and the boy fell several more times as he struggled to reach his father and grandfather. Finally, after what seemed an eternity, but probably covered no more time than the life span of a spring rain squall, the convulsions slackened.

The boy reached his father and grandfather and joined them in attempting to pull his bleeding, unconscious *kahpho*, sister, from beneath a pile of splintered wood. They labored fruitlessly, unable to tug the heavy debris from her body. With each lingering, albeit less violent, heave of the ground, additional parts of the lodge, already weakened by the initial tremors, collapsed. Finally, the boy's grandfather stood and pointed outside.

"We must go," he said.

The boy's father shook his head. No.

The grandfather knelt beside his son and rested a hand on his shoulder. "It is too late. We must leave or we will die."

The shaking of the earth, now no more than dying ripples, at last relented. "It is over," the boy's father said, "finished." He continued his frantic efforts to free his daughter.

The grandfather, with a strength and swiftness belying his age, jerked the man to his feet. "No, it is not finished," he said, his words commanding, forceful. "The flood is coming."

"What flood? There is no water falling from the sky."

"The flood from the great water." The grandfather inclined his head toward the ocean.

Outside, an orange glow filled the night. One or more of the destroyed lodges had apparently caught fire.

"Hurry," the grandfather said.

"Where to?" the boy's father asked, his voice tight with emotion as he stared down at his trapped and injured daughter. Moans and groans from others filled the weakly lit darkness.

"The *canims*," the old man said. The canoes.

"*Mama?*" the boy asked, tugging at his father's breechcloth.

"She's gone," his father said. A tear ran down his cheek. The boy had never seen that before.

He followed his elders outside. They scrambled over piles of sheared and splintered timber, the young Indian blinking back his own tears. Smoke drifted through the ravaged village. The wails of the injured and dying mingled with an eerie chorus of barks, yips, and howls from animals in the nearby forest. The boy grasped his father's hand with a firmness born of fear.

Together they stumbled through the chilly darkness, through their ruined settlement, toward their canoes resting on the mudflats of the river. They slashed through soggy eelgrass and deep depressions and ponds that hadn't been present a short time earlier. The boy's father stopped to look in the direction of the ocean. The boy looked, too. The weak moonlight glistened off wet sand as far as he could see. It appeared as if the tide had receded beyond the horizon, into the depths of the sea.

"See that," the boy's father said, pointing. "The great water has retreated. There is no flood coming, old man." He touched his head in a gesture suggesting the grandfather had lost his senses.

"You are wrong," the grandfather snapped, glaring at his son. "There is a deadly flood coming, one in which the waters will flow uphill. Our ancestors knew of it. They warned us in their stories."

The young boy looked from his father to his grandfather, trying to comprehend.

"I will explain when we get to safety," his grandfather said. "Now we must move quickly."

The boy's father stared back at the remnants of the lodge, then down at his son, as though weighing the consequences of an impending decision.

The old man rested a hand on his son's shoulder. "I am sorry," he said, "but you must live for the one who lives." He shifted his gaze to the boy.

From somewhere distant, well beyond the exposed tidal flats, well out over the depths of the ocean, a hissing, like that of a massive snake, cut through the human and animal cries that suffused the darkness.

"Run," the boy's grandfather commanded.

The boy looked around, not understanding from what they were fleeing. His father grabbed his hand and tugged him toward the canoes. A few residents of the village had already paddled into the stream. But others, ignoring the exhortations of the elders, continued rescue efforts in their crumpled homes, two of which burned with the ferocity of a wildfire.

They reached the canoes. The boy and his grandfather clambered into one. The boy's father pushed the dugout into mid-stream, then climbed into it himself. The two older men began paddling, heading upstream. The sound that had begun as a hiss, grew louder, like rushing water or a breaking wave.

The boy's father and grandfather stroked furiously in a desperate effort to outrun whatever was coming. Initially, the river's course paralleled the shore, but eventually turned inland. The boy had no idea how far they had to go to find a place of safety. He knew only that something evil pursued them. He could hear it clearly now, grinding and chewing its way through the forest and up the river, snapping trees in violent thunderclaps of destruction.

Then he saw it and gasped. A massive surge of black water, not just in the river, but on both sides of it, closing in on them like a beast from the depths of the sea. Within an instant, the surge caught them, lifting the canoe as if it were riding a huge ocean swell.

The men ceased paddling and clung to the gunwales of the canoe, the vessel now merely riding the flood like a chunk of driftwood in a cascading stream. The roiling water, filled with trees, dead animals, and—the boy's gut lurched—two bodies clothed in the garb of his tribe, churned around them in an angry surge.

Even after the initial rush, the water continued to rise, hoisting the canoe ever higher, until it reached the tops of the shorter trees along the now-inundated banks of the river. A whirlpool snatched the dugout and slammed it into a stand of towering spruce, the needled boughs of the trees clawing, like wild animals, at the exposed skin of the Clatsops.

The boy's father grabbed at one of the boughs, caught it, and screamed for help. The grandfather, realizing his son's intent, seized another limb. The canoe jerked to a stop. The men struggled to wrestle the canoe into a position of relative stability as the ocean continued to rush fiercely around them. The boy ventured a peek over the edge of the canoe and tried to guess how far they were above what used to be the ground. He thought six or seven grown men might have to stand on one another's shoulders to reach them. His heart beat so rapidly he feared it would leap from his chest.

After what seemed like forever, but wasn't—the position of the crescent moon had barely shifted—the water began to recede, draining rapidly back toward the sea. The boy relaxed. "It's leaving us," he said, a note of hope tinting his words.

His grandfather shook his head. *No.* "It will return. Once, twice, maybe three times before the sun rises. We must remain here. It will be safe."

So they sat the night in the sheltering upper boughs of a Sitka spruce, in a dugout canoe, as the great flood attacked twice more, backing off only after whatever evil spirit had loosed the destruction seemed satisfied. For warmth, they huddled together in the small boat, but still shivered uncontrollably as chill of the winter night deepened.

Sunrise came dull and muted, the land along the river virtually denuded of life. No animals moved, no bushes swayed in the wind, no grass sprouted from the banks of the stream. All vestiges of anything living had been swept away. Nothing but a debris-littered landscape met the eye: flattened trees, shattered timber, the bloated carcasses of deer and elk, squirrels and raccoons, lynx and bear, and the remains of at least one human. A heavy frost tinged the nightmarish scene in a ghostly whiteness.

Only the small stand of spruce where the men had found shelter remained. With most of the lower limbs of the tree that had offered them safety still intact, they scrambled down from the canoe and reached the ground, now nothing but mushy, salt-encrusted layers of mud and sand topped with a thin layer of ice.

On foot, they trekked toward the village, a laborious journey over frosty, boggy ground that sucked relentlessly at their feet. They encountered rock slides, washouts, and, where the ground had mysteriously sunk into the maws of the earth, gaping depressions filled with downed trees. It seemed as if the land itself had tried to devour whatever had stood upon it.

They moved through a morning mist in strange silence. Their exhalations, thin streaks of vapor, trailed behind them in white gossamer threads. Not even the cries of seabirds, normally abundant, pierced the morning stillness. No sounds of human presence, other than theirs, cut through the brooding hush. No voices of hunters. No thud of elk-antler wedges splitting wood. No laughter of young children.

Nearing exhaustion, they reached the site of the village, or at least where the village had stood. Nothing remained save sand, driftwood, and seaweed, and the limp, lifeless bodies of the crushed and drowned. The boy counted at least twenty corpses, mainly of the elderly and children, littering the beach and river banks. Among the human remains, seagulls pecked dutifully at the carcasses of dogs. The stomach-churning stench of death pervaded everything.

The boy turned from the scene, fearing he would be sick. He didn't wish to display weakness in front of his father. His chest heaved as he fought back waves of gut-wrenching sobs.

A hand came to rest on his shoulder. He looked up into the face of his grandfather whose reddened eyes appeared clouded and misty.

The boy choked back a final incipient sob. "What happened here, *Chope*? Why did the great water and land turn against us?"

The grandfather steered the boy to a barnacled stump that had washed ashore in the immense flood, and they sat. The boy looked once more at the carnage that confronted him. His father walked among the bodies, examining each with the care of a kindred spirit. He flailed his arms and shooed away an inquisitive eagle. He stooped beside each of the dead, laid a hand on them, and appeared to utter a blessing.

Suddenly, the earth vibrated and the boy leapt from the stump, prepared to flee for his life once again. The shaking ceased. His grandfather remained seated. "Don't be afraid," he said. "It's just the final echo of a great battle."

"What battle?" Still harboring trepidation, the young Indian again sat beside his grandfather.

"When I was a boy," the old man said, "there was a tale passed down from generations gone by, over seasons too numerous to number. It was a story that no one I knew had been witness to. Nor had my grandfather's grandfather, or even the generations before them. But it was an account we knew to be true. It has now happened again. I will tell you why. But you must listen closely, so you can tell the story to your offspring."

"Yes, *Chope*."

"In the darkness, the mighty Thunderbird, the most powerful of all spirits, whose eyes shoot lightning and whose wings unleash thunder, snatched Whale from its home in the great water and bore it inland, soaring toward the lofty mountains where Thunderbird's nest awaited. Whale, you see, would provide a fine and long-lasting feast."

The boy nodded.

"But because of the size of Whale, Thunderbird tired and descended to earth several times to rest its wings. Each time it did, a fearful struggle ensued, Whale fighting for its life, Thunderbird battling to subdue it. A final skirmish, violent and prolonged, occurred near Thunderbird's home. The earth shook and deformed, forests sank, masses of rocks tumbled from the mountains. The great water retreated but returned with fearful speed and fury, rising higher than ever before, washing away villages and turning rivers to salt. All this we have witnessed."

The boy nodded again.

The grandfather shifted his position on the stump, blew into his hands to warm them, then continued his story. "The shaking we felt moments ago was Whale in its death throes. Thunderbird, as always, was the victor. Now the earth and great water will let us live in peace for many generations."

"But not forever?"

"The spirit of Thunderbird controls our destinies. In times of tranquility, it is easy to forget that we live on a battleground; that we are at the mercy of earth that trembles and waters that inundate." The elder paused and surveyed the devastation surrounding them.

After a long while, he said, "No, the peacefulness will not endure. That is why you must repeat this tale to those who will follow you, for it is the unseen generations that will grow complacent, thinking all is well, that Thunderbird is sated and delivers only harmless thunder and lightning. But he will grow hungry again, a battle will ensue, and the land will convulse and flood once more. Villages will disappear and people will die."

The boy stared out at the water. "It was so beautiful here, *Chope*," he said softly.

"Yes. Long after we no longer walk this land, people will think that. But they, like so many of us, will not be aware of the danger that lurks. You must warn them with your story. It is yours to hand down now."

The boy stood, wrapping his arms around him for warmth, and turned toward the mountains. He wondered how many generations would pass before Thunderbird took flight once more in search of Whale.

Chapter One

The Ghost Forest

The Copalis River
90 Miles west of Seattle
Monday, March 23 (Present Day)

ROB ELWOOD NOSED the canoe into a muddy bank bordering a tide-water marsh. He turned to his son Timothy seated in the rear of the canoe. "Hand me the shovel."

While Timothy steadied the canoe, Rob chopped away at the bank of the marsh with the shovel. Overhead, seagulls orbited beneath a low-hanging gray overcast. Behind the marsh, bundles of mist, like flannel cotton candy, clung to the tops of a dense stand of Douglas fir and Sitka spruce. A chilly breeze snaked up the narrow, languid river, a reminder that spring had yet to arrive on the Washington coast. The fetor of mud and marine life, both living and dead, permeated the dull morning.

Rob worked at a steady pace, hacking out a vertical cut that exposed layers of silt, mud, and peaty soil. He glanced back at his son. Tim, wool stocking cap pulled low over his brow, kept his paddle jammed into the mucky bottom of the river, stabilizing the small boat. His sullen facial expression conveyed his mood.

"Hey," Rob said, "it was your idea to see what your old man does when he goes to work. You were the guy who wanted to find out what a geologist does in the field."

"Yeah, well I guess I had kind of a different vision."

Rob stopped digging and placed the shovel in the bottom of the boat. "Like what?"

"It's spring break, Dad. I thought we might go somewhere warm, like Hawaii, to study volcanoes. Or Southern Cal. You know, the San Andreas Fault. The Big One. Something like that. Exciting. Not digging in a frigging mud flat."

"It's a tidal marsh." Rob pulled his lightweight anorak tight around his neck, adjusted his wire-rim spectacles, and blew into his hands to keep them warm. "You think I wasn't sixteen once, son?"

Tim squinted at him. "What's that supposed to mean?"

"It means I haven't always been *Doctor* Elwood. It means I know about babes in bikinis on warm beaches during spring vacation. Believe it or not, I've been through the horny-adolescent-male stage."

"Daaad." Tim's cheeks turned the shade of a hearty Merlot. Using his free hand, he yanked his iPhone from his parka and punched at the virtual keyboard with his thumbs. "Hey, guess what? The Trail Blazers won last night." He held up the phone so his dad could view the score.

Rob sighed. "Let's talk about another mystery then. Swing the canoe around so you can see what I've excavated."

Tim pocketed his phone, then pivoted the craft and brought it abeam of the tiny cliff his father had cut into the bank.

"What do you see?" Rob asked.

"Mud. Crap."

"You're going to have to do better than that if you want to be a scientist."

Tim shrugged. "Maybe I'll be a writer."

"Maybe you should think about being something you can actually make a living at."

"Yeah, well . . ."

"Come on, son. Look at the mud. Try to think analytically about what you see."

A ripple of water thunked against the canoe. The boat bobbed up and down.

"Tide's turning," Rob said, "and we've still got stuff to look at on the marsh. So let's step it up. Try doing a little detective work, okay?"

Tim leaned closer to the excavation, making a show of examining it. "Sure," he said, sounding less than enthusiastic. "There're layers of mud, like different colors, different textures. Silt maybe." He squinted. "And it looks like there're little bits of plants and grass stuck in the mud." Indifference etched on his face, he turned toward his father. "What a thrill."

Rob didn't respond immediately. Partially out of frustration, partially in an attempt to come up with a way to engage his son, he paused. After a minute or so, he spoke. "Look again near the bottom of what I hacked out. There's something different, something besides just typical salt-marsh deposits."

Tim moved his gaze back to the excavation. "Oh, yeah. Looks like there're twigs and chunks of bark and stuff in the mud."

"Right. Those are the remains of a spruce forest, a forest that grows only on dry land. But it's not dry here, is it? Kinda weird, huh? But there's something else, too." He extended his right arm, and with his index finger traced over a thin, grainy deposit layered on top of the mud harboring the spruce bits.

Tim sighed, reached out, and took a pinch of the deposit between his thumb and forefinger. "Sand." He looked at his father.

In his son's eyes, Rob detected a nascent question. "Good. So let's think about this. Mud, mud, mud, then suddenly a layer of sand. Where'd that come from?"

Tim shrugged.

"Come on. Pretend you're on *CSI*. Give it a shot. There's a mystery here."

"The sand came in on a high tide."

"Only once? And another thing, we're probably three miles upstream from the mouth of the river. That would suggest something a hell of a lot bigger than a high tide carried this sand inland."

"A storm. A big storm."

"Good. That's a possibility. Let's pull the canoe up onto the grass and take a look around."

They maneuvered the craft onto the slightly raised hummock of the marsh. They secured the boat and clambered out into a field of soggy, tan grass. Beneath the ankle-high growth, thick mud, almost quicksand-like in its consistency, sucked at their boots.

Several meandering tidal streams snaked through the marsh. A great blue heron stalked along the edge of one of the creeks, searching for breakfast. It paused to inspect Rob and Tim. Apparently deciding the slow-moving figures offered no threat, the bird continued its hunt.

Rob watched as Tim surveyed the grassy slough. "Something seem a bit out of place here?" he asked.

"Yeah, kinda. Those things." Tim pointed at the scattered silvery stumps and spires of dead trees. The snags gave the marsh the appearance of a giant pin cushion.

"Good catch, kid. What stood here a long time ago looked just like the thick forest behind it. Spruce, fir, cedar. Now all that remains are grass, some huckleberry bushes, and these dead trees from another age. We call it 'The Ghost Forest.'"

"Ghost Forest?" Tim's voice betrayed a spark of interest.

"These old stumps and trunks are Western red cedar—strong, rot resistant, insect resistant. They remained here long after the rest of the forest died and decayed. Remember the spruce bits in the mud?"

Tim nodded.

"So here's the crux of the puzzle. What killed the trees?"

Tim's face brightened. Engagement. A mystery to be solved. "I like my big storm theory. A saltwater flood from the sea."

"Except seawater would have drained back out to the ocean. The trees would have survived. Try again."

A bald eagle soared above the marsh, working its wings like trim tabs, probably running an armed reconnaissance in search of a mouse or vole.

Tim furrowed his brow, staring at the Ghost Forest. "Hey, I know," he said. "Fire, a forest fire."

Rob motioned him forward, toward the naked snags. They squished across the marsh, in spots brushing through the leathery, serrated leaves of salal bushes. They reached a place where several of the bone-colored spires stood in close proximity to one another.

"See any evidence of fire? Blackened wood? Burn marks?"

Tim walked around the trees. Squish, squish, squish. "Not really," he said finally, sounding a bit dejected.

"So?"

Tim closed his eyes and tilted his head toward the slate-colored cloud deck. He remained in the reflective pose for a moment, then opened his eyes and pivoted toward his dad. "Sink hole," he said decidedly. "A big sink hole formed and allowed salt water to rush in."

"Well, that's not totally correct, but you're close. Good thinking. Here's the deal. Remember the layer of sand covering the mud that contained the spruce forest debris?"

Tim nodded.

"The same thing from about the same time—we know that because of radiocarbon dating—has been discovered all along the coasts of Washington and Oregon. That means something catastrophic happened in the Pacific Northwest a little over three hundred years ago. Something that caused certain areas to subside, or sink, thus allowing tidal marshes to become blanketed in sand."

"Something *catastrophic*?" Tim eyes widened. "What?"

"A massive earthquake, what's known as a megaquake. It caused some spots to suddenly sink, like where we're standing, and unleashed a huge tsunami that swept beach sand inland and permanently flooded those places that had, so to speak, caved in."

"Really?"

Rob could see he had Tim's interest now. "Trouble is, we're not talking something of just historical significance. It's an event, a disaster, that's going to happen again."

Tim stared at his father.

"Remember that movie *The Impossible* that came out a few years ago, the one about the big tsunami in Sumatra?"

"Yeah. That was pretty scary."

"Here," Rob said, his voice dropping to a hoarse whisper, "it'll happen here. In the Northwest. Just like Sumatra. And I don't mean just *here*," he stamped his foot on the soft earth, "I mean everywhere from Vancouver Island to northern California."

Tim smiled. "Come on, Dad, you're yanking my chain."

"Wrong. It's easy to pass off what once happened here as 'ancient' geologic history, something that happened many years before white men reached the western edge of the continent. But it's not. The Earth is restless and sometimes violent.

"Mount St. Helens, for instance. The restlessness didn't cease just because we settled the region and built freeways and skyscrapers and dams. The threat of violent upheavals persists. Just ask the people of Sumatra or Japan. Or if you could, even the Indians who used to live along coasts here."

Tim kept his gaze fixed on his father.

Rob went on. "Earlier you mentioned The Big One on the San Andreas fault. Forget it." He shook his head in slow motion denial.

Tim narrowed his eyes. Skepticism.

"Oh, L. A. will still get *a* Big One," Rob said, "but—and this is something we didn't realize even thirty years ago—it's really Vancouver, Seattle, and Portland that are Ground Zero for *The* Big One, the eight-hundred-pound-gorilla quake."

Tim stood silent for a few moments, perhaps trying to come to grips with the consequences of what his father had just told him. The wind picked up, sighing through the crown of the living evergreens and rattling through the dry bones of the Ghost Forest. Overhead, a squadron of gulls, calling to one another in piercing cries, rode the freshly invigorated wind.

Tim broke out of his reverie. "Hey, there's another canoe." He pointed at the river.

Rob turned. A canoe with single paddler pushed upstream, riding the incoming tide. Not a fisherman. Someone fishing would use a drift boat or cast a line from the shore. A recreational paddler? Maybe, but the boat appeared to be making directly for the marsh.

Rob continued watching. The canoe eased into the bank and stopped. Its single occupant exited, secured the craft, and glided toward Rob and Tim. *Glided* seemed the correct word. The new arrival, decked out in a University of Washington ball cap, Pendleton jacket, and L. L. Bean footwear, moved effortlessly over the boggy land in long, smooth strides and, in a matter of seconds, stood in front of Rob and Tim.

"Hi," she said, and extended her hand. "I'm Cassie."

"Hello," Rob said, shaking hands with her. "I'm Robert Elwood, Rob. And this is my son, Timothy." He nodded at Tim.

"I hope you don't mind me intruding," she said. "But I've read so much about the Ghost Forest I decided I wanted to come see it for myself."

Rob took stock of Cassie. Her slight build seemed the reason she'd been able to move over the marsh with such ease. Beyond that, in a word, she appeared entrancing. Not necessarily beautiful, but beguiling. A ponytail the shade of sugar maple leaves in a New England autumn spilled out from beneath the back of her cap. If eyes, as is often said, are the windows to one's soul, then Cassie's virescent irises suggested something timeless and wise resided deep within her.

To complement that implication, she appeared, well, ageless. Rob had no clue whether she might be in her early thirties or late sixties. Perhaps it depended on how the light hit her, at least what little of it managed to squeeze through the leaden overcast.

"What's your interest in the Ghost Forest?" Rob asked.

"I've been doing research on Native American legends along the north Pacific Coast. Most recently with the Makah and Huu-ay-aht people." She gestured northward. "Before that, with the Snoqualmie, Quileutes, and Duwamish. Within each tribe, oral histories of a 'great shaking of the earth' and a 'massive flood from the ocean' have been handed down over many generations."

"So I've heard," Rob said.

"Originally, researchers categorized the tales as folklore and mythical sagas. For one thing, the timeframes of the stories were impossible to pin down. There were a lot of vague references like 'shortly before the white man's time' or 'four generations before my grandfather's time.' That left a lot of room for interpretation. Maybe the 1700s, maybe the

1600s, if at all. Then, with the discovery of the Ghost Forest, we—"

"And a lot of other research discoveries, too," Rob interjected.

"I'm sure," she said, "but the Ghost Forest was the most high-profile. Anyhow, it was an important part of the evidence that there had indeed once been a 'great shaking of the earth' and 'massive flood' along the coast."

She paused, seeming to allow her thoughts to drift into the past, or maybe the future, then continued. "So, the Native American tales it turns out aren't mythology, they're history."

A gust of wind riffled the dark waters of the Copalis.

"More than that," Rob said. "They're a warning."

Chapter Two

Here be Dragons

The Ghost Forest
90 Miles WSW Of Seattle
Monday, March 23

"A WARNING?" Cassie asked, moving her gaze over the skeletal Ghost Forest. "How so?"

"Because we now know there's a long history of great earthquakes along the Pacific Coast, and that there are more to come."

"*We?*"

"I'm a geologist," Rob said. "My interest is in earthquakes and tsunamis."

"That seems a strange passion," she said. It sounded like a statement that begged a response. Her gaze fell on him with the intensity of an investigator, yet he felt no discomfort. Her curiosity seemed born of genuine intellectual interest.

"I was working under contract in the northeast Indian Ocean," he said, "helping map underwater topography near the Sunda Trench, what used to be called the Java Trench, just prior to the catastrophic Sumatra-Andaman quake and tsunami in 2004. I had come home, back to Oregon, for Christmas vacation. The disaster struck the day after Christmas, Boxing Day. Virtually all of the Indonesian friends I'd made over there—I hung out a lot on the Sumatran coast—lost their lives, along with over two hundred thousand others . . ." His voice trailed off.

"I'm sorry," Cassie said, her words soft and coated with compassion. "I understand loss." She reached out and touched his arm.

"Thank you. Anyhow, the point I was driving at is that the Sumatran tragedy mirrored what happened here over three centuries ago."

"In 1700, right?" Cassie asked.

Rob nodded.

"Really?" Tim said. "How could you know the exact year? The Indians' stories"—he inclined his head toward Cassie—"seem kind of, well, vague."

Rob gestured at an old deadfall lying in repose in the thick marsh grass. "Let's sit. We've got a little while before the tide reaches us."

The heron whose territory they'd invaded studied their movements briefly, then dipped its beak into one of the sluggish streams braiding the marsh. It grabbed a squirming fish, flapped its wings in graceful slow motion, and took flight.

The trio seated itself on the decaying, moss-covered log, Tim to Rob's right, Cassie on the other side. Rob turned to Cassie. "You're from U-Dub?" he said.

"Oh, this." She patted her ball cap. "No, I guess I just like purple and gold. I bought it at a University of Washington bookstore. I'm actually from Troy." She offered an inscrutable smile, something that suggested she might harbor some sort of secret, but Rob found himself unable to decipher what might be involved.

Instead he said, "Troy University? Good school. What's your field?"

"Strategic Communication, but I guess I've morphed into more of a cultural anthropologist. You know, studying the history of Native American tribes in the Northwest. How about you?"

"from the University of Washington, then got my doctorate from Oregon State in geology with a specialization in geophysics and plate tectonics. Have my own company in Portland now."

"Then you really are an expert in all of this?" She moved her gaze over the marsh.

"As much as one can be, I suppose."

She didn't respond right away, but appeared to study him intently, a non-threatening appraisal.

After several moments she said, "You're apprehensive about something. I sense it."

He stared at her, puzzled, and a little surprised.

She shrugged. "It's a gift I have." She looked into the middle distance, seeming to focus on nothing. "Or maybe a curse."

He nodded. "Here's the thing, Cassie. What took place here is not just an interesting geological study of something that happened in the past. It's a canary in a coal mine."

"The past as prologue to the future?"

"Exactly."

"If you've got time, I'd like to hear about it."

"Sure, but bear with me for moment. I have to start with a quick lesson in something called plate tectonics."

A smile crept across her face. "I've been learning all my life. Go ahead."

"Over the past century, we've discovered that the outer shell of the Earth consists of rigid plates, kind of like the cracked-but-not-completely-broken shell of an egg. These plates, seven or eight huge slabs and many smaller ones, 'float' on a viscous mantle beneath them."

"Continental drift," Tim piped up, recognition of the concept flashing in his eyes.

"Well, maybe you got some of your old man's genes after all," Rob exclaimed, raising his gaze skyward in a gesture of praise. "At least it's good to know you haven't been spending all your time thinking about babes in bikinis."

Tim's cheeks flushed again. "Come on." He flicked his gaze in Cassie's direction. *She isn't family.*

Cassie laughed, something melodious and timeless. "Hey, you think babes don't ever think about guys, too?" She redirected the conversation. "So, we've got continental drift which, I gather, isn't always smooth."

"It's not," Rob said. "Around the globe there are a number of 'subduction zones' where one plate is sliding beneath another—subducting. Usually this happens where a heavier oceanic slab is knifing underneath a lighter continental plate. If the plates get locked, that is, stuck together with the subducting plate dragging the edge of the upper plate along with it, then they sometimes 'unlock' in a single, violent event. The result is what geologists call a megathrust earthquake. I was telling my son about that earlier."

"Is that what happened here?" Cassie asked.

"It happened here. It happened in Sumatra in 2004. In Japan in 2011. It'll happen here again. And when I say 'here,' I mean in the Pacific Northwest. That's because there's something called the Cascadia Subduction Zone just offshore. It extends from southern Vancouver Island to northern California. It's where the Juan de Fuca Plate is sliding underneath the North American Plate."

"How far offshore?" Cassie asked.

"From where we are, the leading edge of the zone is maybe fifty miles west. But for all practical purposes, we're standing on it."

Tim stood, tugged the brim of his stocking cap up, and surveyed the area again. "So there was a big quake—"

"Monstrous quake. The shaking would have felt like ocean swells rippling through the earth and probably lasted for several minutes. It would have been difficult to stand. The ground deformed, cracks yawned open, portions of the land suddenly subsided by as much as eight or ten feet. Then the sea invaded, rushing in like a forty- or fifty-foot-high storm surge—the tsunami. The dense grove of trees that had lived here for centuries suddenly found itself swamped in saltwater. They died. Only the skeletons of the cedar trees remained standing to remind us of what happened."

"Don't forget the Native American legends," Cassie said. "They're reminders, too, not just folklore."

Rob nodded.

"So, 1700," Tim said. "How can you be sure?"

"I can narrow it down even more than that. How about January 26th, 1700, at 9 p.m.?"

"Come on, Dad, that's BS. The Indians didn't have calendars or clocks, they didn't write anything down, and apparently weren't very precise in dating their stories." He glanced at Cassie who bobbed her head in agreement.

"Actually, determining the exact date and time of the event is a fascinating detective story. It's one that involves tree growth rings, radiocarbon dating, and knowing how fast a tsunami moves through the ocean. To summarize the tale, by carbon dating the plant material in the mud layer I showed you, scientists were able to narrow down the time frame to between 1690 and 1720. The technique is imprecise.

"But, by studying tree growth rings of these dead trees"—he gestured at the Ghost Forest—"and trees that were still living at the time, 'witness trees,' researchers pinned the time down to late 1699 or early 1700. It was like reading a barcode from Mother Nature."

"So, 1700. And the rest you kinda guessed at?" Tim asked.

"Not at all. Enter the Japanese. They've been keeping written records of earthquakes and tsunamis since the 5th Century."

"During the last years of the Roman Empire," Cassie noted.

Rob shrugged. He didn't know. "Anyhow, the Japanese recorded what they termed an 'Orphan Tsunami' in early 1700. 'Orphan' because it struck without a local earthquake as a precursor. So no one could understand where the tsunami came from. It washed over the Japanese coast around midnight on January 27th.

"Investigators have since determined the 'orphan' could only have been triggered by the same monster quake that created this Ghost Forest and all the others along the coasts of the Northwest."

"How could they know that?" Tim asked, appearing to be fully engaged by the story.

"Good question," Rob said. "Forget being a writer. Work on being a scientist."

Tim smiled and waited for his father to continue.

"Well," Rob said, "given the size of the waves that smashed into Japan, around twelve feet, researchers calculated they must have been spawned by at least a magnitude-nine earthquake. Since there's no evidence of any other megaquake from around 1700, it left only the one that struck here. Then, since scientists also knew it would take about ten hours for a tsunami to race from here to Japan, it pinpointed the time of the quake as 9 p.m. on January 26th."

"That's pretty cool, Dad."

Rob stifled a chuckle. A breakthrough. *My teenaged son thinks science is cool.*

"I'm not sure I know what a magnitude-nine earthquake means," Cassie said. Something caught her eye and interrupted her thoughts. She sprang from the log where they'd been seated and pointed toward the thick forest bordering the marsh. "Look," she exclaimed. A herd of about a dozen elk, females and youngsters, wandered along the verge of the evergreens, grazing on grass and leaves and giving Rob, Tim, and Cassie only a cursory examination.

Rob stood, too. "That's why I love field work. Not too many other jobs have an office environment like this." He glanced at the river. "We'd better be heading back. The tide's coming up quickly now."

They trudged toward their moored canoes. "You asked about magnitude," Rob said to Cassie. "The old Richter Scale has been put out to pasture. We now measure earthquakes with something called the moment magnitude scale. The Richter and moment magnitude are basically similar for smaller convulsions, the quakes in the three to seven range, but for larger ones, the megaquakes, moment magnitude is much better at capturing the total energy released. That's because monster quakes don't necessarily shake harder, they shake longer."

"Could you put this whole idea of magnitude into a context for me?" Cassie asked. "That would help me understand better."

"Me, too," Tim chimed in.

"Sure," Rob said. "The Sumatran megathrust quake was a nine-point-one. The 2011 monster off the coast of Japan was a nine."

"What was the biggest ever?" Tim asked.

"After the advent of the seismograph, that is, when we were actually able to measure the intensity of ground shaking, that would have been a nine-point-five off the coast of Chile in 1960. It claimed over sixteen hundred lives."

"Wasn't there a major quake in Alaska around that same time?" Cassie asked.

"Prince William Sound, 1964, a nine-point-two. Did an immense amount of damage in Anchorage and launched a tsunami that killed a dozen people as far south as Crescent City, California."

"How about quakes in the Lower 48?" Cassie asked.

They reached their canoes. The incoming tide had lifted them almost to the level of the marsh.

"Well, among the more famous, or infamous, the quake that destroyed San Francisco in 1906 was a seven-point-seven. The Bay Area earthquake that occurred during the World Series in 1989 registered a six-point-nine. More recently, the Northridge quake in Southern California in '94 checked in at six-point-eight. None of those, by the way, was a megathrust earthquake. They didn't occur near subduction zones."

"Is there really that much difference between, say, a six-point-eight like Northridge, and a nine-point-one like Sumatra?" Tim asked. "The numbers don't seem very far apart."

"The moment magnitude scale is logarithmic," Rob said. "Have you studied logarithms in school yet?"

"Yeah."

"So you know that each whole-number increase on the scale represents a factor of—"

"Ten," Tim interjected.

"You're right. See, you really do have the makings of a scientist. But here's the deal, for *total* energy released—that's taking into account how long the shaking goes on—each full step in the scale represents a *thirty-fold* increase."

"Still a bit abstract," Cassie said.

"Okay, think of it this way. Weight aside, consider something the diameter of a large pearl. Let that represent the energy in a six-point-eight tremor. Like for Northridge. A lot of damage there, right? Now consider a nine-point-one megathrust. Sumatra. You're talking about something the size of a bowling ball. There's a big difference between the diameter of a pearl and a bowling ball."

"That helps," Cassie said. She stooped to tug her canoe closer. Tim stepped forward to help. "Thank you," she said. She turned to Rob. "So what's the thinking about the magnitude of the 1700 quake?"

"At least a nine. But it wasn't just 1700. I don't have time to go into detail now, but by examining sediments cored from the seafloor off the Pacific coast, researchers have determined there probably have been at least nineteen megathrust earthquakes over the past ten thousand years, and at least that many 'smaller' ones."

"What's the difference?" Tim said, whacking his hands together to get the mud off.

"The megathrust quakes represent a full-length rupture of the Cascadia Subduction Zone, from Vancouver Island to northern California, almost seven hundred miles. The smaller ones, still monsters by any standards, occur when only a portion of Cascadia rips, usually the southern half, from southern Oregon to northern California. Even those quakes probably check in between eight-point-two and eight-point-six."

"Nice," Cassie said. "So there's a sleeping giant under us?"

"Interestingly enough," Rob responded, "Cascadia is essentially a *Doppelgänger* of the Sunda Trench, the subduction zone that triggered the Sumatran disaster." He let the statement hang. The television and YouTube images of the tsunami surging through Thailand's resort areas and Banda Aceh flashed through his mind. A tiny dart of terror knifed into his psyche. He blinked and drew a deep breath, willing the vision to disappear.

"You okay, Dad?" Tim asked, resting a hand on Rob's shoulder.

"Sure. Just a bit tired. Time we get back to Portland. Mom will be worried if we're late."

"We shoulda brought the plane."

"I'm not instrument qualified, remember?" He pointed at the lowering cloud deck. "This is strictly IFR weather." A splatter of rain emphasized his point.

Cassie retrieved her paddle from the canoe, ready to depart. "So I guess the real question is not how bad things might get here, we kind of know that, but when?"

"That's the long pole in the tent. We don't know. We do know the full-length rips in Cascadia, the ones that trigger the biggest quakes, come along every five hundred years or so. But if you tally *all* the quakes, including the so-called smaller ones, the interval is around two hundred and fifty years.

"Here's the catch, though, there's no real rhythm in the intervals. The marsh records and sea sediment cores suggest there have been gaps as short as a hundred years, but also as long as a thousand. There's no predictive value in that. If you look at just the last *five* megaquakes, the intervals have averaged around three hundred and twenty-five years. So does that mean we're due? Or does that mean the stress in the locked plates may have been relieved enough by the more recent convulsions we don't have to worry for another millennium?" He paused. "No one knows for sure."

A seagull coasted overhead and issued a sharp cry.

Cassie prepared to step into her boat. "And even if you knew, who would listen?" Her gaze seemed to drift away again to something distant and unseen. "Oracles of doom never seem to fare well. People don't want to believe dire news. Think about the Old Testament prophets. Isaiah, by some accounts, was sawn in half. Jeremiah, who was reviled and ridiculed, lamented his own birth. Zechariah was murdered."

Rob steadied Cassie as she seated herself in her canoe. "Yeah," he said, "I should probably stay out of the soothsaying business."

"Well, perhaps we'll run into each other again," Cassie said. I'll be working on the Oregon coast through the summer."

"We've got a beach house in Manzanita. So maybe."

With Cassie in the lead and Rob and Tim following, they moved off, paddling against the incoming tide, but riding the lazy seaward drift of the Copalis.

Rob allowed his thoughts to wander. Back to a dark winter night along the Pacific Coast of North America when the earth shook and dogs yowled and seawater surged and people died—the wrath of what must have seemed a mythological beast, angry and fierce and relentless. He looked around and shuddered slightly, knowing it still lurked.

"In medieval times," he said, raising his voice to be heard over the steady slap of their paddles, "maps often carried sketches of dragons to represent the guardians of unexplored territories. In fact, some ancient mapmakers entered the inscription 'Here Be Dragons,' to warn of such dangers."

Cassie looked back.

Rob stopped paddling. "We could stamp that on modern maps of the Pacific Northwest."

Chapter Three

Nightmare

Lake Oswego, Oregon
A Portland Suburb
Wednesday, May 27

"I HAD THAT DREAM again last night," Rob said. Seated at the breakfast table, his hand trembled as he lifted a mug of coffee to his lips. His stomach roiled as he sipped the hot liquid. He considered spitting the coffee back into the mug, but dismissed the idea. Instead, in an unsteady motion, he placed the large ceramic cup back on the tiled table. A dollop of the mug's contents splashed out.

His wife Deborah, standing behind him, massaged his neck and shoulders. He leaned his head back into the maternal comfort of her breasts. She smelled fresh, of soap and perfumed body lotion. Although not drop-dead gorgeous, she was attractive. Tall, tanned, and athletic with green eyes and ebony hair, she'd always drawn second glances.

"I've told you before," she said softly, "you're too damned wrapped up in this earthquake and tsunami business. Let it go for a while. Let's spend a week or two at the coast."

"One dream, maybe a couple, I could understand," he said, ignoring her suggestion. "But the same one over and over again, once or twice a week, each more explicit. It bothers me." He paused. "No, it doesn't bother me, Deb, it terrifies me."

Low-angled morning sunshine streamed into the breakfast nook, illuminating a constellation of tiny dust motes in a shimmering light show. Outside, towering evergreens and verdant rose bushes, alive in an explosion of late-spring blooms, added to the already bucolic mood of the day, a mood that escaped Rob.

"It's a reflection of how tied up you are in your work," Deborah said, her words more forceful now. "You really need to get away, and I mean for more than just a weekend."

"I can't. You don't understand. This dream—this nightmare—I can't ignore it. Intellectually I know I should. I'm a scientist, for Christ's sake. But it's almost like there's a message in there for me." He placed his hand on Deb's and swiveled to face her. "But you're probably right. I've somehow managed to wind myself around the axle worrying about stuff I don't have an iota of control over."

Deborah seated herself across from Rob. "Tell me again about the dream," she said, her voice quiet once more, seeming to reflect genuine interest and concern. It reminded Rob of why he loved her, at least one of the reasons. Her support of his endeavors remained a constant in their relationship, even though she'd staked out boundaries beyond which she would not allow him to venture. Deborah, the practical. Deborah, the level-headed.

He drew a deep breath and looked out the window, squinting into the brightness of the rising sun. After several moments, he turned his gaze back to Deborah.

"It's vivid," he said. "I wouldn't even call it a dream anymore. It's like being embedded in a terrifying virtual reality. I'm on the coast. I can't identify the town. It doesn't matter. It could be anyplace between Vancouver Island and Cape Mendocino. It's everyplace. Every town. They're all under the gun. The quake hits, the ground heaves and pitches like swells in a heavy sea. There's no permanence or solidarity to anything. You might as well be trying to cross the Columbia River Bar on an air mattress. The shaking, violent, like nothing you've ever felt or could even imagine, is unrelenting."

He ceased speaking and stared out the window again. Deborah rested a comforting hand on his forearm. He placed his own hand on hers and resumed.

"Cracks spider web across the ground. Fissures, like crevices in a mountain snowfield, open. Buildings slump and collapse. There's an explosion. A gas line rupture maybe. Finally, after a minute or two, the convulsions diminish. People stagger into the streets. They're dazed, injured, confused. A few realize what has happened and begin to run toward higher ground, away from the ocean. They know what's coming."

"The tsunami." Deborah had heard the narrative before. Her voice sounded far away.

Rob nodded. "We've tried to hammer it into the heads of coastal residents that the only warning they'll get before a huge tsunami slams in is an intense, prolonged quake. That they'll have only a matter of minutes to escape to higher ground before the ocean surges inland. It won't be like a tsunami generated by a distant quake, like in Alaska. We've had those before. You know, when you get several hours to prepare and then the surge ends up being only a couple of feet high."

Deborah furrowed her brow. "You said only a few people ran?"

"Maybe it's the 'Can't Happen Here Syndrome.' People find it hard to believe their homes, their businesses, even their lives are in acute danger and can be snatched away just like that." He snapped his fingers. "Or perhaps they're in shock or just too damned stunned to understand what's happened, what's going to happen."

He tried his coffee again and this time managed to swallow a sip.

Deborah rose from her chair, walked to the window, and adjusted the plantation blinds to deflect the sunlight knifing into the room. She sat again and waited for Rob to go on.

"One or two people point toward the ocean," he said. "They realize the surf has receded to a point they've never seen before. Offshore sandbars and rock formations are exposed. Dogs begin to yowl. Now a handful of additional residents realize the danger. They begin to run and walk rapidly away from the beach. A few jump into their cars."

"They're not supposed to do that," Deborah interjected, "try to evacuate in their vehicles."

"When do folks ever do what they're supposed to? In a sudden crisis, they forget or panic." Rob gazed straight ahead, his eyes focused on a photograph of the Oregon coast on a peaceful, sunny day—the coast that had been his Mayberry growing up as a kid. Now it had become his Banda Aceh in-waiting. Banda Aceh, where the Sumatran tsunami of 2004 had washed away tens of thousands of lives in a matter of minutes.

He continued speaking. "Anyhow, once the automobile exodus begins, it dawns on more and more people that the two-minute warning for their lives has sounded."

"Two minutes?" Deborah's voice registered surprise.

"A metaphor. Football. Maybe they've got ten minutes. Fifteen at most. Whatever it is, they freak out. Suddenly the street is clogged with cars, SUVs, and pickups. But they can't go anyplace because fallen trees and power lines have blocked the roads.

"They look back toward the ocean, but nothing is there, save for sand flats and a thin, white line of surf on the horizon."

"The tsunami?"

Rob tried to answer, but his voice cracked.

Deborah waited.

"It doesn't come in like a huge breaking wave, like those Hollywood tsunamis," he said, finding his vocal footing again. "It floods in like a massive tidal bore, rushing across the beach, surging over berms and seawalls, thundering up streets and sidewalks, swallowing everything in sight. It's thirty feet deep, maybe fifty or sixty, I can't tell. It blasts inland, a swirling gray-green cesspool of debris, choked with vehicles, logs, pieces of homes, people. There's no sound, but there must be. I just can't hear it. Maybe that's for the better. But I know it's there. The roaring water, screams, car alarms, the death rattle of a community . . ." His voice faltered.

"It's just your subconscious stressed out, working overtime," Deborah said. "It's not real."

"That's the problem, Deb. It is real. At least the threat is. That's what nobody wants to believe. If the earthquake and tsunami hit tomorrow, given the state of relative unpreparedness in the Northwest—compared to say, Japan—the death toll would dwarf Katrina or 9/11. That's pretty damn real."

"Still, your dream is just that, honey, a dream," Deborah reminded him.

"Is it?"

"You tell me. You're the scientist."

"But I'm not a psychoanalyst." He toyed with his coffee mug. "Do you think I need to see a shrink?"

"I think, like I said, you need some time off. Let's plan on spending a few weeks in late June and early July at the beach place, okay? We can take the plane, so if you need to, you could fly back to Portland for a few hours if any important business arises. It'll be great, honey. We can play golf, fly kites, go crabbing, take in a Fourth of July parade, or maybe just hang out and turn into beach Buddhas."

"Yeah, the kids would *love* that," Rob said, with more sarcasm that he intended.

"The kids *will* love it because we'll threaten them with boarding school in Tanzania if they don't," Deborah retorted.

He smiled at her. Her quick wit and sense of humor marked another reason he'd fallen for her, long before he found out something else about her: that she came from money. That of course, had set more than a few tongues wagging when they were dating. People couldn't believe he'd actually been smitten by the woman, not her money.

Even after they were married, he'd never asked how much. He knew only that it amounted to enough they could afford things such as a beach home and an airplane. Hardly trappings within reach on a geologist's salary.

Only after they'd dated for almost a year did he find out she came from a family descended from the Bishops who'd built the Pendleton Woolen Mills into an international powerhouse. The iconic shirts and blankets from the company had helped create an obviously healthy trust fund for Deborah.

He and Deborah didn't flaunt their wealth—well, her wealth—but they did enjoy it. A second home in the quiet little coastal town of Manzanita. A membership in Oswego Lake Country Club. A Cessna T182T Turbo Skylane hangared at the Hillsboro Airport just west of Portland. The four-seat, single-engine craft proved perfect for short family trips, and invaluable for Rob's business, the Oregon Geophysical Consortium, of which he was founder and president.

"Okay," he said. "Manzanita. A few weeks around the Fourth. Sounds great." Yet it didn't, though he couldn't pinpoint why. Something about the idea gnawed at him, like a tiny sound you hear in the dead of night but can't identify. Like a warning light deep in your psyche that flickers red then fades before you can fully grasp the meaning of it.

Had there been something in his nightmare—a signal, a sign, a fore-warning—that had slithered from his conscious into his subconscious and now hid there like a parasitic tick? Something ethereal that had fled the logic and reality that come aborning with wakefulness? He'd read somewhere that we all have dreams every night but don't remember most of them after we arise.

But what did it matter? He dealt in hard science, not metaphysics. Deborah more than likely had nailed it, as she often did. His dreams sprang from his obsession with work. They were post-cognitive, not precognitive. They linked to the past, not the future. Bolstering his wife's theory, he remembered exactly when his dreams, his nightmares, had begun. The first of them, like an incubus from the deep, had burrowed its way into his sleep a few days after he and Timothy had returned from their spring-break trip to the Ghost Forest.

Still, the nighttime journeys of his mind nagged at him. While he didn't deem himself religious, he often found wise counsel from a long-time friend, Lewis Warren, a retired Episcopal bishop. Lewis, over the years, had become a sort of father figure to him, always ready to discuss anything—science, history, politics, morality, sports—not just religion, which in fact, they rarely talked about.

Rob considered their discussions refreshing, lively, and informative. Lewis proved to be one of those rare individuals: a well-read intellectual who remained eminently approachable and understandable. He also played a decent game of golf, and Rob more often than not found himself donating to "Lewis's Ministry," whatever that was, when they played for a dollar a hole on Manzanita's little course.

"I need to spend some time with Lewis," Rob said to Deborah, who had busied herself stuffing breakfast dishes into the dishwasher.

"Golf or jabber?"

"Jabber, as you so eloquently put it."

"Yeah, well he's good at that. I always thought of him as a bit of an egghead, though."

Deborah had him pegged. Lewis read voraciously, often on topics of philosophy, psychology, and neurobiology, not just religion.

"He might be able to bring some objectivity to my situation."

"I can't?"

"You can, and I value that. But, as you always tell me, it doesn't hurt to get a second opinion."

"That's in reference to doctors." She wiped her hands on a dishtowel.

"Lewis *is* a doctor. And he always seems to be able to take a universal view of things. You're probably right, Deb, the preoccupation with my work is getting to me. I'm thinking Lewis can probably validate that."

"Ah, ha," Deborah said, shaking a finger at Rob in mock reprimand, "that's just your way of getting cheap counseling."

He smiled. "I don't consider it cheap. Lewis can be a pain in the ass, not to mention a bit obtuse at times. Anyhow, I'll get in touch with him first thing when we get to the coast."

Chapter Four

Shack

Atlanta, Georgia
Friday, June 5

ON GOOGLE, SHAWN McCready typed in the name carefully, making certain he spelled it correctly: Alexis Tamara Williamson. He'd known her as Alex, but that had been twenty-five years ago, when they'd been lovers. No, they'd been more than that. They'd been engaged, and she'd given herself to him fully, body and soul, as they say, to be his forever wife. Young and full of himself, however, he'd thrown her overboard. Looking back through a framework crafted not only by time, but by maturity and experience—though he knew even now some people would argue the maturity point—it had been his greatest failure.

Back then, though, it had been a different world for him, one he ruled. As a shit-hot pilot in the U. S. Air Force flying the fastest fighter in the world, the mach two-point-five F-15, and owning and driving a ZR-1 Corvette, once at 170 mph on an empty stretch of I-64, he'd made the very conscious decision he needn't be reined in by a wedding band. There certainly were plenty of other women in the stable, or, as they were derogatorily referred to by the guys in the squadron, "pussy on the hoof." So many women, so little time.

It had been a good life in those days, or so it had seemed, and he'd earned his nickname, Shack, on a couple of levels. On one, because he'd been the best damn pilot in the First Fighter Wing, rarely missing the target bulls-eye, or "shack," with his missiles and bombs on training runs. On another, because he'd found it almost too easy to "shack up" with some of the more attractive amateur camp followers who hung around air bases. As a six-foot blond 'zoomie,' he'd been to young ladies like 'hunny' to Winnie-the-Pooh.

In retrospect, and to be blunt, he'd been largely a self-serving asshole during the first half of his Air Force career. Not that a lot of young fighter jocks weren't. In spite of his ego-driven shortcomings, however, he had at least managed the verisimilitude of a highly successful officer, making wing commander before retiring as a bird colonel with twenty years. Still, the second half of his tenure in the military had been marred by two failed marriages. Since the collapses had been primarily on his shoulders, he perhaps hadn't been able to distance himself *that* far from the "self-serving asshole" stage.

Now, unable to adjust to the relative stability of civilian life, he'd blown through three jobs in just five years. He'd discovered work in the private sector to be unfulfilling and lacking excitement.

Not that he believed it would really help—he took a dim view of anyone prying his head open and peeking under the hood—but he finally decided to meet with a counselor. *Probably can't screw me up any worse than I am.* The counselor turned out to be a little doughboy of a man with oversized spectacles that made him look like an owl, and who cleared his throat a lot and said "hmmm" about every ninety seconds.

"YOU MOVED AROUND a lot in the Air Force?" the counselor had asked.

"PCS'd about every two years."

"PCS?"

"Permanent Change of Station."

"So there wasn't much geographic stability in your life?"

"I never owned a home."

"Hmmm," Doughboy mumbled, then continued. "I'm wondering how you felt about being, well, shall we say, a vagabond?"

"It was just part of Air Force life." *Obviously this doofus has never been in the military.*

"That's not what I asked. How did you *feel* about it? Name an emotion."

"Multiple choice, okay? Give me some options."

"I'm on your side, Mr. McCready. Help me out here. I just want to know how you felt."

"Jesus. Okay, restless. I felt restless. In truth, I probably wouldn't have minded a little permanence in my life. You know, being able to make a commitment to someplace or someone."

Doughboy glanced at some papers on his desk. "Were you in combat?"

"Yes. Operations Deny Flight and Joint Endeavor in the Bosnian War. I was flying out of Aviano Air Base in Italy then. Later, after Air War College, I was a squadron commander at Bagram Airfield in Afghanistan."

"The assignments you had were exciting?"

"There were very few dull moments."

"Hmmm." The counselor adjusted his glasses and squirmed in his chair like a muffin stuck in a baking tin. "The Air Force pretty much took care of everything then?"

"Except for a wife." Shack meant it to be funny.

The counselor merely flashed him a wan smile. Eventually the session got around to Alex.

"It seems as if something about your relationship with Alex bothered you more than any of the others?" Doughboy said.

"I guess."

Doughboy cleared his throat and waited.

Shack picked up on the cue. "I didn't then. But looking back, I feel badly about how I treated her."

"You regret it?"

Shack nodded. "But truly, and I'm sure it's a failing I have, I've never been much into feelings."

"Feelings can be the fuel to reach a resolution about this."

"Resolution isn't something I've had much of in my life." Shack paused, then lowered his voice and spoke haltingly. "I've probably just avoided it."

"Let's see what we can do something about that. Tell me more about you and Alex."

"I'd given her an engagement ring before I went TDY to Aviano."

"TDY?"

"Temporary Duty. But after Aviano, I was PCS'd directly to Spangdahlem Air Base in Germany."

"What did you tell Alex?"

"Nothing."

"Nothing?"

"I never saw her again. Never contacted her after Aviano. We traded a couple of letters when I first got over there, but after that, well . . ."

"You didn't go back to the states after Aviano?"

"No. Like I said, I went directly to Germany. It's not like I had a household or family to pack up and move."

"Did she try to contact you?"

"She sent a few letters to me when I was in Aviano. I just ignored them. Never even bothered to open them. After I got to Germany, I never heard from her again."

"So she didn't even know where you went?"

"Probably not."

Doughboy's eyes narrowed; he remained silent.

"I know. I was a jerk. I honestly feel bad about that now. She was a good woman. Of all those I . . . met,"—he'd thought about saying "bedded," but passed—"she was far and away the best. Intelligent, funny, honest, and a looker." He paused. "Hey, doc, is there something else going on here? Is it just that maybe you never get over the first one? Or perhaps there's some sort of nostalgia for the 'Camelot of youth'?"

"What do you think?"

"I think I'd somehow like to atone for what I did to her. Maybe just say 'I'm sorry' if nothing else." He looked down at his hands, which he had clasped tightly together in his lap. "I guess I'd like to know, too, that she's okay. That she got on with her life and that I didn't leave her with permanent emotional scars." He looked up at the counselor. "Here's the thing, doc. I was a shithead for what I did to Alex, forcing her to walk the plank without even a life preserver, but I feel like *I'm* the one who's drowning now."

Doughboy leaned forward and stared through his owlish spectacles directly at Shack. He spoke softly and deliberately. "Sometimes we can't patch up the present until we patch up the past."

Shack blinked. The guy had actually said something that made sense, given him a direction that might lead to a way out of the guilt-infested jungle in which he'd been wandering.

THUS HAD BEEN born the notion of contacting Alex, not to "reignite the fire," too much time had flowed through their lives for that, but to apologize for his egotistical, self-serving behavior. He genuinely wished to atone for his actions, for sneaking out of her life, their life, like a thief in the night. He owed her that much. But he owed it to himself, too. He needed salve for his own soul.

He understood his Google search could be in vain. He knew Alex only by her maiden name, Williamson, and she undoubtedly had married since then. A woman like her wouldn't have remained single, she had too much going for her. When they'd met, she'd been a newly minted attorney just out of William and Mary. She worked at a small law firm in Hampton, Virginia, home to the headquarters of Air Combat Command at Langley Air Force Base where he'd been stationed.

Besides being smart, Alex had been physically attractive, statuesque in a word. She didn't flaunt her beauty, though; she didn't have to. She had the same allure for men that Shack did for women. So perhaps their union had been preordained. They'd met at a Friday night "happy hour" at the officers' club. Two weeks later they became lovers. To call their affair steamy would have been like calling an F-15 fast. The first night, they "did it" four times.

"Jesus, Shack," Alex had said after the third time, "what were they serving at the bar tonight, testosterone on the rocks?"

"No. All I needed was you."

Shack looked away from his computer and stared out the window of his den into a late afternoon cloudburst drenching the Atlanta landscape. He could still smell Alex's perfume, *Fendi*, after all these years—notes of rose and orange sprinkled with pepper.

How difficult, he wondered, after a quarter of a century, would it be to track her down? He fully understood he might have to hire a private investigator. Most of the "people finder" websites, so widely advertised on the Internet, searched only through databases of public records that might or might not be up to date. Assuming she now went by a married name, a search of such databases might be useless. He harbored his doubts.

Anyway, why not start with Google and go from there? He hovered his index finger over the enter key.

"Okay, Alex. Here I come." He hit the key.

"Wow," he whispered as Google's search engine filled the screen with candidates.

Over a dozen entries for Alexis T. Williamson popped up. *Maybe not the right lady.*

He clicked on the first entry. A website appeared. Alexis T. Williamson, Attorney-at-Law. The site featured a photograph of Ms. Williamson. Shack stared at it, but not for long. There was no mistaking who it was: Alex. A little older. A bit fuller in the face. Raven hair streaked with silver. And a smile that still turbocharged his heart rate. After twenty-five years she remained stunning.

"Wow," he whispered again.

He couldn't believe his good fortune. He'd found her with almost no effort. No people-finder sites, no private detectives. He figured she would be located somewhere nearby, that is, in the Southeast or Mid-Atlantic states. After all, she'd grown up in Richmond and attended the University of Virginia as an undergrad before entering William and Mary. Surely she wouldn't have strayed far from her roots. Perhaps she'd remained in the Hampton Roads area.

He scrolled through the site, searching for an address, at least her business address. He found it quickly.

"Oregon?" he exclaimed. She couldn't have wandered *farther* from her roots. But there it was, someplace called Manzanita where she specialized in family law, estate planning, real estate transactions, and environmental issues. *Environmental? Well, yes. In Oregon, what else?*

He Googled Manzanita, found it to be a tiny town, population about seven hundred, on the north Oregon coast, roughly sixty miles west of Portland as the crow flies. Or maybe as the Seahawk flies, he wasn't sure of the standard out there.

And her name? That surprised him more than anything. Why still her maiden name? Had she never married? Impossible. Perhaps she'd divorced and reverted to her maiden name. Or, more likely, she'd merely retained her birth name as her business appellation. People in the entertainment and television industries did that all the time, he knew, for "branding" purposes. If she'd established a solid reputation as a lawyer under Alexis Williamson, she'd have wanted to keep that.

She had phone numbers listed, but Shack had already made a decision not to make his apology by telephone. It would be too easy for her to dismiss him by just hanging up. He wanted a chance to express his regrets , explain his actions, if that were possible, in person. A least a face-to-face encounter would afford him the opportunity to get his foot in the door, literally, if he had to. He understood Alex might be less than thrilled to see him again, but all he wanted were a few moments to get the words "I'm sorry" out of his mouth. If that came at the expense of a crushed foot, so be it.

Invigorated by his easy discovery of Alex, Shack jumped into trip-planning mode. First, he called up the Delta Air Lines website on his computer and discovered there were more than three dozen flights a day from Atlanta to Portland, Oregon, the nearest major city to Manzanita. Only four were nonstoppers, however, which is what he wanted. He missed flying as a pilot, but hated flying as a passenger. He trusted no one in a cockpit other than himself. The less time spent airborne in sardine class, the better.

Next, he'd need a place to stay. He typed in "motels, Manzanita" on Google and discovered the town had four. "Four?" he muttered. "The place must be a vacation mecca." Finally, he thought about *when* to go. Over the Fourth of July holiday? *Yeah, that might work. Maybe they'll have a spectacular sparkler display on the beach.* He decided he'd best arrive a few days prior to the Fourth to make certain Alex's office would be open. *But that could be a problem, couldn't it? What if she's on vacation or something?*

Easy enough to find out. He went to her website, scrolled down to her contact information, and punched in her office number on his cell. Almost immediately, he realized the mistake he'd made, almost made, and disconnected the call. "Shit," he said. He'd forgotten about caller ID.

So back to the Internet, fount of all knowledge. He discovered that by hitting *67 followed by the number to be called, your name and phone number would not appear on the callee's phone.

He punched in Alex's number again, this time with his ID blocked. She answered on the third ring.

"This is Alexis Williamson," she said. Apparently in a burg as small as Manzanita, attorneys answered their own phones, no assistants or paralegals required.

Shack shook his head. *West Bumfuck, the end of the continent.* "Attorney Alexis Williamson?" Shack asked, a potential client wanting to make certain he had the right individual. He forced himself to speak more softly than usual and enunciated his words with great clarity, not wanting to give Alex a chance, as small as it might be, to recognize his voice as belonging to someone out of her misty, and perhaps not fondly remembered, past.

"Yes," she said, "I'm an attorney at law. To whom do I have the pleasure of speaking?"

If you knew, it might not be a pleasure. "My name is Roger Davenport. I'm calling from Atlanta, Georgia." Better to be truthful here, he'd decided. An area code could always be linked to a geographical region.

"How may I be of service, Mr. Davenport?"

His heart thumping, he listened closely to her voice. She'd lost virtually any hint of the Southern lilt she'd carried when he knew her. Then again, it never had been deeply ingrained in her speech.

"A friend of mine recommended you," he said, "well, sort of. He remembered doing some work with an Alexis Williamson many years ago at a small law office in Norfolk, Virginia, I think it was."

"Oh?" She paused as though taken aback.

He swallowed hard. Had he overplayed his hand?

"That *was* a long time ago and it was in Hampton, Virginia. What's your friend's name?"

He answered her question, one he'd prepared for, with a made-up name. "Dan Ortino."

"Umm, I don't remember anyone by that name."

"Well, like you said, it was a long time ago. But he must have been impressed by your work. When I mentioned to him I was thinking of contacting an Alexis Williamson in Oregon who did real estate work, that's when he told me he'd done business with someone by that name way back when, and if you were the same Ms. Williamson, I couldn't go wrong."

"I didn't handle real estate cases in Virginia."

I know. "He never said what type of work it was, just that you were good."

"How nice he remembered after all these years. At any rate, what can I do for you, Mr. Davenport?"

"I'm considering buying some property in Manzanita, and wanted to get some legal advice relative to that."

"I see. Are you interested in making an appointment, or were you thinking of a phone consultation?"

"I'll be in Manzanita in early July. I was hoping you might be available to meet with me then."

She was. Shack scheduled an appointment with her for July first at two p.m.

"Thank you, Ms. Williamson," he said as they concluded their conversation. "I look forward to seeing you."

"Yes." She paused. "You said you were from Georgia?"

"Yes, Atlanta. Although I grew up in Florida and then moved around a lot after that."

"Ever been to Tidewater, Virginia?"

Shit. With a ballpoint pen he tapped out a furious, nervous staccato on his desk. *Was she onto him?* "No," he lied. "Why do you ask?"

"Oh, nothing." She laughed lightly, dismissing her question. "Your voice vaguely reminded me of someone."

"Really?" He almost choked on the word, his heart rate suddenly in afterburner.

"Well, not so much your voice as the cadence of your words. At any rate, it's not important, Mr. Davenport. You're on my calendar for July first."

They hung up. He'd been barely able to say goodbye as he fought to control his breathing. She'd always been sharp, and she'd obviously picked up on the fact that his speech had a distinct beat: an occasional brief pause in the middle of a sentence as though he'd reached a period, something hard to disguise. Now he wondered who would spring a surprise on whom.

No matter. He'd committed himself to reaching out to Alex and would follow through. So he proceeded with his preparations. The next step, he figured, would be a snap. Securing a place to stay in what he deemed "Hooterville." Only it turned out not to be a snap. The first three motels he called were fully booked through the first week of July. So was the next one.

"What in the heck is going on out there. Is there some kind of convention in town?" he asked at the end of his fourth call, though he couldn't really imagine such a thing in a hamlet that had fewer residents than the subdivision he lived in.

"It's the Fourth of July, sir, it's always packed then," the reservationist answered. She seemed a pleasant enough woman, but she'd answered the phone with "It's a beautiful day on the Oregon coast" even though he'd heard on The Weather Channel that gale warnings had been posted. It made him question her veracity. But maybe Oregonians loved storms.

"How about vacancies in nearby towns?" he asked.

"It's the same all up and down the coast. The Fourth is a big deal."

He thought about changing his meeting with Alex, but now that he had the appointment, he decided to press on.

"Do you have a wait list, you know, in case somebody cancels?"

"We do, but it's pretty long already. Your best bet might be to try to find a rental home. There may be a few of those available."

He agreed and she gave him the phone numbers of several agencies that handled vacation rentals. Within twenty minutes he'd secured "a cute condo that sleeps two and is just a short walk to the beach." He didn't care about that, but he did care that he'd have to shell out for a minimum stay of a week even though he'd planned on being there only three days. Total tally: over a thousand bucks. The price of penance, he figured. If he had to spend a week in Hooterville, he'd spend a week in Hooterville.

Next, he booked a flight to Portland, leaving June twenty-eighth, returning July fifth; economy comfort so he'd have a bit of extra legroom and not have to travel straitjacketed into an upright bed of nails.

Finally, he reserved a rental car. He was told it would be about an hour-and-a-half drive from Portland International Airport to Manzanita.

Finished, he brought up Alex's website again and stared at her photograph. He stood and walked to the window. The rain had ceased, but the trees and bushes still ran with water, dripping from leaves like spring tears. He returned to his computer and looked once more at Alex's photo.

"Why Oregon?" he asked aloud, as though her image might respond.

Chapter Five

Neahkahnie Mountain

Neahkahnie Mountain
Near Manzanita, Oregon
Monday, June 8

JONATHAN RAYMOND strode along a hiking trail on the south side of Neahkahnie Mountain, just north of Manzanita. He moved somewhat slower than usual, stepping around or kicking out of the way twigs and branches, debris from Friday's late-season storm. Ahead of him, Zurich, a great bear of a dog, led the way.

Zurry, as Jonathan called him, looked back frequently, making sure his master remained close. Zurry's tri-colored coat—black, white, and rust—glistened in the bright spring sun. They had reached the steepest part of the trail and climbed steadily now, Jonathan beginning to sweat. The smell of damp earth and coastal wildflowers filled the air.

At just under seventeen hundred feet, Neahkahnie didn't qualify as a big mountain, but it appeared imposing, rising as it did from sea level less than a half mile away. It didn't offer a challenging hike, but in spots the trail inclined sharply. Near the summit, to reach the absolute top of Neahkahnie, one had to scramble hand over foot up a pile of boulders. But in clear weather, such as today, Jonathan knew those who reached the pinnacle would be rewarded by a breathtaking view south from Manzanita all the way to Tillamook Bay.

He had traversed the trail numerous times, searching, as had thousands before him, for alleged buried treasure, the Lost Treasure of Neahkahnie Mountain—that probably didn't exist except as legend. He knew that, but at age seventy-five the hunt filled his days and offered Zurry vigorous and necessary workouts.

The trail proved firm and hard-packed where the sun had warmed it, but muddy and slippery where it had remained in the shadow of the spruce and fir that crowded Neahkahnie's slopes. Beneath the evergreens, wild lilies of the valley and giant trilliums offered a peaceful counter-point to the often windswept forest. No wonder, Jonathan mused, coastal Indians had considered the mountain "the place of supreme deity."

He'd been probing for the "lost" treasure for over a decade, but had never come across anything of interest. Nor, apparently, had anyone else, despite a few rumors to the contrary. Unregulated excava-tion had been prohibited after searchers, along with loggers, had come close to denuding the mountain in the mid-20th Century. Still, in the wake of big storms, such as the one of a few days ago, new avenues of exploration sometimes opened near uprooted trees.

Zurry halted abruptly and wheeled, looking back down the trail behind Jonathan. The dog didn't bark or growl, merely stood silently as a protective sentinel. Jonathan turned and squinted into the morning sun, looking for what Zurry had sensed, not necessarily seen. Out of a halo of light, a slight figure appeared and raised a hand in greeting. "Hello," a woman's voice called.

Jonathan waited for her. Panting slightly, she approached. A tangle of red hair spilled out from beneath a University of Washington ball cap. "I'm Cassie," she said and extended her hand.

"Miss Cassie, pleased to meet you. I'm Jonathan." He shook her hand. "This is Zurich." He dropped his gaze to Zurry.

"Oh, my. What a gorgeous dog! May I pet him?"

Jonathan nodded.

She knelt and ruffled Zurry's fur. Given Zurry's size, they ended up nose to nose. He licked Cassie's cheek.

"What is he?" she asked.

"A Bernese Mountain Dog. A working breed, but he's very gentle."

Still petting him, she stood. "You said your name is Jonathan. I've heard about you."

Jonathan gave her a weak smile.

"You're the one they call Neahkahnie Johnny."

"I'd be hard to misidentify, wouldn't I? A six-foot-two black man with snow on the roof." Not only that, Jonathan knew, but African Americans were truly a tiny minority in Oregon, outnumbered not only by whites, but by Hispanics and Asians, as well.

Cassie laughed. "Dead giveaway."

"So you've heard the stories about me?"

• Cassie shrugged. "What? That you're a Vietnam vet suffering from

PTSD, or a stoned-out ex-hippie, or a former medical doctor addicted to prescription drugs?"

"Yeah, those."

"Not to pry, but is there a smidgen of truth to any of them?"

"Probably."

She waited, apparently expecting him to say more, but he'd already allowed his mind to drift away from her question, and didn't bother to follow up. Overhead, a hawk circled, a dark smudge against a turquoise sky.

"So," Cassie said, "I understand you've been poking around for the treasure supposedly buried up here?"

"Yeah, me and a hundred thousand others over the years."

"But there's nothing, right?"

He studied Cassie, attempting to divine what her interest might be in him, in Neahkahnie, in hidden riches. But he lost his focus and merely shrugged. "Probably just a legend," he said.

"Oh, I don't know. Maybe not."

She caught his interest. "Why do you say that?"

"I'm a researcher," she said, stroking Zurry's head as he sat patiently beside Jonathan. "I'm investigating Native American legends along the north Pacific Coast. The last few weeks I've been talking to Chinooks and Clatsops, what few descendants of the original people I could find, anyhow. The tribes were pretty much wiped out by disease and battles after explorers and traders began to settle near the mouth of the Columbia."

"As I understand it, the legend of the lost treasure began with the Clatsops," Jonathan said.

Cassie nodded. "And I gather that pretty much everyone in Oregon has heard the tale. That a great 'winged canoe' visited here in the late 1600s and white men toting a large chest came ashore and buried whatever they were carrying. The 'winged canoe' was probably a Manila galleon from the Philippines, although variations of the story suggest it could have been an English or French privateer. Anyhow, it's unclear whether the ship wrecked or merely anchored here temporarily."

"As the Indians told it," Jonathan added, "the sailors were accompanied by a giant, dark-skinned man whom they killed and buried with the chest, believing his spirit would protect it until they could return for it."

"Probably a slave from west Africa or the Caribbean," Cassie noted.

"Now you understand part of my interest in the treasure, or whatever it was," Jonathan said.

She didn't respond immediately, appearing to analyze his words. "I see," she said softly. "One of your forebears may have been buried on this mountain." She reached out and touched the sleeve of his shirt. "I'm sorry."

His thoughts floated away again. He pictured the mariners and the black man struggling up the forested slopes of Neahkahnie, lugging the chest, digging a deep hole, then lowering the crate into it. He grimaced at the next image: the sailors running a sword through the black man— "thanks for your help"—and finally, after he'd gasped his last breaths, tossing his body, like the carcass of an elk, into the hole to be its forever guardian.

Zurry nudged his huge head into his master's hip, bringing Jonathan back to the present. "So you think the Clatsops' tale may have some credence?" Jonathan asked.

"Yes. There is evidence that a Spanish galleon shipwrecked near this coast around 1693. That would have put white men and maybe even 'pieces of eight' here in the late 17th Century, supporting the Native American stories."

"What about the buried treasure tales?"

Cassie adjusted her ball cap. She edged out of the shadow of a towering Sitka spruce into a shaft of sunlight, and seemed to transform from a middle-aged woman into a young girl not yet thirty. It was as if a seasoned field researcher were morphing into a college cheerleader.

"All along the north Pacific Coast, Native American tribes possess oral histories of great battles between a massive thunderbird, a benevolent protector of the tribes, and a giant killer whale, the spirit of evil. The battles were said to have caused the earth to tremble and enormous floods to be unleashed from the ocean. Sometimes the Indians would flee the floods in their canoes. But many were killed."

Jonathan waited patiently, sensing Cassie would get to the point. He watched her eyes intently.

"We now know," she continued, "that many of these stories relate to a huge earthquake and tsunami that devastated the coast here in 1700. Some of the tales may predate that. There were other great quakes and tsunamis prior to 1700. The point is, these so-called Native American *legends* turned out to be based on fact, on something that actually happened. So why not the one about buried treasure?" She paused a beat. "Oh, and the part about burying a dead man with the treasure. While Spanish mariners didn't do that, pirates did, and that's something the Indians couldn't have known, so it's unlikely they made it up."

Jonathan shrugged. "But no evidence of treasure has ever been found."

"That's because it isn't here."

Jonathan stared at her. "Say that again."

She pointed at a large boulder embedded in a fern-covered slope adjacent to the trail. "Let's sit a while."

Zurry stood and bounded up the path, slobber flying from his lips. He appeared happy and eager to be on the move again. But when Jonathan and Cassie stopped and seated themselves, Zurry returned, his tail lowered in a sign of disappointment. He plopped down at their feet, raising a small cloud of dust.

"I found one descendent of the Clatsops," Cassie said, "who remembers a story handed down by his grandfather, and probably his grandfather's grandfather, and so on through many generations."

"All orally?"

"Yes. The Clatsop language was Chinook Jargon, or *Chinuk Wawa*, a trade language used by many tribes in the Northwest. Think of it as the Chinook equivalent of pidgin English, which means the tales passed from generation to generation probably lacked detail. Anyhow, here's the essence of what I've been able to glean."

She related to Jonathan the legend of a great battle between Thunderbird and Whale, and the death and destruction it had wreaked upon the coastal tribes when the earth shook and the ocean surged inland.

"And you think that relates to the 1700 quake and tsunami?" Jonathan said. He struggled to remain focused on Cassie's narrative.

Cassie nodded. "As I mentioned earlier, some tales may predate even that event. But here's what's really important. There's an addendum to the most recent version of the legend, that is, if you consider three centuries past *recent*."

Jonathan hung on every word, hoping Cassie would get to the treasure, or whatever might have been buried near here.

"The account goes on to tell of the chest the white men had buried on Neahkahnie Mountain being unearthed by a 'river of mud,' a landslide, I suppose, and being swept down to the beach where it lay half-buried in the sand for several generations. The Indians, of course, refused to go near it, fearful of the 'giant black spirit' that guarded it."

"Always scared of the black dudes," Jonathan said quietly.

"Any spirit of the dead, white or black," Cassie added.

"But the chest, what happened to it? It wasn't just left there. Somebody would have found it by now."

Zurry lifted his head and looked around as if he sensed something. "It was found."

Jonathan ignored Zurry. "When? By whom?" His voice, though he harbored considerable skepticism, betrayed a note of excitement.

"As the Clatsops tell it, or at least *Clatsop*—it's a single-source narrative—after three or four generations, white men from the 'Great River' discovered the chest, dug it up, and carried it northward."

"The Great River? The Columbia?" Jonathan fixed his attention on Cassie.

Zurry stood and took off down the trail at a rapid trot.

"Probably the mouth of the Columbia," Cassie answered. "Anyhow, the Indians, from deep within the forest, watched the white men as they carried the chest away."

"To where?"

"Now we get to the part that's hard to interpret. The white men, traders I guess—"

"If the chest lay undiscovered for three or four generations," interrupted Jonathan, "that means whoever found it could have been from the Lewis and Clark Expedition. The explorers spent the winter of 1805-06 near the mouth of the Columbia, and we know they ventured as far south as here."

"Yes, I suppose they could have been from the Expedition. At any rate, they headed back toward the river with the unearthed box."

Zurry, from somewhere down the trail, erupted into a spate of furious barking. Jonathan stood to get a better view. He caught a flash of black as a bear, not much larger than Zurry, sprinted across the trail and down a steep slope into the safety of a dense cluster of salal and spruce. Jonathan whistled for Zurry who, reluctantly it seemed, returned to his master and Cassie.

"Sorry," Jonathan said, "Zurry gets excited if he thinks I'm being threatened. The bear could care less about us, but Zurry doesn't know that." He petted the now-panting dog who once more lay at his feet, his huge head resting on paws the size of small snow shoes.

"It's good to have someone looking out for you," Cassie said.

"Yes. He's not only my protector but my best friend." He paused. "Go back to your story if you would, Miss Cassie. I'd like to hear the part you said was difficult to interpret."

Cassie adjusted her position on the boulder. "The Clatsops, as I mentioned, watched the white men from a distance. And, according to the tale, the men reburied the chest. But *where* is the part that's obscure to me."

Jonathan stopped stroking Zurry's head and fixed his gaze on Cassie. "What were you told?"

"That the box was buried once more, this time just inland from the stone fins of the great Whale and the towering sea lodge of the warrior Thunderbird, on the side of a short mountain." She shrugged. "I don't know what that means, nor did the storyteller, a young man who's a student at Western Oregon University. He only repeated the tale as he'd heard it from his grandfather."

Jonathan lifted his gaze toward the sky and squeezed his eyes shut, trying to make sense of the description. The topography and geology of the north Oregon coast, where he'd spent so many of his years, flashed through his mind. To Cassie or anyone who hadn't spent much time here, the description wouldn't have made sense, at least in terms of landmarks and their modern names.

His heart fluttered as a clear image formed in his mind. He opened his eyes and turned toward Cassie. "I know where to look," he said, suddenly abandoning his doubts as to the veracity of the tale.

Cassie stood. "Well, I must be on my way. Good luck with your search. I enjoyed meeting you." She started back down the trail, but stopped and turned. "Yes, I think you *do* know where to look." She waved and disappeared into a shadow cast by the forest.

Chapter Six

Cannon Beach

Cannon Beach, Oregon
Tuesday, June 9

JONATHAN STUDIED the towering sea stack, a vertical column of rock formed by erosion that sat just offshore from Cannon Beach. The monolith's iconic shape, that of a giant haystack, gave it its name, Haystack Rock. The tide, at low ebb, allowed Jonathan to scout the perimeter of the rock. Because it rose over two hundred feet above the wash of the Pacific, Jonathan understood why the Clatsops could have envisioned it as the sea lodge of the warrior Thunderbird. The concept of a haystack would have been unfamiliar to Native Americans.

As he and Zurry trudged around the rock in spongy, gray sand, Jonathan studied the tidal pools surrounding its base. Filled with marine life—starfish, crabs, anemones—the tiny ponds sparkled in the morning sun like they might have at the dawn of creation.

Several other early risers, a few bearing clam shovels, reconnoitered the moss- and lichen-flecked rock with Jonathan. A half-dozen seagulls waddled beside them. But not for long. Zurry lit out after them in an explosion of wet sand and officious barking. Overhead, feathery cirrus clouds floated lazily near the stratosphere. Despite the nearly clear skies and brilliant sunshine, the air remained cool. So unlike Middle Georgia where Jonathan had grown up, where a June day would have dawned warm and sticky, and any thought of needing a jacket would have seemed laughable.

Now, however, Jonathan cinched his windbreaker more tightly around his neck, warding off the coastal chill. He walked away from the reach of the tide into the softer sand of the upper beach. He turned and looked back at the rock, the Indians' warrior lodge for the fabled Thunderbird. Beside it stood several smaller rocks, The Needles. Viewed at a distance, one could imagine them as the stone fins of a whale, or *the* great Whale, as the Clatsops had.

So, if this indeed was the spot referenced in Cassie's narrative, the white men would have buried the box just inland from here "on the side of a short mountain." Not a very precise description in terms of distance or direction. Jonathan turned again, this time to gaze inland, looking for a small hill or "mountain."

It wasn't hard to spot. A forested hump of land, probably no higher than Haystack Rock itself, rose immediately behind the beach. Its contemporary designation: Haystack Hill State Park. Jonathan had hiked it once. The path through the evergreens and brambles had been steep, rugged, and unmarked—a place unlikely to draw many visitors. But he recalled being rewarded by a spectacular view of the beach and Haystack Rock once he beat his way to the top of the hillock.

He knew, however, that the men with the chest—traders, trappers, explorers, whoever they were—wouldn't have dragged a heavy wooden box very far up the hill. Nor would they have dug a hole for it on the beach. They would have had enough sense to keep the chest out of reach of storm tides, and therefore buried it a bit inland, probably just beyond the driftwood and small rocks that marked the narrow transition zone between sand and forest.

Except that now, more than forest lay beyond the beach. Civilization had taken over. Roads had been carved through the trees. Homes and cottages lay nestled among the beach pines and salal. Boardwalks led from paved parking areas to the fine-grained sand of the beach. Jonathan shook his head in disappointment. The task of finding any "buried treasure" would be virtually impossible, assuming, and it remained a *huge* assumption, that it *had* been buried here or nearby and hadn't been removed. As far as Jonathan knew, there were no reports, either historical or modern, that a "treasure chest" had ever been discovered near Cannon Beach.

He realized he was piling conjecture upon conjecture and embarking on a pursuit of an apparition at the end of a rainbow. He peered down and addressed Zurry. "And that's the fatal flaw of dreamers, isn't it?"

Zurry wagged his tail.

Even beyond all the speculation lay a mystery. *Why would the men have buried the chest here in the first place?* Jonathan considered that and formulated an answer. *If the men were from the mouth of the Columbia, as seemed likely if they were members of the Lewis and Clark Expedition, or even if they were trappers who came later, getting back to the river would have been a long, difficult slog with heavy cargo.*

Or maybe whoever found the box didn't want anyone else to know. So why not stick it in the ground here, near easily recognizable landmarks, and hope to get back to it someday? Except—conjecture again—*they didn't. The Corps of Discovery, the Expedition, had pulled out in 1806 after wintering over. The fur trade blossomed a few years after that, but it was rough business in primitive country, and who knows what the life span of a trapper or trader might have been.*

Zurry remained by Jonathan's side. Jonathan lowered his hand to Zurry's head and ruffled his fur. "Looks pretty hopeless, doesn't it, old boy?" The dog woofed softly, perhaps agreeing with his master. "Well, if nothing else, I'm a determined son of a bitch." *Obsessed, my friends would say.* Zurry woofed again.

Jonathan knew that his buddies, the few he had, and detractors, too, considered him three sacks short of a full load. And maybe he was. He'd been shot up pretty bad as a Marine Corps rifleman in 'Nam. But being in the Marines had been a damn sight better than the existence he'd come from, and a whole lot better than where he would have ended up had he stayed in the South.

He'd been one of seven kids growing up in a tin-roof shotgun shack in the piney woods of Georgia where his father had carved out a tiny subsistence peanut farm. Jonathan, his siblings, and his pop had labored from before sunup to after sunset day after miserable day in an attempt to make ends meet. But they never did.

Schooling—segregated, of course—in a run-down, three-room, termite-riddled building had been hit and miss. Mostly "miss" because of the vast amount of time spent working the fields.

As soon as Jonathan had turned seventeen, he'd hightailed it to Macon and joined the military. "Best decision I ever made," he said to Zurry, who cocked his head at him. "That's how I got here. Ended up at Fort Lewis and fell in love with the Northwest. Of course, being a black man here I was really a fish out of water, but folks pretty much let me be."

He knelt in front of Zurry. "I know we live in kind of a dump, but maybe I can remedy that someday." He stood and moved his gaze blankly over the landscape. He knew it would come back to him, but for the moment, the reason for his being here, on this beach, had abandoned him. Buying time in an attempt to get refocused, he found a piece of driftwood among the scattered tangles of seaweed and orphaned sand dollars that dotted the water's edge. He picked up the stick and hurled it. "Get it," he yelled, and Zurry was off like a great, furry whippet.

He trotted back with the quarry in his mouth. He dropped it at Jonathan's feet. Jonathan stared at it, a smooth, bone-white piece of wood. He looked at the residences lining the edge of the beach. The legend came back to him. A treasure chest. A black man buried with it. Only a skeleton now.

"We'll get started tomorrow, Zurry. Off to the land of Oz." He picked up the stick and tossed it again. "Get it, boy!"

HE AND ZURRY spent the next week in a futile search for the buried chest. Jonathan's initial approach took him up and down South Hemlock Street, the main drag running south from the center of boutiquey Cannon Beach. He fully understood he'd likely embarked on a fool's errand. That if there were treasure buried in the vicinity, it was a good bet it might now rest beneath a road, the foundation of a home, or a parking lot.

After he'd explored South Hemlock to no avail, he ventured into side streets, trying to appear casual as he swung his two-box, pro-style metal detector back and forth along the shoulders of the roads. He'd set the discriminator and sensitivity of the detector at optimum levels in hopes of locating caches well below the surface, while at the same time eliminating pings on such things as tin cans, construction nails, and scrap metal.

Over an old Marine fatigue cap, he wore expensive, padded head-phones to be better able to concentrate on the few returns his detector broadcast. The headphones blocked ambient noise and allowed him to hear the often whispery signals returned from objects far below the surface.

On his back he'd strapped a long-handled digger—a T-handled, serrated shovel over a yard in length—and a small pack. The pack held a short-handled digger by Lesche that was basically a specialized trowel, a few energy bars, and water for both him and Zurry. Zurry strolled beside him, occasionally nudging Jonathan's hip to warn of approaching automobiles.

Jonathan, wishing to avoid the appearance of trespassing, found it virtually impossible to explore the yards of the homes and cabins that fronted the streets. Once in a great while, however, if he was certain nobody was around, he'd step off the road and make a couple of quick passes with the metal detector over someone's front yard. He never got any hits.

On Saturday, a Cannon Beach police vehicle, a sporty-looking white SUV with a black brush guard over its front grill, pulled up beside Jonathan.

The officer driving the SUV didn't get out. He merely rolled down his window. "How's hunting?"

Jonathan pulled off his headphones. "Pardon?"

"Are you finding anything?"

"Junk."

"Looking for anything specific?"

"Just targets of opportunity." Jonathan knew a local resident, or residents, had probably called 911. Not surprising. Here he was, a black man wandering the streets of a white neighborhood with homes running upward to a million bucks. Cause for wariness.

The officer nodded at the metal detector. "Pretty fancy rig for street work. Mainly see those on the beach."

"I've done a lot of exploring on Neahkahnie Mountain."

Zurry padded over to the SUV and stuck his head through the open window. The cop petted him. "Magnificent animal."

"His name's Zurry."

"He accompanies you when you're on Neahkahnie?"

"He does."

The cop, a youngish man with a square jaw and a buzz cut studied Jonathan and Zurry for a moment. A glint of recognition flickered in his eyes. "You're the guy they call Neahkahnie Johnny?"

Jonathan nodded.

The officer gestured at the surrounding homes. "Just some nervous neighbors, you understand."

"I'm familiar with the drill."

"Sorry. Anyhow, are you really hunting for targets of opportunity or something else?" The cop furrowed his brow. Circumspection.

Jonathan shrugged. "Let's just say there might be a little more to the old legend than first thought."

The officer smiled. "Well, you'd better keep that to yourself or this place will be overrun with treasure hunters before you know it. Our little secret, okay?"

"Obliged." Jonathan tipped his cap and the cop drove off.

Jonathan spent the remainder of the weekend working the side streets near the base of Haystack Hill, but turned up nothing.

HALFWAY THROUGH the second week of his search, on a bleak, drizzly morning, Jonathan worked his way into a shallow swale adjacent to the beach. He thrashed through blackberry bushes, bracken fern, and wild grass, his hands protected by heavy-duty contractor gloves. He swung the detector from side to side, at least as much as the underbrush and a scattering of gnarly pines would allow. As he approached the ocean side of the hollow, he received a strong signal.

"Whoa." He marked the spot with a sturdy twig and ripped off his headphones. The soft thunder of the Pacific surf filled his ears. But was it only the surf? His heart rate accelerated. He drew a deep breath to steady himself, then unslung the long-handled digger and removed his backpack.

"It's not too deep, whatever it is," he said to Zurry. The dog peered at the twig stuck in the ground, perhaps wondering if his master would throw it for him to retrieve.

Instead, Jonathan plucked it from the damp soil and, using the digging tool, went to work in the spot he'd removed it from. It didn't take long before the shovel registered a solid thunk. Jonathan slowed his efforts and carefully scooped chunks of earth away from the top of whatever he'd hit. His heart continued to hammer in quickstep time.

Finally, he knelt and, using his hands, brushed the remaining loose dirt away from his discovery. Gradually, it came into a view. Not large. Maybe the size of a small toolbox with a carrying handle on top. Metal, probably aluminum. Not a material that would have been used in the 17th Century. His heart rate decelerated. He pulled the object from the ground.

"Shit." He held it up for Zurry to see. "It's a tackle box." He opened it, but there were no surprises inside. Only lead weights, shiny lures, and thin fishing leader. He replaced the box in the hole.

He stood and brushed dirt and mud from his clothes, cleaned the digging tool, then shouldered it and the backpack. Disgusted with the futility of his search, he inhaled deeply, and followed it with a long, slow exhalation. "Come on, Zurry," he said, "let's call it a day."

They walked back to Jonathan's car, an old Pontiac beater, scarred, dented, and rusted, with over three hundred thousand miles on it. Jonathan threw his pack into the trunk, opened the back door for Zurry, and plopped into the driver's seat that threatened to swallow him like quicksand.

He turned to Zurry. "What say we take a break for a bit. I need to rethink my whole approach to this. You know, come up with a real plan and quit wandering around just hoping to get lucky." Zurry, already sound asleep on the seat, didn't respond.

"All right, I'm glad you agree." He cranked the engine. It sputtered and coughed then settled into a raspy purr. "I'll figure out a better scheme. We'll return on the Fourth of July weekend. Most people will be off attending parades or festivals then, so we should be able to poke around in yards without ruffling feathers."

He slipped the Pontiac into gear and headed back to Manzanita.

Chapter Seven

Laneda Avenue

Manzanita, Oregon
Sunday, June 28

IN THE PREDAWN darkness, Rob sat in an Adirondack chair on the deck of the family's beach house and stared out at an ocean he couldn't yet see, only hear. The gentle wash of the surf seemed at once both soothing and ominous, like the Grim Reaper speaking in a calming tone while reaching behind his back for a razor-edged scythe.

Rob, in sweatshirt and jeans, had been up for almost two hours, unable to sleep, terrified by the vivid nightmare that had awakened him. It had returned after an absence of almost a month. He reached for a mug of coffee that sat on a table beside him, but his hand trembled uncontrollably and he found himself unable to grasp the cup. No matter. The coffee had likely cooled to an undrinkable level anyhow. He rested his hand in his lap and leaned back in the chair. His eyes closed involuntarily, but he snapped them open, forcing himself to remain alert, fearful of being dragged back into the violence and chaos of the dream world from which he had escaped.

Dream world? It had been more than that, more than a dream. It had been an alternate reality, too palpable, too emotional, too real to have been something manufactured by his subconscious mind. *But if not that, what? What was its genesis? What did it mean? Am I going crazy, or have I been led to the banks of a Rubicon on whose opposite shore awaits enormous danger?*

He drew a long, deep breath, inhaling the salty coolness of the Pacific air, its freshness acting to calm his thoughts. The sigh of decaying combers sliding up the beach, stalling, then coasting back into the surf offered a tranquil counterpoint to the fears that had surrounded him and now launched jabbing attacks.

The click and thunk of the slider to the deck opening and shutting interrupted the fleeting peace he'd found. He turned. Deborah, still in her pajamas, walked toward him.

"You had that nightmare again, didn't you?" she said.

He didn't answer.

"Have you called Lewis yet?" she asked. "You said you would. You said you needed to talk to somebody." Concern threaded her voice.

"We just got here." They'd come from Portland yesterday, he and Tim flying the Cessna into Nehalem Bay State Airport, a short airstrip just south of Manzanita, and Deborah and his daughter Maria driving down in the Range Rover.

"So call him this morning."

"It's Sunday. He sleeps in."

"He's retired. He'll be up with sun."

"What time is it?"

"Five thirty, give or take." Deborah stepped back into the house and flipped on the deck spotlights. A raccoon broke cover from beneath the deck and scuttled into a thick knot of wild huckleberry bushes between the house and a small bluff overlooking the beach.

"I'll call him after breakfast," Jonathan said. "The sun isn't even up yet."

"I'll fix you some eggs."

"Wait," he said, standing.

Deborah fixed her gaze on him.

"I think you and Maria should go home before the Fourth."

Deborah waited, not saying anything.

Rob stared past her. "I think something bad is going to happen."

She smiled. "I'll get the eggs started. You'll feel better after you get something in your stomach."

"You aren't taking me seriously?"

"You're having nightmares. You're overworked. Stressed out." She paused. "Obsessed with this earthquake-tsunami bullshit."

"It's not bullshit." But his own words failed to convince him. He retreated into the corner of his mind that held out hope he was merely harboring some sort of deep anxiety reaction to his life's work.

Deborah stepped toward him, her palm extended in a conciliatory gesture. "I'm sorry. I know it's not bullshit. Let's go over the dream again."

He shook his head. "I need to talk with Lewis first."

SHACK MCCREADY strolled along Manzanita's main street, Laneda Avenue. He had to admit, the tiny town possessed a certain Spartan, weather-beaten appeal. It seemed to exude a laid-back stolidness as though trumpeting the fact it had avoided the commercial excesses of some of the more popular seaside towns in the Southeast, such as Myrtle Beach in South Carolina or Florida's Panama City Beach. At the same time, it clearly lacked the more sophisticated, high-end appeal offered by locales like St. Simons Island, Georgia, or Highlands, North Carolina.

Shack guessed Manzanita might be the kind of place people go to "get away from it all," but maybe not get lost. Had Alex done that?

He continued his stroll along Laneda. The sidewalks, while busy, weren't crowded enough to require him to elbow his way through throngs of people. Since he knew the town had a permanent population of only a few hundred, he decided most of the foot traffic had to be visitors. Ice cream cones and hot dogs appeared popular with them, as were bicycles, and on the beach, kites. In the distance, a half-dozen kites dipped and darted in a busy breeze near the breaking surf.

Several blocks up from the beach, Shack reached a graying, shake-sided building with a large picture window. On the window, in large, gold letters: ALEXIS WILLIAMSON, ATTORNEY-AT-LAW. He stopped. Knowing it was Sunday, he assumed her office would be empty. He cupped his hands on either side of his face and peered through the glass. It looked, he had to admit, like any other lawyer's office with shelves of law books, framed certificates, a large desk, and leather chairs. It appeared cozy rather than intimidating. Stepping back from the window, he allowed his thoughts to drift away on a raft of nostalgia, to an afternoon on another beach in another time.

He and Alex had been lazing in the sun on the warm sands of a military beach in Dam Neck, Virginia. Their conversation had turned to what their life would be like after marriage. One thing she wanted, she stated quite firmly, was a beach house. Her comment struck terror deep into Shack's psyche. Suddenly, all he could envision was a tiny, white-washed seaside cottage with a picket fence and screaming, snotty-nosed kids swarming around a minivan parked in the driveway. It wasn't where he wanted his life to go, wasn't an image with which he could identify.

Had that been the moment, the catalyst that triggered his decision for a no-notice bailout on Alex? With the great clarity of hindsight, he understood what an immature, chicken-shit action it had been. At the time, however, it had seemed only like "the great escape" to him.

He continued his walk down Laneda and tilted his face up to catch the sunshine.

"Give me a chance to atone," he whispered, though he didn't really know to whom he directed the appeal.

ROB, AFTER SCHEDULING a visit with his friend Lewis, stepped into his house a little after four p.m. The home sat several blocks back from the ocean in a copse of beach pines and Sitka spruce. Its interior, cluttered but neat, seemed dimly lit with the late afternoon sun forced not only to beat through the stand of evergreens, but windows thick with the residue of a hundred winter storms.

In the living room, a threadbare sofa and several semi-tattered easy chairs sat in a haphazard formation around a coffee table hewn from Western red cedar. Lewis, tall and lanky, wore a thin cardigan deserving of several Purple Hearts. He moved in a slightly bent-over fashion that made him look somewhat like a scarecrow walking against a stiff wind. He set a bottle of Jim Beam and two glasses on the table, then sank into a chair and gestured for Rob to sit, too.

Lewis, with the usual impish twinkle in his green eyes, pointed at the bottle. "Two fingers or three?"

Rob sat in a chair opposite Lewis. "Better make it three."

Lewis nodded and poured.

They picked up their glasses. "Bless the pagans," Lewis said, and they both drank.

Lewis, with his glass still in hand, pointed at Rob's. "You've still got two fingers left."

"Don't worry, I'll take care of it."

"Okay," Lewis said, "tell me about these dreams you've been having."

"Nightmares," Rob corrected. "They started back in March, after Tim and I visited the Ghost Forest . . . I've told you about that, right?"

Lewis nodded.

"In late May, the dreams stopped. Then last night they . . . it . . . returned, but worse."

"How do you mean, worse?"

Rob took a sip of Beam, then spoke. "It was more vivid than those past. More real. Like I was part of it. I had no sense I was dreaming, no sense of disconnectedness, no feeling of being outside looking in." He looked directly into his friend's eyes. "I was there, Lewis. I swear to God, I was there."

"I believe you. But let's start with the earlier dreams, the earlier nightmares. Tell me about those."

Rob spent the next twenty minutes describing them in as much detail as he could recall. Lewis took notes, occasionally wetting his lips with the bourbon.

After Rob had finished, Lewis sat in silence, studying his notes. Rob waited. Lewis jotted some additional items with a pencil, then said, "Now tell me about last night's nightmare. Take your time." He sat back in his chair.

Rob took another swallow of his Jim Beam, then began. "It's the Fourth of July. I'm walking along Laneda with Deb and Tim and Maria."

Lewis interrupted. "How did you know it's the Fourth?"

"There's red, white, and blue bunting on all the stores and shops. A banner draped across Laneda is puffed out in the wind beneath an overcast. I can read its lettering clearly. It's advertising the parade. The street is filled with people, bundled up, waiting for it. I can hear it in the distance, at least the bagpipes and drums."

Lewis nodded and wrote something on his pad. "Okay, go on."

"It's funny, though. The music, the pipers, seem to be getting farther away, their notes floating off on the wind." Rob chuckled, silently, to himself. "I guess dogs don't like bagpipes. Several are tugging at their leashes, tails tucked between their legs, trying to get away."

"Maybe they don't like crowds," Lewis offered.

Rob shrugged. "Deb and I stop to get some coffee to go. The kids continue walking up Laneda. Abruptly, there's a strange silence. I can't hear the pipers any longer. Even the wash of the surf seems to have diminished. Suddenly, several small earth tremors ripple through town, each shake growing in intensity. Within a matter of seconds, they morph into huge undulations, up and down, brutal sinusoidal waves."

Lewis interrupted again. "You mean like ocean swells?"

"Yes. Huge ones. I see fear in the eyes of the people near me. The ground they've always thought of as solid, stable, and permanent, the bedrock of their physical existence, has become nothing more than quivering Jell-O." He reached for his bourbon again, then thought better of it.

"The coffee Deb and I have slops out of our cups. Deb loses her balance and staggers against the side of a building. I pull her erect and we start to run up Laneda, looking for Tim and Maria. But it's hard to remain upright. It's like trying to sprint on a trampoline."

"You're frightened?" Lewis asked.

"Strangely not. I know what's coming. I just want to get my family to safety."

"What's happening around you? What are other people doing?"

"Milling around. Some look stunned. Others seem to be staring at me."

"Yes?"

Rob toyed with the glass on the table, sending the bourbon into a cyclonic swirl. "It's weird. I'm wondering why they aren't running, trying to get to higher ground. The shockwaves keep coming. A few buildings crack and slump, then more and more. Utility poles topple. Still, many people appear frozen in place. Instead of fleeing, they cluster around me, blocking my path. I see Tim and Maria ahead of me. I wave. They wave back, then point behind me. I turn, look back down Laneda. The water is coming. A surge of ocean sweeping inland, growing deeper and deeper, popping buildings and homes from their foundations, picking up cars and trucks as if they were bathtub toys." Rob stopped talking, gripped the glass, tipped it to his lips and drained it.

"Then?" Lewis asked.

"Then I knew we were going to die." Rob barely got the words out, his chest tight with emotion.

Lewis waited for him to continue.

"That was it," Rob said. "Next thing I remember, I'm sitting up in bed, sweating, shaking, drained. It wasn't like I'd awakened from a dream, though. More like I'd escaped from a terrifying reality into the safety of another."

Lewis sat silently, tapping his pencil on the table. He appeared lost in thought, as if trying to digest and analyze what he'd heard.

Rob fixed his gaze on him. "What the hell is going on, Lewis?" he asked, his voice soft and raspy. "This is just some sort of stress reaction to my work, right? I'm not going crazy, am I?"

"No." Lewis stood and walked to a window. He pulled its curtains open to allow more light into the room. He returned to his chair and stood next to it. "I'll tell you one more thing."

"Yes?"

"You aren't having dreams."

Rob snapped his head up, stunned by the words, and stared at Lewis.

Chapter Eight

Visions

Manzanita
Sunday, June 28

ROB SLID HIS EMPTY glass toward Lewis. "I think I need a refill."

"Maybe Starbucks instead of Beam," Lewis said. He disappeared into the kitchen.

"So, if I'm not having dreams," Rob called after him, "what am I having? You trying to tell me nightmares aren't dreams?"

"No." The hiss of a Keurig issued from the kitchen.

"What? I'm nuts then?"

"No. I already told you that. Whaddaya want in your coffee?"

"Black's fine."

Moments later Lewis returned to the living room with two mugs of coffee. He handed one to Rob and kept the other. "Let me tell you why I think you aren't having dreams," he said.

Rob set his mug on the coffee table, scooted forward in his chair, and leaned toward Lewis.

Lewis blew on his coffee, then took a cautious sip. "Hot," he exclaimed. He placed the mug on the table next to Rob's, then sat back in his chair. "There are lots of theories about dreams—what causes them, what they mean, what's the neurobiology behind them—but the modern view is that they're connected to the unconscious mind.

"In contrast, the ancient Hebrews believed dreams were the voice of God alone. Early Christians mostly shared those beliefs, some still do, and considered dreams as being of a supernatural character. The Old Testament includes many stories of dreams serving as divine inspiration or prophesy, like Pharaoh's dream that Joseph interpreted, or Nebuchadnezzar's that Daniel decoded."

Rob picked up his mug, hovered his lips over it, then placed it back on the table. "Ancient history. What about the 21st Century?"

"Fair question. The modern prevailing hypotheses link dreams to our brain, not to God. They seem to be more post-cognitive than precognitive."

"Translation, please."

"We dream about things past, not something that might happen in the future. The concerns, anxieties, frustrations, angers—all of the pressures that gang up on us in everyday life—can be the catalysts for our dreams. But the images and vignettes that visit us in our sleep are never straightforward or clear. They may be bizarre, surreal, or metaphorical. More often than not we don't have a clue what they mean."

"Yea, verily," Rob said. "Being chased by monsters. Forgetting my pants in public. Getting lost in familiar locations."

Lewis swilled some coffee, raised an eyebrow, and looked askance at Rob. "Really? No pants? Maybe we should explore this further, Rob. I don't want you slipping any deeper into sexual deviancy." He chuckled. His emerald eyes danced in ribald merriment.

Rob allowed Lewis his moment—perhaps his friend had been a widower too long, over seven years— then said, "This is all very interesting, but you said I wasn't having dreams."

"Exactly. The point I'm driving at is that there's nothing metaphorical, nothing puzzling, nothing phantasmagorical about what's been terrorizing you in your sleep."

"No?"

"It's pretty damn straightforward. It's Cascadia letting go in a full-rip megaquake and unleashing a devastating tsunami. There's nothing post-cognitive about that. You're seeing the future, Rob." He paused, then said quite firmly, "It's a *vision*, not a dream."

A tightness coiled around Rob's chest. Lewis's proclamation wasn't what he wanted to hear. He clutched the arms of his chair in a fierce grip and inhaled deeply to steady his breathing. He tipped his head back and gazed at the ceiling. "Jesus, Rev, you told me I wasn't going loopy. Visions?" His voice rose. "That's the kind of shit that gets you stuffed into a rubber room."

Lewis stood and walked to him. He rested a hand on his shoulder. "No, it isn't. Calm down. We'll work through this."

"We? I'm the one flying over the cuckoo's nest. Or do you think God is my copilot?"

"That's the real quandary, isn't it? 'The Lord spoke to me,' are the words of the insane and prophets of God. So which are you? Looney

Tunes or the Lord's Lieutenant?" Lewis retreated to his chair.

Rob's respiration rate slowed, and he fastened his gaze on Lewis. "*You* told me you didn't think I was off my rocker."

Lewis shook his head. "Don't pay any attention to me. What do *you* think?"

Rob remained silent, pondering the ramifications of his response.

"Come on," Lewis said, "there's no right or wrong answer here."

"Oh, I think there is," Rob said. He leaned forward, his elbows on his knees, his hands grasping one another. "I just don't know which is which."

Lewis waited, not moving or uttering a sound.

Rob took a sip of coffee, leaned back embracing the warmth of the mug, and closed his eyes. "I don't think I've punched my ticket for the asylum yet, but I don't like where that leaves me."

Lewis adjusted the sleeve of his tattered cardigan and cleared his throat. "There's a school of thought," he said, his voice low, "that believes consciousness may be as much a fundamental property of matter as such things as mass, spin, and charge—"

"Whoa," Rob interrupted, "where are you—"

"Hear me out," Lewis said, raising a hand to signal Rob to give him a chance to finish. "I'm not going to lead you down a metaphysical rabbit hole. I just want you to consider something."

Rob shrugged and nodded.

"Spirituality is essentially a subjective experience," Lewis continued. "It's basically a polar opposite to the scientific method that we, especially scientists such as yourself, are so enamored with. I'm not saying that's good or bad, I'm just setting a stage."

"Go on."

"Okay. If you can accept there might be some validity to the notion that a universal consciousness exists, I would argue that such a phenomenon could complement what hard science tells us about the world. And here's my key point: It might not be clergy or theologians who are best attuned to such an eventuality. It more likely would be artists, musicians, and scientists who are tuned in to this, well, let's call it 'virtual reality.'"

"You lost me, Rev."

"Sorry. I'll try to sum it up in a simple sentence or two. What I'm getting at is that it may be people like yourself, with a foot in religion and a foot in science, who experience dreams with a vision of the future. That's because your mind envisions the past, present, and future as a single, timeless eternity."

"Sure I can't have another shot of Beam?" Rob asked.

"No. So here's the wrap. You aren't bat-shit crazy and you aren't an oracle of the Lord."

"So where does that leave me?"

"That really is the bigger question, isn't it?" Lewis stood and began pacing. "It leaves you, really, in an untenable position."

Rob rolled his eyes. "I know that. That's why I'm here." His gaze followed Lewis as he stalked around the room.

Lewis remained silent.

Growing impatient, Rob asked, "What would you do?"

Lewis stopped pacing, rested his hands on the back of his chair, and stood behind it. "Let's go for a walk."

They stepped outside into a cool swirling wind and summer sunshine battling with fragmented stratus clouds. They moved up Manzanita Avenue, a street running parallel to Laneda. Children on bicycles coasted past them. Families carrying picnic baskets and blankets trudged along the shoulders of the road, presumably heading back to their vehicles or rental homes after a day on the beach.

Side by side, Rob matched Lewis's long, shambling strides.

"I can't really tell you what to do," Lewis said. "It's a dilemma unique to you, your background, your beliefs, your values."

"I know," Rob responded, his voice subdued. "There are no easy answers, nothing in black and white."

Lewis slowed his pace. "The problem is, there are just too damn many factors involved, and there's too much subjectivity, all tied directly to you."

Rob kicked a pine cone along the street. He waited for Lewis to continue, hoping he had more to bring to the table than just how complex the situation was.

"Look," Lewis said, after holding his thoughts for some time, "if I told you to go public with your—let's call it a premonition—and everything goes south, then I've ruined your reputation and career. On the other hand, if I advise you to clam up, and a megaquake and tsunami slam the coast, then we'd both live out our days knowing we could have saved hundreds, maybe thousands of lives, but didn't act."

"We'd feel like Noah would have if he hadn't built the ark."

"I can't help but think Noah was more certain of his course," Lewis mumbled. "I think he had a hotline to God, or vice versa." He turned his head toward Rob and spoke with more authority. "Anyhow,

I think I *can* bring some perspective to your dilemma."

A dune buggy clattered by them. One of its occupants, a sunburned young man, called out to Lewis. "Hey, Rev, wanna take a ride on the beach?"

Lewis smiled and waved him off, then addressed Rob. "I think in the end, it boils down to a cost-benefit analysis."

"I've done a few of those for my business."

"This one's different, though. The stakes are human, not monetary."

Rob stuffed his hands into the back pockets of his jeans and kept walking, head down, listening intently to Lewis.

"Let's assume you decide to remain silent, and no earthquake occurs. You've made a good decision. Your reputation, and the Pacific Northwest, remain intact. There is no cost.

"But what if the 'Big One' hits and the Oregon Coast has its 'Banda Aceh Moment'? The cost is horrendous, in terms of lives lost, in terms of what the impact is on you, knowing if you'd had the guts to speak up, many people could have been saved."

"Thanks for laying that on me, Lewis."

"I'm just defining the grid here. Nothing more. So let's consider your other option: going public, speaking up. If you do, and nothing happens, the cost is also horrendous, but only to you. You become an object of scorn and ridicule, the Chicken Little of the geological world. Your reputation is in the toilet and so is your business. Basically, you're ruined."

Instead of responding, Rob merely drew a deep breath. Fresh sea air. Sunshine. Life.

"Finally," Lewis said, "if you go public with your concerns, and your visions prove prophetic, you're a hero. Not everyone will believe you, of course, maybe very few. But you will have at least triggered awareness in the back alleys of people's minds. They'll have escape options and contingency plans within reach whether they acknowledge it or not. Others will actually prepare for the disaster by staying away from the coast or by taking protective actions and laying in emergency supplies. Sure, there will still be deaths, but not to the extent there would have been had you failed to speak out. So there's a reduced cost in terms of fatalities, and maybe a positive return for you."

They neared Highway 101 at the upper end of the street. The two men halted. Rob turned to Lewis. "But everything hinges on the validity of my vision."

"Yes, it does. Unfortunately, that's something we won't know until after the fact."

Rob extended his hand. "Thank you, Lewis. I appreciate your insights. I really do."

Lewis accepted the proffered hand and gripped it firmly. "I wish I could help more. I know you're bearing a heavy load."

"I need to talk with Deb."

"One thing," Lewis said.

"Yes?"

"If you decide to go public, whatever you do, don't say God has given you a revelation. That would mark you as a Looney Tunes nut job right out of the starting gate."

Chapter Nine

A Prophet in His Own Land

Manzanita
Monday, June 29

IN THE MANZANITA Community Center, Rob sat adjacent to the podium preparing to talk at a hastily called press conference. He'd made his decision to "go public" late the previous day. As suggested by Lewis, he'd weighed the costs and benefits of speaking out, and then discussed them with Deb.

The back and forth with Deb hadn't gone well. She'd pointed out the general public and media would not understand the concepts that had factored into his decision, abstractions such as "universal consciousness" and "virtual reality."

"They aren't going to get it," she'd said, her voice firm. "They won't give a shit about the philosophical and psychoanalytical nuances of how you reached your conclusion. All they're going to hear is that an expert in the field believes a big quake and tsunami are going to hit on the Fourth of July. They aren't going to give a damn about the uncertainties involved, or the doubts you wrestled with."

"So you're saying what?"

"Keep it low key and close-hold. Don't go public. Talk to emergency managers, police, mayors, and maybe that Coastal Threats Expert guy."

"Pete Cameron?"

"Yeah. Let the decision makers make the call about how to handle your concerns. If you broadcast your *visions*,"—she hit the word hard—"and they don't materialize, you'll be pilloried in the media. Please, please, please don't risk everything you've worked so hard to achieve."

He'd remained silent for a long while, reanalyzing, reevaluating, and reweighing the consequences of acting or not acting on his vision, or whatever it had been. Finally, he'd reached for Deborah's hand and grasped it.

"Your idea isn't bad," he'd said softly, "but, if I'm right,"—and he knew he'd never be sure if he was or wasn't until it was too late—"there's not enough time left for the 'decision makers,' as you call them, to act. Bureaucracies, while they may mean well, function in environments filled with sludge and molasses wrapped in red duct tape. I need to launch a rocket."

Deb had glared at him, yanked her hand from his, and stalked from the room.

Now he surveyed the people filing into the community center and noted Deborah's absence. He also noted, save for a small station from Coos Bay, there were no TV cameras present. Nor did there seem to be any representation from the large daily newspapers in the state such as *The Oregonian* or *Register-Guard*.

A reporter he knew from the *Daily Astorian* had seated herself in the front row, but the only other news hounds in the room seemed to be from the small weekly and biweekly presses that dotted the coast. Obviously, the short lead time for the conference had not allowed the bigger media outlets, such as those in Seattle and Portland, to dispatch correspondents. Or maybe they just weren't interested. Rob knew their thinking could well have run along the lines of *It's just another whacko announcing the End Times.*

The vast majority of attendees appeared to be emergency managers, police, and municipal officials, mainly from towns along the North Coast. They included the city manager of Manzanita, a beer-bellied, aging autocrat who crashed down in a chair and glowered at Rob.

Pete Cameron, the Coastal Threats Expert, entered the room, gave Rob a quizzical what-the-fuck look, and seated himself next to the newspaperwoman from Astoria. They apparently knew each other. The lady took out an iPad and began taking notes as Pete whispered to her.

As Rob continued to wait for the conference to begin, the woman named Cassie, whom he and his son had met in the Ghost Forest several months ago, slipped into the community center. She stood against a rear wall and nodded almost imperceptibly at Rob.

The room appeared about three-quarters full as Lewis stood to introduce Rob. He concluded his introduction with a plea. "I ask that you listen to Dr. Elwood with an open mind. What he's about to tell you is in no way to be construed as a warning with a scientific basis.

Absolutely not." Lewis paused, and allowed the words to hover over the audience.

After a moment, he continued. "What he's going to present, as you will hear, is something that borders on being . . . well, metaphysical, and not based on hard science. But, we, he and I, after long consideration, decided it was important enough to shine a public spotlight on. If you'll listen carefully and objectively, I believe you'll understand the doctor's concerns, and mine, and thus be able to report or act on them as you see fit. Each of you will have to weigh the pros and cons of action or inaction."

Pete Cameron, the Threats Expert, stood. "If Dr. Elwood's concerns are not based on science, then isn't this press conference an exercise in futility? How can you expect anyone to develop a responsible initiative to something that's apparently been stirred up with 'eye of newt and toe of frog'?"

Rob glared at Pete, a little fireplug of a man who seemed constantly in motion, perhaps burning off nervous energy. He'd counted on Pete, with whom he had a casual, professionally based friendship, as an ally. After all, they both harbored apprehensions about the same thing: coastal preparedness for earthquakes and tsunamis. *But now? Here I am, taxiing for takeoff and I've already got engine trouble.*

Lewis took a step toward Pete and went on the offensive. "Thanks for keeping an open mind, Dr. Cameron." The phrase, wrapped in sarcasm, came out like a lance hurled by a white knight. "I'm sure others here are impressed with your professional credentials and reverence for science. Perhaps your concerns will turn out to have merit, but I respectfully request you curb your acerbic prejudgment and allow Dr. Elwood a fair hearing."

Although Lewis towered over Pete like a gangly scarecrow, Pete held his ground. "I don't think—"

Lewis interrupted. "Maybe that's the problem, sir."

To the accompaniment of scattered snickers and muffled laughs, Pete sat and didn't attempt another retort. But the look on his face told Rob that Lewis's jibe had scored a hit and that he wouldn't be getting any support from Pete.

Rob walked to the podium and began his presentation. As he talked, rehashing and condensing what he and Lewis had discussed the previous day, he watched the facial expressions of those in the audience. He realized then, Deborah had been right. They weren't getting it. They obviously understood his fear regarding the immanency of a catastrophic event, but they weren't buying into the genesis of his apprehensiveness.

He finished his explanation in about twenty-five minutes and then, with growing trepidation, asked for questions.

Pete Cameron went first. "With all due respect, Dr. Elwood, and I've known and respected you for quite some time, what you've presented isn't even pseudoscience, it's witchcraft. There isn't one iota of evidence, physical or statistical, that Cascadia is more likely to rupture on the Fourth of July than on any other date."

Rob returned fire. "That's my point, Pete. But maybe you were too busy formulating your own prejudged negative response to catch it. I said, pay attention now, there is no scientific way to predict earthquakes. So maybe we have to look at other options when it comes to divining the future in the discipline of seismology. Maybe we shouldn't be afraid of dipping our toe into the waters of the metaphysical."

"Dipping our toe?" Pete snapped. "Pardon my French, but bullshit. You just dove in headfirst and buck naked."

A few chuckles floated through the room.

Rob rolled his eyes. "Maybe so. But to follow up on your metaphor, it was a plunge I felt I had to take. The consequences, if I didn't speak out and a full-rip nine hit followed by a forty-foot surge, seemed more than I could accept."

Pete began pacing back and forth in front of the first row of chairs. "God, you just don't get it, do you? You just don't understand the irreparable harm you'll do when your forecast—"

"It's not a forecast."

"Okay, okay. It's not a forecast, it's a scenario. Does that satisfy your silly semantics?"

Rob nodded and smiled. At the same time, he pictured dragging Pete behind a commercial trawler through Tillamook Bay.

"All right," Pete continued, smirking. "Do you understand the immense damage you'll do when your scenario busts? Not only to your reputation and career, but to all the work that's been done in attempting to educate the public regarding earthquake and tsunami preparedness?

"When the holiday comes and goes and there is no disaster, the response of anyone who bought into your *scenario*"—the word came out the vocal equivalent of a sneer—"will be, 'These guys are smoking dope. Why should we ever listen to them again?'"

Rob didn't believe that necessarily would be the case, but he had no evidence it wouldn't. "You're presupposing failure," he countered. A weak response. The image of Pete and Tillamook Bay returned. He wondered how long a guy would survive being keelhauled by a fishing boat.

"Of course I am." Pete pivoted to face the assemblage. "I don't want anyone in this room to think I'm endorsing Dr. Elwood's vision. I'm not. Maybe he's not a charlatan, or maybe he is, I don't know, but he is grievously misguided, and I don't want him misguiding you." He spread both arms in front of him like a preacher blessing a congregation.

An emergency manager whom Rob recognized from an adjacent county stood and addressed a question to Pete. "Is there any way to supplement Dr. Elwood's vision with real science? I mean, I've heard that an earthquake prediction system is in the works."

"There is no proven method of predicting when and where an earthquake will strike," Pete answered. He seemed to relish taking over the stage from Rob. "What you may have heard about is an early warning system that's being tested by the Pacific Northwest Seismic Network. Understand it doesn't *predict* quakes, it only triggers a warning after one is detected.

"The system is not operational, and even if and when it is, which is probably a year or two down the road, it would provide alerts with only small lead times."

"How small?" someone in back asked.

"Worst case for Cascadia, maybe thirty seconds. Best case, up to four minutes."

A murmur of disappointment rippled through the community center.

An elderly man seated near the edge of the crowd stood. "Hold on here. I've lived on the North Coast most of my life. We've had tsunami warnings before and they always were put out in plenty of time, like hours ahead of the wave, not that they ever amounted to much. I don't get it. What's so different now?"

"The difference," Rob said, "is that the tsunamis we've experienced in the recent past, your lifetime, were *distant* tsunamis, caused by megaquakes hundreds or even thousands of miles from the Oregon coast. Places such as Alaska or Japan. The fact they were so far from us gave us adequate time to issue warnings. Also, by the time the tsunamis arrived here, they were always significantly diminished with the water rises amounting to only a few feet.

"If Cascadia ruptures, that happens right here." He tapped the floor firmly with his foot. "It won't occur hundreds of miles from here. The time between the quake and arrival of the tsunami will be a matter of minutes, not hours. And it won't be diminished. We're talking forty feet, maybe fifty, not four or five."

The reaction from the attendees seemed subdued, which didn't surprise Rob: Most of them were in the emergency preparedness business and already knew the difference between distant and local tsunamis.

"Dr. Elwood," a woman in the audience said, "how certain are you that the event you described, what some people have called 'The Big One,' is really going to happen?"

"Absolutely positive." He waited a beat, then added, "But that's not the question you meant to ask. Scientists know that destructive quakes and tsunamis have hit here repeatedly over the centuries, and that they will again. We just aren't sure when."

"But *you* claim to know," someone shouted, his words accusatory and wrapped in cynicism.

"No, I don't *know*. I strongly *suspect*, however, and I've tried to illuminate as clearly as I could my reasons for that suspicion. Look, I'm not a hundred percent sure, or even eighty percent. Believe me, I've got my doubts, too. Remember, I'm a scientist, not a mystic. Let me repeat, for all the arguments I laid out earlier, I felt compelled to make my concerns public, and then let the public decide what actions, if any, should be taken."

"That's a cop-out, sir," a burly emergency manager from Seaside growled. "We're not the experts here, you are. The trouble is, we're not hearing a geologist, we're hearing a witch doctor."

And so it went for more than forty-five minutes: legitimate questions, vitriolic attacks, and scattered expressions of support. Overall, the audience seemed evenly split among believers, skeptics, and outright doubters. Rob figured that's about as good as he could have expected.

Pete accosted him after the session ended. The newspaperwoman from Astoria accompanied him.

"Jesus, Rob," he questioned, "how could you pull a stunt like this?" He shook his head in an obvious sign of disapproval and disgust. "You've really stepped on your flopper big time with this one."

The female reporter arched her eyebrows and blinked, then turned a pale shade of red.

"Better make that 'stepped on your poncho' for print purposes," Rob suggested.

Lewis injected himself into the conversation, approaching Pete. "You don't even want to give him a *chance*?" He words carried a veneer of venom.

"He would have been more credible if he'd used a Ouija board for his presentation." Pete rocked back and forth, like a toy metronome, from his left foot to his right. "Let me warn you, doctor, when I'm asked by the media what I thought of this little dog and pony show, I'll have a one-word response—crap." He wheeled and stalked away, followed by the reporter.

Cassie had worked her way from the back of the room to the podium and now stood in front of Rob.

"Hi," she said, "I'm Cassie. Remember me? We met a few months—"

"Of course, I remember." They shook hands. "I remember something else, too. That you warned me of the fates a few of the Old Testament prophets, 'oracles of doom' I think you termed them, met. If I had to guess, I'd say I'm about to rediscover their demises, at least figuratively."

She smiled, an expression that seemed both understanding and, ironically, sad. "Yes. Not only that, but you seem to have stumbled into the 'prophet in his own land' syndrome, too. In Manzanita, you see,"—she swept her arm around the room—"you're just one of the gang who went a little whacko."

Rob expelled a long breath, allowing his shoulders to sag. "You sound almost as if you've been down this road yourself."

"It's a long, hazardous path," she said softly. "The trouble is, even if you're certain you're right, few if any listeners believe you."

He studied her for a moment, then blurted out a question that had formed in his mind, but that he hadn't meant to articulate. "Who are you?"

"Just someone who's interested in ancient cultures." She turned to leave. "I'll be around for a few more weeks. We'll probably see each other again."

She slipped from the room, almost as if she were a fairy tale character, ephemeral yet eternal.

Chapter Ten

Reunion

Manzanita
Wednesday, July 1

AT PRECISELY TWO p.m., as scheduled, at least for the fictional Mr. Davenport, Shack stepped into the office of ALEXIS WILLIAMSON, ATTORNEY-AT-LAW. A puff of wind, bearing scents of salt and seaweed, accompanied him into the small building. No one greeted him.

"Have a seat, I'll be right out, Mr. Davenport," a voice said. It came from somewhere in back, and somewhere in the faraway past. Shack recognized it instantly. Barely detectable were the honey threads of the Deep South that once had been subtly woven into Alex's words. Words, a few of which, he suspected, she now regretted. He glanced toward the exit. *I still have time to make a run for it.* Instead, he seated himself in a comfortable leather chair and surveyed the room.

Above a set of long, low wooden shelves crammed with law books and journals, broad shafts of sunlight reflected off a dozen or so framed certificates, photos, and awards mounted on a pine-paneled wall. Alex being awarded her law degree. Alex speaking at a gathering of some sort. Alex hiking along a forested trail. Alex standing next to a young woman, perhaps her daughter. *So she did marry. Good. Maybe I didn't irreparably screw up her life.* He continued to study the pictures. Oddly, no shots of Alex with a man. Meaning what? Maybe nothing.

An interior door clicked open, and a few bars of Benny Goodman's "Big John's Special" wafted into the room. Shack had forgotten how much Alex loved big bands and swing music. But then, he'd probably forgotten a lot of things about her. He rose as she entered the room.

He swallowed hard. He'd also forgotten how striking she could appear. Statuesque fit the bill, but perhaps that wasn't appropriate for an attorney. His mind struggled for a description. *Professional seductiveness?* Maybe. Her midnight-black hair, now streaked with silver, reminded him how old she was, how old they both were, how much time had passed.

She halted, open mouthed, when she spotted Shack. Her hazel eyes fixed him in a withering gaze. "You," she said, the word tinged in a hard frost.

He remained rooted in place, taken aback by her icy greeting, unable to formulate a response. Finally, he found a few words. "Yes. I hope you don't mind me showing up this way."

"I do," she snapped, "I really do." She didn't suggest he be seated again.

"Alex—"

"So I assume you didn't change your name to Davenport and that you really don't have any legitimate business with me?"

He paused before responding. "Maybe I do. If you'll give me a chance."

"I gave you a chance twenty-five years ago, you bastard. I think that told me all I needed to know about you."

When he'd been a young Air Force lieutenant, he'd been dressed down by senior officers more than once, but never with as much vitriol as loosed by Alex. He raised his arms in submission. "I come in peace. But if you want to vivisect my character, you've every right."

"You're damn right I do." Her eyes flashed an angry message, of an old wound not forgotten.

Still, the depth of her ire puzzled him. In one sense, she seemed to have moved on with her life, created professional success and built self-worth, maybe to a greater degree than he had. Yet, after a quarter of a century, she still burned with profound anger over a personal slight. Okay, maybe not so "slight." But he found the intensity of her indignation puzzling after all these years.

"Look," he said, "I came, believe it or not, to apologize for what I did to you, for the way I just kicked you to the side of the road. Yes, I was an asshole, a shithead, a bastard. I have no defense for that. All I can say now is that I'm sorry. I didn't show up here hoping to repair our relationship." He lowered his head. "More than anything, I think I just wanted to assuage my own guilt by making sure you were okay."

"Better late than never, huh?" Her words shot out edged in venom.

"Yes," he answered firmly, lifting his gaze to meet hers. A tiny counterattack.

"So, you've spoken your piece."

"And?"

"You're free to get the hell out of here."

He stared outside, looking through the backward lettering on her window into a sun-speckled afternoon where pre-holiday clusters of pedestrians strolled up and down Laneda Avenue.

"I didn't mean to upset you, well, any more than I ever did, by showing up here," he said. "I wish there's something I could do to at least calm the waters between us."

"Maybe there is." She walked from behind her desk to where he stood.

"Anything," he said.

Before his mind could register a defensive response, she swung her right arm in a looping roundhouse hook and landed her open palm on the side of his face. A pop like a small caliber gun discharging reverberated through the room. His head snapped sideways from the force of the blow. Red and blue stars flitted across a black tapestry that draped over his field of vision.

"Shit," he said.

"You bet," Alex responded. "There's a phone on my desk if you want to call the cops and charge me with battery. You can probably get me disbarred."

He massaged his throbbing check and stared at Alex through watering eyes. "In the movies, isn't this the part where'd I grab you and we'd lock lips?"

"Yes, in the movies. In real life, this is where you exit mine forever." She nodded at the door.

He stood his ground, realizing how badly he wanted to unearth whatever lay buried in her psyche that had produced such enduring pain.

"I don't want to leave it like this," he said, his hand still resting on the side of his face. He could feel it beginning to swell.

"How do you want to leave it?" A curt question.

"Dinner. I want us to smoke a peace pipe over dinner."

"You're dreaming."

"Maybe."

"No."

"Alex, please."

"No. If you want to smoke something, walk up the street to the cannabis shop. Recreational pot is legal in Oregon now. We're done here."

"I'm begging."

She didn't respond.

"The best restaurant in town," he said.

She glowered at him in silence.

"I need a cold steak to slap on my face," he added.

"You probably just need another slap, period."

"I'd rather have dinner."

"What part of *no* do you not understand?"

"Come on, Alex—"

"Out. Now. Goodbye. *Auf Wiedersehen. Arrivederci. Das vendanya.*" She herded him toward the door.

He backed out, still holding a hand to his face. "You're a hard woman, Ms. Williamson."

"You ought to see me in court." She slammed the door, rattling the glass in it.

He stood on the sidewalk staring at the door, staring at nothing. *How could I have hurt her that much?* His ego throbbed more intensely than his cheek. He pivoted and shuffled up the street toward a Mexican place that advertised pitchers of margaritas, half price before five p.m. As an old fighter pilot, he knew how to attack his problems.

He nursed his way through half a pitcher, having to restrain himself from polishing off the remaining half in a few big gulps. He tossed a ten on the bar and walked back out into the sunshine. Yes, fighter pilots know how to attack their problems. If you don't get your target the first time, you go after it again.

To kill time before his next strafing run, he wandered in and out of the shops and galleries lining Laneda. At five o'clock, he returned to Alex's office. She looked up from her desk as he entered. Another Benny Goodman piece, one he recognized but couldn't name, tumbled softly from hidden speakers.

She glared at Shack and shook her head in apparent disbelief. "Early Alzheimer's?"

He sat in the leather chair in front of her desk.

"What in the hell do I have to do?" she barked. "Call the cops and tell them I'm being harassed? Stalked?"

"I think we've probably got a Mexican standoff there." He patted his now-swollen and still aching cheek.

"Okay, you called my bluff. Now what?"

"Have dinner with me."

"Do you recognize the tune that's playing?"

"I recognize it but can't name it."

"It's the 'Jersey Bounce.' Does that give you a hint what I'd like to do to you?"

"You aren't from Jersey."

"A girl can change."

"Good. Have dinner with me."

"No."

"We played that scene already. Let's try something different."

"How about *maybe*?"

"How about *yes*? I'm only in town for a few days. Then I'll be out of your life."

"Forever?"

"If that's how you want it."

"Gee, what gave you the first clue?"

He waited.

She twirled a strand of her shoulder-length hair around her forefinger and gazed at the ceiling. "Okay," she said after a minute or so, "small penance if it'll get you off my case. There's a new place in town a couple of blocks up Laneda toward 101. It's called the Jolly Roger. Meet me there tomorrow at eight."

"Eight?"

"Yeah. Maybe it'll put you back on the road to keeping commitments."

He stood and walked to the door. He noticed a fully loaded backpack resting on the floor next to the exit. "Planning a hiking trip?"

"It's my go-bag," Alex said, offering no further explanation.

"Your go-bag?"

"A lot of people on the coast have them."

"Yes?"

"In case there's a big earthquake, we know we'll get slammed by a tsunami within a matter of minutes. We grab the bag—it has emergency supplies—and go. Run to safety."

"Really? That happens a lot around here?"

"Every five hundred years or so."

"Right." He stepped into the street and turned his gaze toward the ocean, a few blocks from where he stood. *Strange country.*

Manzanita
Thursday, July 2

SHACK ARRIVED fifteen minutes prior to eight p.m. and secured a booth in a back corner of the Jolly Roger, a restaurant that seemed fresh and upscale. The establishment's decor, not surprisingly, reflected a pirate theme. Lithographs and paintings of pirate vessels—sloops, schooners, brigantines, and square-riggers—adorned the walls. Interspersed among them: swords, sabers, and cutlasses. An obligatory treasure chest, drooling phony pieces of eight, hung suspended from the ceiling, as did a cannon that looked as though it really had been dredged from Davy Jones's Locker. Additional decorations appeared to be of a more general marine nature: fishing nets, large glass balls—floats for the nets, Shack assumed—and photographs of commercial trawlers and cabin cruisers.

Shack, attempting to respond to the spirit of the restaurant's motif, sipped a drink called Pure Ol' Pirate's Piss. Mostly dark rum, he was told, with a touch of vodka, curaçao, and pineapple juice.

"Kind of a sissy drink, isn't it?" Alex slid into the booth opposite Shack.

Shack stood. "They didn't have any Jeremiah Weed."

"What's that?"

"A hundred-proof fighter pilots' drink."

"Are you still an immature fighter jock or do you just behave like one?"

He ignored the jibe, seated himself, and took stock of the woman he'd dumped a quarter-century ago. He had to admit, she looked stunning. *Damn her.* A black pant suit accentuated her still-viable physical assets, while a white silk blouse revealed just enough cleavage to trap an unguarded glance.

She caught *his* unguarded glance. "You haven't changed, have you?" she said, a hardness in her voice.

"And if I hadn't noticed," he responded, "would you have been disappointed?"

"I'm past that."

"Sure you are. That's why you walked in here decked out like you were going to junior officers' night at the O-club."

She colored slightly. He'd finally scored a point.

"Okay," he said. "Forget it." He leaned toward her and caught a scent of *Fendi*. He found himself swept back to a seemingly endless summer of so long ago. Naked bodies glistening in perspiration, rumpled bedsheets, soft cries and moans in the night. "I was a prick for what I did to you, I acknowledge that. But I truly, truly apologize. Words are weak, I know, but they're heartfelt.

"And, if it makes any difference, it wasn't you. Wasn't anything you did or didn't do. You were just in the wrong place at the wrong time in *my* life. My state of mind then—and it was totally screwed up—was that I didn't need to be tied to any one woman. Again, I didn't mean to hurt—"

"You don't know how much you wounded me," she snapped. Her eyes flashed in hardened resentment.

"Do you want to talk about it?"

"No. Let's just call a truce and try to enjoy our dinner. Then you can beat feet."

Shack had no option but to agree. He ordered Chinook salmon stuffed with Dungeness crab. She had a bowl of seafood chowder and a plate piled high with steamers (clams harvested from local beaches and harbors). They shared a bottle of Oregon chardonnay.

"I taste pears," Shack said.

"I taste victory," Alex responded and raised her glass.

Shack noted the absence of a wedding band.

"So, you aren't married?" he asked.

"Not now."

"In the past?"

"Yes, for about ten years."

"I assume the young lady I saw in the photograph in your office is your daughter?"

"Yes." Alex didn't look up from extracting a razor clam from its shell.

"She lives with you?"

"She's in her final year of law school at Willamette."

"Where?"

"Willamette University. It's in Salem."

"You're proud of her?"

"Very." She changed the subject. "And you? Wife? Kids?"

He shook his head. "A couple of brief marriages. Neither lasted very long. No children."

"The old commitment bugaboo again, huh?" She smiled, an expression suggesting she'd landed another punch.

They managed to get through the remainder of the dinner in

relative peace, mostly by making small talk about Manzanita, the upcoming parade, and rumors of a big earthquake and tsunami supposedly poised to strike on the Fourth.

"Are you worried?" Shack asked.

"No," she said. "It doesn't make any difference. You're either prepared or you're not." She looked around the restaurant. "It looks like the doomsday forecast scared off a few people, though. Normally, this place would be packed a couple of days prior to a holiday."

Shack counted four empty tables and booths.

They finished their meal, Shack covered the tab, and they exited the Jolly Roger together.

"May I walk you home?" Shack asked.

"Not on your life."

"Oh, come on, Alex. I'm just trying to be a gentleman. I know I've come up short in that arena in the past, but I don't have an ulterior motive. I'm not going to ask to come in, grope you, or steal a kiss. Just walk. Okay?"

She sighed heavily. "Sure. It's about a four-block stroll."

They walked side by side, mostly in silence, Shack with his arms wrapped around himself to ward off the surprising chill, an antithesis to summers along the Southeast coasts, and Alex nodding and saying good evening to people she knew, which appeared to be quite a few.

They reached her home in short order. In the late-lingering twilight, it appeared weather-beaten but modern with graying cedar siding and an abundance of glass. The soft thunder of Pacific surf, perhaps a block or two distant, filled the incipient night. A dark blur, a bat perhaps, flashed past their heads.

"Thank you," Alex said. "Have a good life." She turned and started toward her front door.

"Alex."

She stopped.

"I *am* sorry," he said.

"Yes. Well . . ."

"It was good seeing you."

She didn't respond.

"What's your daughter's name?"

"Skylar. Good night."

"I'll be around until Sunday. Maybe we'll see each other at the parade."

"I hope not." She entered her house and shut the door firmly.

LATER, IN HIS RENTAL condo, Shack lay on his bed staring at the ceiling, staring at nothing. Muted rock music filtered through a wall shared with an adjoining unit. He replayed the events of the evening repeatedly in his mind. He knew he'd injured Alex emotionally by jettisoning her from his life without so much as a "thirty-day notice," but he couldn't come to grips with the staying power and magnitude of her indignation. Most people, he thought, would just get on with their lives. He could understand if he weren't warmly welcomed by her, but to be met with open hostility?

By midnight, an idea, a possibility, maybe just a fantasy, had blossomed somewhere deep within his mind. And although the notion probably held no more credence than a fairy tale, it seemed something that demanded he follow up on with Alex. He'd have to contravene his promise not to see her again, however.

He fell asleep with the soft wash of distant breakers the only sound in the room.

Chapter Eleven

Encounter

Manzanita
Friday, July 3

ROB AND LEWIS trudged along a sidewalk adjacent to Laneda Avenue. Rob shifted his gaze skyward. Puffy white clouds, like cotton-ball schooners riding a stiff breeze, sailed over the tiny town on an inverted cobalt sea. "A perfect summer day," he noted.

Lewis squinted into the morning sun and brushed a shock of hair from his brow. "Is it?"

"Hardly," Rob mumbled.

Lewis grasped Rob's upper arm and brought him to a halt. "You did what you thought was right," he said, his voice firm. "You did what you had to do. You knew the potential cost."

Rob nodded, but the resolve he'd initially harbored for his decision to "go public" a few days earlier had withered under a relentless barrage of criticism.

They walked in silence until they reached 5th Street. Rob stopped and gestured at the street sign. "If people can get this far from the beach, they should survive."

Lewis looked back down the avenue, toward the ocean. "We're lucky here, in Manzanita. It's only a few blocks to safety."

Rob followed Lewis's gaze, then turned to look up Laneda in the direction of Highway 101. "Not like Seaside or Rockaway," he said, his voice soft.

"I know," Lewis responded. "What've they got in those towns, a half mile, maybe a three-quarter-mile dash to safety?"

"More than that in Seaside. If it's a big tsunami, probably over a mile. A lot of older and handicapped folks won't make it. At a good walking speed, a healthy person can cover a mile in twenty minutes or so. They might have a chance. But twenty minutes is probably the most they'll have."

Rob brought his gaze back to Lewis. "But what the hell. Maybe we'll get lucky. Maybe the quake won't be powerful enough to knock down bridges and buildings and block streets. Maybe the tsunami will be four feet instead of fifty or sixty."

"Ya think?"

Rob looked away from Lewis and didn't answer.

The streets had begun to fill with Fourth of July tourists. License plates identified visitors not only from Oregon, but many from Washington, as well. Others told of wayfarers from California, Idaho, and Utah. The overall mood, despite Rob's public pronouncement, seemed light-hearted and celebratory with little apprehension over a potential disaster.

Rob, of course, didn't share in the ebullient atmosphere. On Monday, in the wake of his press conference, it had become clear rather quickly that his reputation and career were already circling the drain.

"Rob's Revelation," as it had come to be known, had been met with an immediate salvo of scorn and ridicule from both his peers and the public. Fellow geologists labeled him a charlatan. An editorial in *The Oregonian*, which apparently had picked up details of the press conference via a stringer, stated that "somewhere in America, a village finds itself short an idiot this morning. But not to fear, we've found him in Oregon."

Even heavier flak had come via social media—Facebook and Twitter. A noted earthquake and tsunami specialist stated, "The Dr. Robert Elwood Traveling Medicine Show has arrived in town selling a brand of snake oil that's right out of the 19th Century."

Rob and Lewis continued up Laneda, away from the beach toward 101. Rob halted and looked back down the avenue. Squat, weathered buildings, sharing space with storm-whipped pines and Sitka spruce, lined the street. Free of popular franchises such as Starbucks and McDonald's, boutiques, art galleries, and mom and pop stores flourished in Manzanita. Flourished, Rob knew, as much as any retail operation could in a town with a full-time population of only six or seven hundred. Tourism drove the economy.

So he understood why so many of the verbal assaults on him, from the very people he'd summered with for over two decades, bore a toxic level of vitriol. "Rob's Revelation" they said, would drive away a huge chunk of the coast's typical holiday traffic, their lifeblood.

He stepped into the street so he could get a better sightline back to the beach, perhaps sixty feet lower and a third of a mile distant from where he and Lewis stood. The Pacific surf, flat and gentle, glided up the sand in shallow surges, then slid back toward the breakers leaving skinny trails of sparkling sea foam, like strings of diamonds, in its wake.

Sandpipers darted along the beach while screeching gulls wheeled overhead, riding the wind like tiny paragliders. Beachcombers, many bundled in sweatshirts or light jackets to ward off the morning coolness, strolled along the surf line. One or two carried metal detectors, searching for whatever mundane treasures might be buried in the sand. A few others toted clam shovels, perhaps hoping for targets of opportunity.

Rob and Lewis resumed their stroll. The aroma of scrambled eggs, bacon, and griddle cakes from the nearby Dungeness Diner mingled with the salt air and traces of wood smoke.

Rob studied the foot traffic along their route, unconvinced the gaggle of teenagers and families pressing into town constituted a substantially smaller crowd than on any other Fourth of July weekend. It seemed as if the derision heaped onto his revelation had been effective, rendering it essentially null and void.

"Uh, oh," Lewis whispered, and pointed up the street in the direction of 101.

A young blonde trailed by a television cameraman had locked onto Rob like a heat-seeking missile and appeared about to launch an attack.

Rob executed a quick search for an escape route, but Lewis rested a restraining hand on his shoulder.

"Don't bother. They operate in a pack, like hyenas. If one doesn't get you, the next one will. Let's stand our ground."

Thirty seconds later, the warhead of the missile, a handheld microphone sheathed in a wind shield, slammed to a stop inches in front of Rob's nose.

"Amanda Jeffries, KGW-TV," the blonde holding the warhead announced. "May I have a word with you, Dr. Elwood?"

"Don't you have to graduate from high school before—?"

A sharp sideways kick into Rob's ankle from Lewis halted his snide retort before he could complete it.

"Sorry," Rob said. "Yes, Ms. Jeffries, I'd be glad to speak with you."

She lowered the mic from his face. "I understand I look young,

Dr. Elwood. I'm sorry, but I can't help it. I graduated with a master's degree in journalism from Northwestern three years ago."

Rob nodded. "I stand appropriately rebuked. Let's begin again."

Amanda flashed him a smile that he guessed had probably disarmed a significant number of her interviewees, at least those of the male gender. She raised the mic to its previous position and glanced at some notes in her free hand. "You've issued a warning for a devastating earthquake and massive tsunami—"

Rob shook his head. "I didn't issue a *warning*. I issued a statement."

"Yes," Amanda said without missing a beat, "a statement warning of a—"

"I *warned* of nothing," Rob snapped. "Let's get away from that term."

"Okay," she sighed, "you issued a statement saying that a huge earthquake and tsunami would hit—"

"I didn't say 'would,' Ms. Jeffries. In my statement, I explained that what I was presenting was not based on hard science. It was based on something that could be interpreted as metaphysical or, if you're religious, perhaps divine, but it was nothing springing from traditional science."

The breeze plastered several strands of Amanda's straw-colored hair over her eyes. In a deft motion likely born of much practice, she brushed them away, then continued her interrogation.

"Divine? Do you consider yourself religious, Dr. Elwood?"

Lewis intervened. "If I may," he said.

Amanda pointed the mic at him. "And you are?"

"Bishop Lewis Warren. I'm a long-time friend of Dr. Elwood's, and I want to make it crystal clear to you and your viewers that it is not Dr. Elwood's religious beliefs or even his scientific credentials that are under scrutiny here. He explained in detail where his concern sprang from and went to great lengths to point out it was born of neither religious zeal nor some secret scientific knowledge. It's for each individual to evaluate that concern and decide for himself how much credence to put into it."

Fire in her eyes, Amanda took the offensive. "Dr. Elwood is a respected geologist. He's studied big quakes and large tsunamis for many years. He's established himself as a recognized authority. How could people *not* view his . . ."—she paused, apparently searching for the right term—"*concern* as carrying a certain amount of scientific gravitas? I believe it's disingenuous to try to pass off Dr. Elwood's pronouncement as being based on some sort of metaphysical experience and not true science. To the general public, that's a distinction without a difference."

"Is there a question in there, Ms. Jeffries?" Rob asked.

A small crowd, watching the proceedings, unexpected entertainment, had gathered around Rob, Lewis, and the TV crew. Cell phones and digital cameras snapped photo after photo.

Amanda seemed to revel in the attention. "Yes," she said. "You've, if not *warned*, have at least put people in the Pacific Northwest on high alert for a catastrophic event, even though that *alert*, you tell us, has no scientific basis. So here's my question: Why should the public view you as anything other than an irresponsible fear-monger? Or a Chicken Little standing on a street corner with a sign proclaiming THE END IS NEAR?"

Rob drew a deep breath, looked away from Amanda and tried to zero in on something distant . . . something amorphous, bucolic, calming. After a moment, he found his emotional footing, focused his thoughts, and turned back to Amanda.

"I've laid out the reasons for my pronouncement as clearly as I could. I've explained what it is and what it is not. I'm sorry I can't cast my concern in absolute or even probabilistic terms. I've no basis for doing that. I can only relay my experience to the public and let each individual draw his or her own conclusion as to the viability of it."

"Then we're back to the voodoo nature of your, shall we call it, prophecy?" She framed her sentence as a question, but clearly meant it as a declaration, and didn't give Rob a chance to respond. By using the term *voodoo*, she had essentially impugned his sanity.

She turned and faced the camera, self-satisfaction gleaming in her eyes. "For KGW News Channel 8, this is Amanda Jeffries in Manzanita, Oregon."

"Shoot some B-roll of the town," she said to the cameraman after she'd signed off. "Then we'll find some shop owners to interview." She turned back to Rob. "Thank you for your time, Dr. Elwood."

"Thank *you* for your fair and balanced coverage, young lady. Have you ever considered working for Bill O'Reilly?"

She tossed her head, flinging another tumble of hair from her eyes, and flounced off, but not far. Less than half a block away, she encountered the town's city manager, Hector Springer. Hector, elderly and obese, his pants supported by suspenders not quite up to the job, seemed more than happy to embrace his "fifteen minutes of fame," which for most people usually turned out to be a few seconds of air time. Rob had always thought of Hector as overweight, overbearing, and overdramatic, so his performance came as no surprise.

In response to a question from Amanda, Hector gestured at the sky, almost knocking an ill-fitting toupee from his head in the process. "It's a beautiful day on the Oregon coast. It's going to be a gorgeous weekend. Don't let the scare tactics of some moron, who should be tarred and feathered and lugged out of town on a rail, keep you from visiting."

"So," Amanda said, "you're not concerned about the threat of a massive earthquake and tsunami this weekend?"

"The threat, young lady, is no greater now that it has been on any other day during the past several hundred years." He spotted Rob in the surrounding onlookers. "Let me say this, if we do find the crowds this year are significantly reduced from those of previous years, the good doctor,"—he pointed at Rob—"is going to find himself snowed under by a boatload of civil suits." He paused, then addressed Rob directly, "Think of that, my friend."

Rob stared back at Hector, but didn't verbalize his retort. *Mixed metaphors aside, maybe* you *should think of the* lives *that might be saved.*

Lewis, instead, responded. "Why don't you save your threats until after the Fourth, Mr. Springer? You know, just in case Rob is right."

"Maybe you should spend more time with the *Bible* and less with Dr. Elwood," Hector snapped. "As it states in Proverbs, 'Do not congratulate yourself about tomorrow, since you do not know what today will bring.' Dr. Elwood is a fool."

"I think not," Lewis shot back. "But ponder this: 'The greatest lesson in life is to know that even fools are right sometimes.'"

"Proverbs?" Hector asked.

"No, Winston Churchill. He held a somewhat higher office than you."

Hector snorted, wheeled, and waddled away from the interview, clamping a hand on his toupee as a gust of wind churned up Laneda sending dust and stray pieces of paper slithering along the pavement.

Now, in the open and taking unrelenting fire from the media, the public, and even people he once considered as friends, a mushroom cloud of regret about "going public" exploded within Rob. He clenched his jaw and stared at Lewis without seeing him.

Lewis caught his expression. "We discussed it at length, my friend. It was a fully informed decision. Stand by it and I'll stand with you. We don't know that you're wrong."

"We don't know that I'm right."

"And we won't until tomorrow. I think you're right for all the reasons we talked about. As I told you, the gift of prophecy comes with a heavy burden."

"Bullshit! It's a not a gift. And I fully understand, more than ever now, it's not just a burden, it's a damned millstone."

ROB ARRIVED BACK at his beach home to find Deborah packing.

"What's this?" he asked, although he had a pretty good idea.

"Maria and I are going home."

"Because of the tsunami threat?"

"No. Because I can't stand to watch any more public humiliation of you. It's too painful."

He looked away, staring out a window into the midday brightness. "Even my wife has lost faith?"

"Faith in what?" she fired back. "I understand the genesis of your nightmares, Rob, and I'm glad you went to see Lewis. But all I wanted you to do was get a little counseling, a few insights. I didn't expect you to go on stage in front of the world and do a frigging Noah routine. The only thing I've got faith in now are my fears. I'm terrified, Rob."

"Of what?"

"Of you losing everything. Your reputation. Your profession. Your business. And when I say you, I really mean all of us. Me, Tim, and Maria included."

"Why not give me a chance?"

She stepped toward him, hands on hips. "You don't get it, do you? You've just bet our entire future on a dream. This isn't some metaphysical-intellectual exercise. It's real life."

"It wasn't a dream, it was—"

"A *vision*, I know. Well, you said everyone should make their own decision about how to react to your *concerns* springing from that vision. So I made mine."

"Yes?"

"It's that I think my husband took off on a magic carpet ride with his buddy, Lewis, and left me scared to death. And more than a little pissed off." She zipped shut the suitcase she'd been filling. "See you in Portland."

She left Rob standing alone in the bedroom. *A prophet in my own land.*

Chapter Twelve

The Fourth

Cannon Beach
Saturday, July 4

THE FOURTH DAWNED clear and sparkling, the sky a steely blue, so deep and intense it looked as if it might have been rendered by a master painter. The air, exhibiting barely a breath of wind, presaged an unusually warm day.

Jonathan, accompanied by Zurry, returned to Cannon Beach as previously planned, hoping the holiday would lure people away from their homes to parades and municipal festivities, thus giving him more freedom to explore for the "lost treasure."

"Probably lost and gone forever, or maybe never was," he said to Zurry. He knelt in front of the dog and placed his hands on either side of the animal's huge head, looking him in the face. "I got an idea, old boy. I think whoever buried the box, assuming it *was* buried around here, would have taken a path of least resistance up the hill. So they probably followed a creek. Easy travel, an easy location to remember. I have an idea where to search." He stood. "Come on."

He'd studied topo maps of the area over the past few days and had identified a narrow gully, perhaps an old creek bed, running up the side of Haystack Hill. He led Zurry toward the beach, thinking to begin his exploration near the sand, then work his way inland.

He quickly discovered one of his hunches already wrong. It appeared that while a few people may have headed off for the holiday, even more, judging by the plethora of vehicles parked in driveways, seemed to have invited guests for the Fourth.

"Oh, well," he said to Zurry, "we'll press on anyhow."

The gully he planned on following began at the upper edge of the beach and appeared to mark the property dividing line between housing lots, essentially running through the backyards of about a dozen homes. He motioned for Zurry to follow and moved into the depression behind the homes, hoping, due to the early hour, most people wouldn't be up yet and therefore wouldn't spot a man and dog slogging along an old creek bed. If they did get noticed, maybe they'd be dismissed as harmless.

He understood the risk. If someone complained about a trespasser, he could be ticketed and his equipment, confiscated. Despite knowing that, he decided to take the chance.

It proved a good gamble. No one challenged their presence. They spent almost an hour in the gully, slashing their way through eel grass, brambles, and scruffy pines, but discovered nothing of interest. The metal detector remained sullenly silent. They reached South Hemlock Street, the main route paralleling the beach.

On the other side of the road, the gully continued up Haystack Hill. It would be a difficult hike, however. No more backyards, just forest and underbrush. If nothing else, Jonathan considered, the depression would offer a good escape route if the earthquake and tsunami that had everyone abuzz materialized.

Jonathan, like most people it seemed, put little stock in the prediction, if that's what it was, and went about his business as usual. The prophecy—he'd heard that term used, too—had reportedly scared off a few tourists, but the majority apparently looked upon the eventuality of a cataclysm as more of a fantasy than a real threat. After all, such events were the stuff of history and of other parts of the world.

"We'll be fine," Jonathan said, and crossed the road with Zurry in trail. "Besides, animals always know before humans if a monster quake is coming, right?" Zurry didn't seem to acknowledge the question, or maybe just wished to ignore the burden. Jonathan moved back into the dense undergrowth and began beating his way uphill.

He found it difficult to swing the metal detector in a wide arc, so spent what he considered far too much time hacking away at brambles and branches with a small bush machete to clear areas wide enough to work the two-box detector. By noon, he'd labored only about a hundred feet up the gully. He'd gotten a couple of "growls" on the detector, but both turned out to be from scrap metal.

He found a mossy deadfall adjacent to the old creek bed and, exhausted, seated himself on it. Sweat poured off him in salty rivulets. He fanned himself with his ball cap. Zurry plopped to the ground beside him.

"Getting too friggin' old for this," Jonathan said. Zurry remained motionless. "I promise, this will be our last hurrah. If we don't find nuthin' here, it's back to the mountain, okay?" Zurry gave him a puzzled stare.

Semi-recovered, he poured a bowl of water for Zurry, placed two large dog biscuits beside it, then dug through his backpack and fished out a banana, an apple, and bag of trail mix for himself. He washed everything down with what remained in the bottle he'd poured Zurry's drink from.

A ground-shaking rumble startled him. He stood. Zurry jumped up, alert. But tranquility quickly returned. Songbirds sang, jays scolded, dogs barked.

"Just a big truck on the main road, boy," Jonathan said. He remained standing, soaking in the natural melodies of life and, for a moment, forgetting where he was and why. He looked around and spotted the metal detector resting against the fallen log.

"Ah, yes, that's it," he said, barely above a whisper. He re-shouldered his pack, retrieved the detector, and moved back into the gully. "Let's finish up and get out of here." Zurry plodded behind him.

Manzanita

ROB, LEWIS, AND Timothy threaded their way along Laneda, weaving in and out of the crowds lining the sidewalks, waiting for the parade to begin.

"There should be more people here," a voice behind them growled.

Rob pivoted to see Hector, the town manager, waddling in their wake.

"Why should there be more people here?" Lewis retorted. "So you can see more people get killed?"

Hector snorted in derision. He attempted to tug his pants up, but they continued to hang like a misshapen sack beneath his ample belly. "Nobody's gonna get killed today, you morons. I called the director of the Pacific Northwest Seismic Network this morning to see if anything was brewing. He told me everything is quiet."

"Of course it is," Rob snapped, repelling the urge to grab Hector by one of his chins and attempt to shake some sense into him. "I've told people repeatedly, I've told *you* repeatedly, there probably won't be a precursor before Cascadia lets go. It's not like a winter storm we can model and track and issue warnings on. It's more like a terrorist with an explosive belt who sneaks into a crowded mall or theater and blows himself and everybody around him to kingdom come. Probably the only warning you'd get then is when he yells *Allahu Akbar.*"

Hector made another unsuccessful try at wiggling his pants into place. "We aren't talking about terrorists—"

"Damn right we aren't," Rob snapped. "We're talking about something a hell of a lot more deadly. Why don't you give it a rest until the end of the day? Then, if Manzanita is still here, you can bust my balls all you want." He turned to his son and lowered his voice. "You didn't hear me say that."

Tim grinned. "Bust balls? Cool, Dad."

Hector sputtered something unintelligible and stalked off.

Rob, Lewis, and Tim continued up Laneda. As they passed Manzanita News & Expresso, Lewis pointed ahead. "The electronic vultures have come to roost."

At the upper end of Laneda, near its intersection with Highway 101, half a dozen television satellite trucks from Portland and Seattle sat with their antennae deployed. Cameramen and reporters milled around outside the vehicles.

"I don't suppose they're here for the parade," Rob ventured.

"Unlikely," Lewis responded.

"Well, as long as they stay near 101, they'll be safe from the tsunami, presuming they make it through the quake."

"You aren't wishing them ill are you?" Lewis laid a hand on Rob's shoulder and they stopped walking.

"No." Rob issued a long sigh. "I know they're just doing their job. And I understand it's a win-win setup for them here in Manzanita. If the quake and tsunami hit, the nation will see it live. If nothing happens—"

"I'm virtually certain something *will* happen," Lewis said. "The visions you experienced are not without meaning. We went over all the reasons why."

"I remain a scientist," Rob countered. "It's damn hard for me to believe one hundred percent in a prediction. So, I'm just saying, if nothing happens, then *I* become the story. Like I said, win-win for them. They'll be on me like buzzards on roadkill."

They resumed walking, but only for a short time. Rob halted when they reached Division Street. "I suspect we better not get any closer to the buzzards' nests."

Lewis shielded his eyes from the sun with his hand and peered toward the sat trucks. "Yeah, they look like they're anxious to pick at a carcass."

"So this is probably a good time for me to make myself scarce. Tim and I are going to head over to the airstrip and hang around near the plane today. If the quake hits—"

"*When* the quake hits," Lewis said, sounding like a teacher correcting a student who had misspoken.

"I wish I had your faith, my friend. Okay, *when* the quake hits, I wanna get in the air as fast as I can and get out of here. The airstrip will be one of the first places to go underwater when the tsunami strikes."

"Be careful, you two," Lewis said.

"Ditto for you," Rob said. "You know what to do, if . . . when—"

"I won't be far from my go-bag today," Lewis interjected. "When the time comes, I know the drill—grab it and run like hell."

"I wish everyone were as prepared as you. A lot of residents are, I know, but there're way too many out-of-towners in the mix today. It could get ugly."

"You can lead a horse to water . . .," Lewis said. "Look, we did as much as we could. If people don't feel compelled to at least make contingency plans, it's hard to feel empathy for them."

"The thing of it is, even if I'm right, it'll be a hollow victory."

"Without victory, there is no survival."

"Churchill again?"

Lewis nodded. "Whether it's a hollow win or not, doesn't matter. You made a tough call. You get the bull's ears. See ya after the Apocalypse. Get going."

Rob and Tim headed along Division toward the air strip. In the middle distance, the sound of bagpipers warming up filled the morning with melodic discordance.

SHACK HAD SPENT the previous day trying to make contact with Alex, but his efforts proved unsuccessful. He found a sign on her office saying it was closed for the holiday weekend. When he went to her home, no one answered the doorbell. As he stepped back into the street, a neighbor said, "I think she went to visit her daughter for a couple of days."

"Did she say when she'd be back?"

"Nope."

"Do you know where her daughter lives?"

The neighbor paused, as though weighing a response, but ended up saying, "Don't know that I do."

Shack thought the neighbor did, but knew he couldn't press the issue. Now he walked up and down Laneda and along Ocean Road, hoping that Alex might have returned for the parade and that he would spot her in the crowds lining the route of march. Well, crowds such as they were. Certainly by Atlanta standards they weren't. Here, what passed for multitudes, seemed to be clumps of spectators perhaps two or three people deep waiting patiently for the parade to begin.

They munched on pretzels and hot dogs, played catch with Frisbees in the street, and snapped selfies. By noon, Shack had covered the parade route twice but hadn't seen Alex. He noted that no one seemed particularly concerned about the possibility of a megaquake or deadly tsunami, or if they were, it wasn't apparent in the outward expressions of merriment and gaiety.

That changed abruptly. Shortly before the parade's scheduled kick-off, a distant rumble hushed the spectators. Some looked uneasily toward the ocean, others peered skyward, and still others gazed apprehensively at those standing next to them. A few began edging away from the ocean. The rumble morphed into a roar and the ground seemed to vibrate ever so subtly. Not quite sure how to react, Shack watched those around him for a key. If this were the prelude to an earthquake, should he run, seek shelter, make peace with God?

It became a moot point. The source of the roar materialized from the south. A vintage warplane, a P-51 Mustang, arguably the greatest piston-driven fighter ever built, screamed into view, flying inverted just above the beach. It flashed by in a blur of red, white, and blue markings on a shimmering aluminum fuselage. It rolled upright and climbed into the azure sky, its two-thousand-horsepower engine—if Shack remembered correctly—bellowing like a wild bull.

As an old fighter jock, Shack couldn't help but admire the sleek, almost sexy, aircraft. As it disappeared into the haze at altitude, a lump formed in his throat. His heart thumped in his chest as he heard the Mustang begin a dive back toward Manzanita. As if the classic fighter were on a strafing run over the battlefields of World War II Europe, it thundered in low over Laneda in an ear-splitting roar. Shack guessed its speed at close to 400 mph. The mini-crowd waved flags and cheered, though their acclamation couldn't be heard over the scream of the aircraft's engine.

Shack watched in admiration, and just a bit of jealousy, as the P-51 flashed past. In honor of his brothers who had flown the Mustang in combat so many decades before, he snapped off a smart salute. In a matter of seconds, the great old fighter was gone, climbing once again into the wild blue over the Oregon coast and thundering toward home, wherever that was.

The parade began, led by a Manzanita police SUV with its siren and rumbler on full blast. What followed seemed classic small-town America. Shack had to admit, he found it appealing. Clowns, a guy in a gorilla suit, fire trucks, EMS vehicles, a volunteer marching band, a drum and bugle corps, bagpipers, vintage cars, a classic Austin-Healy, a sharp-looking Corvette, pretty girls astride handsome horses, a library cart drill team, and a steam calliope. Shack wondered where that came from. Everything seemed decked out in red, white, and blue bunting. And almost everyone seemed adorned in a saggy Uncle Sam stovepipe hat.

The march continued for almost two hours, but there remained no sign of Alex. Shack, discouraged, trudged back to his condo.

Cannon Beach

JONATHAN, SWEATING profusely in the unusual coastal heat, continued to thrash through thick underbrush as he hacked his way up the dry creek bed. It required maximum effort to clear enough space for him to work the metal detector without smacking it into something.

By mid-afternoon, Jonathan slumped to his knees, his energy and will sapped. Zurry plodded over to him and licked his face in apparent sympathy. Jonathan checked his watch and stroked the dog's head. "Okay, boy, one more hour, then we'll bag it."

He struggled to his feet and resumed his efforts, but with a decided lack of enthusiasm. As his one-hour deadline approached, a solid, high-pitched signal rippled through his headset. He swung the detector in a small arc along one side of the old creek bed. A robust "bonging" persisted.

"Well, let's see," he said. He unslung his pack, unsheathed the long-handled digger, and went to work, hacking at the ever-damp soil, roots, and rocks. Driven by a fresh surge of adrenaline, he labored with renewed vigor. Within a half hour, he'd cleared away almost eighteen inches of dirt and stones. Then, with a firm *thunk*, the digger hit something solid, not rock or root.

Jonathan grabbed his short-handled digging tool and, almost in a frenzy, cleared away the remaining soil covering whatever he'd hit. When he'd moved enough dirt to identify it, he whooped, causing Zurry to jump back with a startled *woof.*

Chapter Thirteen

Discovery

Cannon Beach
Saturday, July 4

JONATHAN KNEELED over the hole he'd carved out and reached toward the top of the object he'd unearthed. He brushed at it with his hand, clearing away the thin layer of dirt that remained. It appeared to be the lid of a chest or trunk of some sort, wooden—perhaps mahogany or teak—and secured by leather straps that had rotted and cracked over time. He eyeballed its measurements, perhaps two feet by three feet.

He removed his gloves and rapped on the lid with his knuckles. Solid. Firm. He stood, grabbed the long-handled digger, and drove its pointed, steel-tempered end down hard at the lid. The tool merely bounced off it. His heart hammering like a row of cherry bombs igniting, he retrieved the shorter digger once more and went to work clearing the dirt packed against the sides of the box.

After an extended effort, he'd removed enough soil from the front of the chest to see a pair of rusted iron locks secured to metal hasps and loops fastening the lid firmly in place. He jiggled the locks. Rusted as they were, they showed no weakness, no tendency to crack or break.

He continued digging around the ends of the chest and found leather hand straps, rotted beyond use, on both ends. He cleared the soil at the rear of the trunk, then attempted to rock it back and forth. It barely budged.

He sat back, drained of energy and now even adrenaline. His shirt and pants, saturated with perspiration and stained in mud, clung to him like damp work rags. Zurry stood beside him and he draped his arm over the dog's shoulders.

"I'm whipped, partner," he said. "There's no way I can get this thing out of the ground." Zurry licked Jonathan's face, seeming to enjoy the salty sheen.

"We're going to have to come back and attack it tomorrow. I need some different tools so I can break into it." Zurry cocked his head, as though listening.

Jonathan remained at the edge of the hole, his arm across Zurry's back, and listened to a light breeze sigh through the crown of the forest, to birds twitter and chirp as they fluttered from branch to branch, to a pair of hawks issue piercing shrieks as they circled high overhead, dark forms against a deep blue sky.

He became lost in the soft symphony of nature and dozed off, his head drooping against Zurry's. When he awoke, he found himself, at least for a moment, unable to recall where he was or why. He stared at the hole, the semi-unearthed chest, the rotted straps, and remembered.

He struggled to his feet. "Gotta fill this hole, Zurry. Don't want anybody else finding it." He had to admit, that seemed unlikely, as far off the beaten path as they'd hiked and the fact it already was late afternoon.

His task completed, he stood over the hole and looked around, marking its location by drawing a line in his mind's eye between a moss-covered boulder and the trunk of a massive Douglas fir, and estimating the chest to be about a third of the way from the rock to the tree. He wondered if whoever had buried the box here had flagged the spot using the same landmarks.

He gathered his equipment, slung the pack over his back, and set off downhill, tracking along the gully. "We'll be back tomorrow with the right stuff," he said to Zurry, who moseyed behind him.

He reached his car parked on a low bluff near the beach. He gazed out over the ocean, remembering the dire warnings of an earthquake and tsunami. Even though the day technically had another six hours left, Jonathan felt as though another "end-of-the-world prophecy" had bitten the dust.

"Good thing," he said, verbalizing his thoughts. "I'm too damned bushed to run away from anything." He opened the car door for Zurry who scrambled into the passenger seat and flopped down. The meaty odors of cookouts and barbecues wafted through the open windows of the Pontiac. It seemed as if the residents of Cannon Beach had dismissed, much as Jonathan had, any concerns of a natural catastrophe, and instead had focused on enjoying a perfect end to a nearly perfect Fourth of July.

As Jonathan cruised south on 101 toward Manzanita, visions of shipwrecked mariners, a tall black man, Clatsop Indians, and a chest filled with unknown plunder filled his mind. His heart beat just a bit faster.

Nehalem Bay State Airport

"DAD, MAYBE IT'S time we head back to town." Tim arose from where he'd been seated beneath the wing of the Cessna Skylane. "It's getting dark."

Rob, who'd been pacing in circles around the aircraft, grunted in agreement. He found it difficult to speak, his gut hollowed by impending defeat. His *vision*, as Lewis had termed it, had always been set in daylight, not dusk or dawn or dead of night. And now the day, the Fourth of July, that had seemed the obvious candidate for his prophesied earthquake and tsunami drained into the growing darkness. *Like my reputation, my career, my future.* He thought of Deb. *Maybe my marriage.* He brushed at a mistiness attempting to fill his eyes. He hoped Tim didn't notice.

He motioned for Tim to follow and they set off for Manzanita.

"It's okay, Dad. You did what you thought was right," Tim said, obviously noting his father's distress.

"What was right, son, would have been to have kept my mouth shut."

"Really? Then why didn't you?"

Rob didn't answer.

"Because," Tim continued, "at the time, you thought speaking out was the correct course. Like you always told me, you try something or say something because you think it's right. If it isn't, then you suck it up and admit you blew it. That doesn't make you a bad person. That's what you preach to me, Dad."

Rob reached out and draped his arm over Tim's shoulders. "Fathers are supposed to buck up their sons, not the other way around."

"I can see you're hurting, Dad. I just wanted to help."

A lump in his throat interdicted Rob's response. A tear slid down his cheek. He didn't attempt to blink it back.

A light, a flashlight beam, materialized out of the dusk. Lewis strode toward them, swinging the light in an arc over the gravel taxiway leading to the tie down pads. "Come on, you guys. Time to get home. The fireworks are about to start."

Lewis stopped in front of Rob.

"I screwed the pooch, didn't I?" Rob said, his voice almost a whisper.

Lewis exhaled a long, low breath and looked Rob in the eye. "I'm not so sure about that. I still think there's validity and truth in what you saw, what you felt, what you *experienced*."

Rob shook his head. "No. Deb was right. I was stressed out, obsessed, consumed by my work. It got to me. I just needed to get away from it and get my head straight. I didn't do that. Instead, it got to me, and now I'm paying the piper."

"Look," Lewis said, "get some rest tonight. Then let's sit down in the morning and go over things again. I really feel we missed something, misinterpreted some element of your vision. Let's figure it out."

"Damn it, Lewis. There's nothing to figure out. It wasn't a vision. It was a hallucination. I made my bed, now I have to lie in it. My time is past. Nobody's going to listen to Chicken Little redux."

"My place," Lewis commanded, "eight a.m. I'm not letting go of this without a fight. More to the point, I'm not letting go of you. If you don't show up, I'll break down your frigging door and drag you out of bed."

Manzanita

ROB'S CELL PHONE rang shortly before midnight. Caller ID showed Deborah.

"Go on," he said when he answered, "say it."

"No," she responded, "I won't. I'm not calling to rub it in."

"So why are you?" His words came out encased in curtness. Her abrupt departure the previous day still stung.

She didn't answer immediately, but eventually said, "Because I'm just so damned pissed."

"Really? Well, I'm a little pissed, too."

"You?" she snapped. "Why should you be?"

"Because the person I'd counted on most wouldn't stand beside me." A hard edge remained in his voice.

"It's kinda hard to support someone making a fool of himself and gutting the success and credibility he'd taken years to establish. I was frightened. Now I'm just ticked, really ticked."

"I did what I thought was right."

"Right? Right for whom? Certainly not your family, or your reputation, or your business—all the things in life you've worked so hard for, all the things that are circling the drain now. No, wait. I just heard a gurgling sound. They're gone, Rob. In the sewer."

He slipped into a defensive mode. "Deb, listen—"

"No, you listen. You know what one TV commentator called you tonight? The Seismology Shyster. He went on to rail against the mainstream media for giving a platform to guys like you, 'pseudo-scientific nut cases.' Let 'em blather on Facebook or Twitter, he said, at least there they'll be with their own kind."

"He might have bitten the hand that feeds him."

"I doubt it. I'm sure he had the full blessing of his station. They know which way the popular wind is blowing."

Rob, deflated, slumped into an easy chair. He wanted to be angry, but found himself unable to focus his ire. Sure, he was the prime target, but he wanted a co-conspirator. Maybe Lewis, for leading him down the primrose path. Or Deb, for failing to be supportive. No. It all came back to him.

"I fucked up," he said softly into the phone.

"Yes, you did."

"So now what?"

She expelled a long, slow breath. "We'll talk about it when you get home."

"What's that mean?"

"It means we'll talk about when you get home." She hung up.

A string of firecrackers exploded in the street outside the condo, but failed to startle Rob. He found himself half hoping it might have been an assassin's attempt on his life.

SHACK, ALONG WITH several thousand others near the beach, had watched the sun, wrapped in cloaks of gold and orange and salmon, sink into the sea with the grace of a dowager bidding adieu to the world. Now, he paced along Ocean Road, to the rear of the crowd that had seated itself on beach blankets, sand chairs, and driftwood to await the town's annual fireworks extravaganza. He hoped against hope to spot Alex, but time verged on running out. In the growing darkness, it would soon be impossible to spot anyone. And the questions he had would go unanswered, at least on a face-to-face basis.

So, maybe one more recon sweep past her house. He trudged toward Manzanita Avenue, the street he thought would take him to Alex's. He hadn't gone more than a few steps when she appeared, striding toward the beach on the opposite side of the road. She apparently hadn't spotted him, or at least recognized him in the dusk, for she didn't slow or acknowledge his presence as she drew abeam of him.

"Alex?"

She halted and squinted in his direction.

"It's me, Shack."

"Oh. I thought you'd be packing. Don't you have to leave for Portland early in the morning?"

"It's good to see you, too."

"Yeah, well . . ."

He moved across the narrow road, now devoid of traffic. "Alex—"

"Hey, we had deal, remember? Dinner, then you'd be out of my life forever. That was the agreement." She stood with her hands on her hips, daring him to come closer.

He stopped. "I've been trying to find you for the last couple of days."

"I was out of town. My daughter invited me to a barbecue last night."

"Did she come back with you?"

"What is this? A criminal investigation?"

"Why are you so damn hostile, Alex? I came here to apologize. I know I treated you badly. Let's at least try to part in peace."

"Good idea." She made a peace sign with her right hand. "Peace. Good bye."

"Why Skylar?"

"What?"

"Why did you name your daughter *Sky*lar?" He put a slight emphasis on *Sky*.

She hesitated, then retorted, "Why not?"

"How old is she?"

Alex pivoted away from him and stepped off the road into the sand dunes.

"Twenty-four, twenty-five?" he called after her.

She halted, glaring at him. She stripped off her sandals and held them in her hand. "One more step, and I swear to God I *will* call the cops. Stalking. If you want to challenge me on my home turf for battery, fine. Give it a go, and good luck."

"Tell me, Alex. I have a right to know." The words came out harsh and commanding.

"You abdicated your rights, you bastard."

"She's my daughter, too, isn't she?" he yelled.

The fireworks display launched with a sudden series of artillery-like explosions that rocked the night. Skyrockets detonated overhead, showering the beach in multi-colored pyrotechnics. A second fusillade of sharp, loud bangs followed, echoing through the gloaming as fiery stars wobbled from the sky, tumbling onto the sand like drunken butterflies.

Alex sprinted into the crowd.

Shack called after her, but she'd disappeared, swallowed by the spectators, the noise, the man-made lightning.

"Skylar," he whispered to himself. Alex's reaction had validated his hypothesis. He had his answer. He had a daughter.

Chapter Fourteen

Two Hours

Manzanita
Sunday, July 5

ROB ARRIVED AT Lewis's shortly after eight in the morning. Lewis already had coffee on the table along with a half-dozen bagels and two tubs of cream cheese, different flavors. Rob mumbled a thank-you and took a seat. He welcomed the coffee. The typical summer chill of the Oregon coast had returned. A flannel overcast hid the top of Neahkahnie Mountain, and gulls, fighting a stiff headwind, hovered stationary over the beach.

Lewis sat across from Rob and took out a notepad, the same one he'd used a week earlier. He studied it as he sipped coffee. Rob remained silent, staring out a window into the gloomy-looking morning, the scene matching his mood.

"In your dream," Lewis said after several minutes, dabbing at his mouth with a napkin, "you said it appeared to be the Fourth of July."

Rob nodded.

"You mentioned you could see a banner advertising the parade flapping in the wind."

Rob shrugged. "Yeah."

"And people bundled up, waiting for the parade, you thought."

"I could hear bagpipers, too."

"But not see them. You said the sounds seemed to be growing more distant."

"Yes." Rob couldn't figure out where Lewis was going with this.

"My point is, maybe the people weren't waiting for the parade, maybe it had gone by already. You said the sound of the pipers faded away completely. So I think, in your dream, the parade wasn't approaching, it was leaving, gone; the fading music being metaphorical."

Rob took a bite of a pumpernickel bagel and chewed on it before answering. Finished, he said, "So what? Coming, going? What's the difference? There was no quake and tsunami yesterday. I got it wrong."

Lewis looked down at his notepad again, then tapped his forefinger on something he'd written. "You said the people in your dream were bundled up." He waited for Rob to respond.

"Jackets and sweatshirts, yes."

"The day was cool and windy then?"

Rob closed his eyes and tried to re-imagine his dream, his nightmare, his vision, whatever it had been. "So it seemed."

"And overcast, you mentioned."

"You took pretty damned detailed notes."

"Something I got used to doing when I was involved in counseling."

"So what's with the forensic reconstruction of the weather?" Rob took another bite of his bagel.

"Think about yesterday. Not the one in your dream, the one we enjoyed in reality. Sunny, warm, almost calm. Kind of unusual for the coast."

"What's your point?"

"A member of my congregations, oh, maybe ten or fifteen years ago in Portland, was a meteorologist. One of the excuses he liked to use when he missed a forecast was 'right forecast, wrong day.'" Lewis let the statement hang.

Rob nodded his head slowly, understanding dawning on him. "So you think I got the day wrong. What about all the people I saw on Laneda? That was a holiday crowd."

"Today's still part of the holiday. The streets will be jammed. And today, unlike yesterday, folks will be decked out in jackets and sweatshirts, just like in your dream."

"I dunno, Lewis." Still smarting from yesterday's disappointment, Rob stood and walked to the window.

"Look out there," Lewis said. "Cloudy, breezy, exactly what you described to me." He rose from his chair and moved next to Rob. "Your vision, what you experienced in your dream, is valid, I strongly believe that. We just misinterpreted the timing."

"Yeah. What if it's next year's holiday, or the year after that?" He paused. "Once burned . . ."

Lewis lowered his chin to his chest, as though contemplating Rob's concern. "Okay, how about this?" he said after a moment. "In your dream, you said your kids, Tim and Maria, were with you. How did they look? Any different from what they do today, like older or more mature? They're at an age where a year or two can make a huge difference in appearance."

"They didn't seem any different. I certainly didn't have the sense they were older. It seemed to me everything was happening as if it were today."

"There. You put your finger on it. Today."

Rob wheeled. "You really think?" His heart rate suddenly ticked a few beats faster. He wanted to believe, but his scientific-objective-skeptical nature jumped to the forefront, shaking a cautionary finger at him, and crying, "No, no, no."

"Yes," Lewis said. "I really think."

"I don't know. Even if that's correct, what do I do? Go public again? Say, 'Oops, sorry. I didn't get it quite right the first time around. The end of the world wasn't yesterday, it's today!'? I'm not sure *I'd* believe me."

Lewis stared at the floor, seemingly mulling over various options.

"I've got an idea," he said finally. "Why don't we sit down with just one reporter instead of going in front of the pack? One correspondent of our choosing. That way we—you—don't get torn apart in a feeding frenzy."

"Who are you thinking of?"

"Amanda Jeffries, that gal from KGW-TV."

"Oh, yeah. That went well, didn't it? She and I hit it off famously. Lewis, I love you to death, but sometimes, I swear, you just go stupid on me."

"No, listen to me. You locked horns. Big deal. She's skeptical, as a journalist should be, but she's also smart. I think we can plead our case with her. She'll listen, give us a fair hearing."

"I doubt it."

"Come on. Let's try it."

"No."

"No? You're going against advice of clergy?"

Rob rolled his eyes. "You're retired."

"That makes my wisdom less valuable?"

"Wisdom, really?"

"Here's the thing, Rob. You believed in your vision twenty-four hours ago. You told me it seemed so real you sensed you were there. Nothing fundamental has changed since then except our interpretation regarding the timing of the event. The event itself, your vision, is still valid. We can only lose by sitting on it."

"I'll think about it."

Lewis shook his head. "Don't. You'll only come to the wrong conclusion. Besides, the clock is ticking."

Rob reran the nightmare through his mind. It remained powerful, palpable: the shaking, the surge, the black water, the fear, the inevitability of tragedy.

"I don't suppose I can trash myself any worse than I have already," he said.

"I'll call the station in Portland," Lewis said. "They'll put us in touch with Ms. Jeffries."

A HALF HOUR later, Amanda Jeffries knocked on the door of Lewis's house. Lewis opened the door for her and her cameraman. Outside, the KGW-TV communications truck sat on the side of the street.

"Coffee?" Lewis asked, as the two news people entered the house.

"No, thank you," Amanda said. "I'd prefer to wrap up our interview as quickly as possible so we can get back to Portland. My news director said you had some additional information for us?"

"We do."

"An apology, perhaps?" There seemed a note of triumph in her voice.

Rob stepped forward. "No, an explanation."

"About why your prophecy blew up?"

Rob evaluated her question. "In part," he said. "But also an explanation about why the danger hasn't passed."

"*Really.*" The word came out coated in skepticism and sarcasm.

"Give us ten minutes," Lewis said. "Then *you* decide whether to go ahead and do an interview."

Amanda looked at her cameraman, who shrugged. "Okay," she said, "ten minutes."

The cameraman seated himself on a sofa while Amanda, Rob, and Lewis sat around the table. Rob and Lewis recapped the analysis and discussion they'd had earlier before Amanda arrived. She sat silently, listening and jotting notes on an iPad.

After they'd finished, she remained quiet, drumming her fingers on the table. She stood and paced to the window where she looked out at the truck. She turned. "Sorry," she said, "I'm afraid I'm not a true believer. I just don't see where the credibility is. You'll have to admit, it was pretty flaky stuff to begin with."

"Not flaky," Lewis countered. "Different, certainly, but not off the wall."

"Difference of opinion then," Amanda said. "It's still basically black magic and not scientific. I work for a *news* organization. You probably should get in touch with the *National Enquirer* or *Globe* with your concerns."

"Lives are at stake," Lewis said. "This is time sensitive, not a joke. We asked for you because we thought you'd give us a fair hearing."

"I did. What I heard is the same stuff I heard Friday. And that didn't work out. You unnecessarily frightened a lot of people."

"Apparently not that many," Rob said. "The streets looked pretty damned crowded yesterday."

"And maybe we didn't frighten people as much as we raised their awareness," Lewis added.

"It's still all based on a vision, a dream," Amanda said. "What are you going to do? Come out every day with an updated interpretation? Martin Luther King, Jr., had a dream, and more than fifty years later it still hasn't come to fruition." She turned to her cameraman. "Come on, Dawson. Let's get out of here." She flicked her head, a dismissive gesture, tossing her hair out of her eyes.

"If it's news you want," Rob said, a bit more sharply than he intended, "maybe you should hang around for a couple of hours. You'll get an exclusive."

"A couple of hours?" Amanda said. "What happens in a couple of hours?"

Supplementing her query, Lewis shot Rob a "what's up" look.

"In my dream," Rob said, "my wife and I had stopped for coffee. We don't drink coffee in the afternoon."

A deathly stillness filled the room. The quiet seemed to settle over everyone as if it had weight.

Amanda broke the hush. "It's just before ten. So two, three hours at the most?"

Rob nodded.

"I don't know." She turned to her cameraman, Dawson. "All the other trucks have left, haven't they?"

"Probably."

Amanda stared hard at Rob. "Okay, I know you believe even if I don't. I'll give you a three-hour benefit of the doubt, just on the slim chance we'll score a news coup."

"You suddenly believe?" Lewis whispered to Rob.

"Yeah, for some strange reason I do. At least for the next few hours."

"You need to get something on the air," Lewis said to Amanda, his voice authoritative, as if coming from a pulpit.

"Not gonna happen," she shot back. "It's still all smoke and mirrors without a credible, scientific foundation."

"It's okay, Lewis," Rob said. "She's right."

"You're on her side now?"

Amanda flashed Rob one of her disarming smiles, and opened the door to leave. "Where should we position ourselves?"

"Go back to the upper end of Laneda. You'll at least be out of the tsunami zone there."

She nodded and stepped out into the cool, gray morning. Dawson followed.

Lewis turned to Rob. "We should have pressed harder to get an alert broadcast."

"I don't think so. She wasn't going to capitulate. But the mere fact a news crew is hanging around with a sat truck may raise a few questions and start some buzz going." He looked out onto the road, beginning to fill with people heading to church, to breakfast, maybe for an early walk on the beach.

"Besides," Rob continued, "if people aren't already prepared for something to happen, they aren't going to be in three hours." He paused. "Or three minutes."

Cannon Beach

JONATHAN ARRIVED early at the old creek bed to resume his efforts to open the locked box he'd unearthed the previous day. Zurry trotted by his side, stopping occasionally to sniff at doggie points of interest. Jonathan wore a lightweight vest to ward off the morning coolness, and a carpenter's tool belt from which he'd slung a heavy-duty bolt cutter, hatchet, hammer, several large chisels, and a pair of locking-jaw pliers—all items he thought might be useful in breaching the chest. He'd also brought along, in his backpack, several empty boxes and a dozen or so canvas bags . . . just in case. "I know," he said to Zurry, "counting my loot before opening the treasure chest." *If that's what it is.*

He found the landmarks, the Doug fir and mossy boulder, easily enough, and within a matter of seconds spotted the location where'd he'd been working, undisturbed from the way he'd left it.

He unsheathed the digging tool and once more uncovered the chest. He dropped to his knees and studied it. Slicing through the rusted iron padlocks seemed to offer the best opportunity of breaking into the box. He retrieved the bolt cutter and fitted the cutting blades over the shackle of the lock on the left. He stood, bent over the hole, and muscled the yard-long handles of the cutter together. The corroded lock proved no match for the leverage supplied by the heavy-duty tool, and the shackle split with a satisfying *crunch*.

"Yesss," Jonathan hissed.

He fit the cutter over the shackle of the second lock. He squeezed the cutter's handles together, and the lock popped apart with ease.

He knelt, pulled the severed locks from the chest and placed them in one of the pockets of his vest. He reached down, put his hands on either side of the now-unbound lid and tugged upward. It didn't budge. Again he tried, again it didn't move. *Crap*.

He examined the chest more closely and discovered the rim of the lid to be trimmed in iron, as was the brim of the chest. Rusted together, fused as if soldered.

There didn't appear to be enough room between the chest and surrounding soil to hammer one of the chisels into the rusted seam. And the chest itself, as Jonathan had discovered yesterday, couldn't be lifted from the ground.

"Oh, well, old-fashioned way then." He stood, plucked the hatchet from his tool belt and went to work on the hardwood lid.

The cover seemed impervious to the first few blows, the hatchet merely leaving dents in the wood. The sound of chopping rang through the woods and sent several squirrels into a scolding frenzy. In the middle distance, a dog yapped. Zurry's ears pricked up.

Jonathan kept at it, pacing his hatchet swings so as not to tire quickly. Gradually, the dents became scars, then cracks. At last, one of the cracks ruptured. The hatchet jammed itself into the fissure. Jonathan jimmied it out, then slammed it into the wood several more times. After about ten minutes, he'd managed to hack out an opening roughly a foot long and several inches wide. He peered into the breach, but the dim light prevented him from identifying anything. He could tell only that there seemed to be "stuff" in there.

He took a breather, then went back to work. Hack, hack, hack. He feared the noise would draw unwanted attention, but other than rebukes from the local denizens—squirrels and birds—no one showed up.

After another half hour of chopping, he had enough wood splintered and slashed to be able to yank the pieces from the lid. After clearing the debris away, he leaned over the chest.

"Hol-lee shit," he said softly, drawing the phrase out. Zurry stood beside him and stared into the hole, perhaps hoping to find plundered dog treats.

Manzanita

SHACK, WITH AN early afternoon departure on Delta from Portland to Atlanta, knew he didn't have much time. It would take at least a couple of hours to drive to Portland International. First, however, he wanted to talk with Alex. He *needed* to talk with Alex. He packed the car, left his house key in the condo, and drove through the sunless morning to Alex's.

He rapped on her front door. No answer. He rang the doorbell. Again, no response. With virtually no traffic, vehicular or foot, in the neighborhood, he decided to walk around the house to see if he could spot Alex through a window. First, he checked the garage and saw her car. That confirmed her presence.

He set off along the side of the residence, following a narrow path through seagrass, salal, and blackberry brambles, so unlike the neat Bermuda grass lawns that carpeted Atlanta subdivisions. He peaked into a couple of windows, trying not to appear like a cat burglar, but drawn Roman shades blocked his view.

At the rear of the house, he found a cedar deck with a built-in spa tub. He stepped onto the deck and moved cautiously toward a set of glass doors leading to the interior of the home. He placed his hands on either side of his face to block outside light, pressed his nose against the glass, and stared into what appeared to be a sunroom. He caught, or thought he did, a glimpse of motion in an adjacent hallway. He tapped on the glass and called Alex's name. His efforts went unanswered.

Discouraged and a little bit angry, he moved back to the front of Alex's house. He couldn't phone her because he didn't have her personal number, but she probably wouldn't have answered anyhow. He stood beside his car trying to figure out what to do next when a Manzanita police SUV drove up.

"Shit, Alex," Shack muttered to himself.

The officer, a kid who didn't appear to be out of his twenties, climbed from the vehicle and approached Shack. "Sir, what's going on here?"

"I was just trying to contact Alex . . . Ms. Williamson."

"You're Mr. McCready, I assume?" The cop stopped several yards in front of Shack and looked him up and down, a careful, practiced procedure.

"Yes."

"Well, you were trespassing, Mr. McCready. And Ms. Williamson apparently doesn't want to see you."

Unsure of what to say, and taken aback by Alex's determination to have no further dealings with him, Shack merely nodded.

"We can resolve this peacefully if you agree to leave the area now and not return. Ms. Williamson doesn't wish to press charges." He paused. "I understand you're scheduled to leave town today?"

"I have a one p.m. flight out of Portland."

The cop checked his wristwatch. "It might be a good idea to get on the road then. The traffic can get heavy going back to Portland on a Sunday."

"Am I permitted to have breakfast first?"

The young officer squinted at him, perhaps trying for a Clint Eastwood glare. "Yeah, sure. Try The Big Wave up on 101. But if you come back here, I *will* arrest you. *Capiche?*"

Shack almost burst out laughing, but decided he might get the bum's rush if he did. *Capiche? Really?* Instead he said, "Got it."

Chapter Fifteen

Warnings

Manzanita
Sunday, July 5

ROB LEFT LEWIS'S place and headed back to the beach house to roust Tim out of bed. Like most teenagers, Timothy loved to sleep in on his "days off," which amounted to most of summer vacation. They needed to get over to the airstrip again, so if—when—the earthquake struck they could get the Skylane airborne as quickly as possible.

As Rob trudged through the loose gravel on the shoulder of the macadam road, he heard footsteps behind him. He stopped and turned.

"Oh, I didn't mean to startle you," Cassie said.

"You didn't. Just kind of snuck up on me, I guess."

They continued walking, and she fell in beside him, her lush red hair, as usual, tumbling from beneath a ball cap. And as usual, Rob had no clue as to how old she might be. She seemed . . . ageless.

"So today's the day, I guess," she said.

"What?" The question surprised him. How could anyone have picked up on that so rapidly?

"The TV satellite truck, it's still here," she said. "There's not much reason for it to stick around except . . . ." She stared at him, and he read a timeless wisdom in her eyes, and a thought as bizarre as his "vision" flashed through his mind.

"No," he said slowly. "You didn't need any physical clues to figure this out." He stopped walking and faced her. "You know, don't you?"

She shrugged. "Maybe I sense it, that's all. I'm just a university researcher."

"From Troy?"

"Yes."

"In Alabama?"

"Everyone has to be from someplace." She laughed. "Look, I just wanted to get in touch with you and say goodbye."

"I thought you said you'd be around for a few weeks yet?"

"My work is finished. I need to get home." She moved her gaze toward the ocean as though seeing something unseeable, then looked again at Rob. "You've done well, Dr. Elwood. You've stayed true to your principles and beliefs, spoke the truth in your prophecies, and weathered the curses." She touched him lightly on the arm. "I know about curses."

"How?"

"It comes with the territory."

"What territory?"

"You'll figure it out." She stepped away from him. "I need to get going. Don't wanna get caught in a tsunami."

The sudden yapping of a large dog in a nearby yard drew Rob's attention from Cassie. When he turned back to say goodbye, she was gone. He caught a glimpse of her lithe figure fading into a soft ocean haze as she walked toward Laneda. He tracked her visually until she turned a corner, heading up Laneda toward 101.

Yes, I figured it out. I know who you are. But I don't believe it.

More dogs joined the initial yapper. Then yowling cats. Their barks and cries melded quickly into an urgent chorus of concern filling the morning.

Rob broke into a sprint toward the beach house.

Cannon Beach

JONATHAN STARED into the opening he'd hacked out in the lid of the chest. His breathing became rapid and shallow, pure excitement. Zurry looked from the box to Jonathan and back again, puzzled, obviously not understanding his master's exhilaration.

Jonathan surveyed the contents of the box, although as yet they were only partially visible. He spotted small leather pouches secured with twine, porcelain objects, bundles of silk, chunks of something that looked like beeswax, and in the bottom. . . . He reached into the chest and thrust aside the other objects. Ingots! He counted them, six, each about a foot long.

He withdrew his hand from the chest and stared at Zurry. "Jesus, can you believe this, old boy? Gold. No-bullshit-real-deal gold." He couldn't be certain of it, of course, but what else could the bars be?

Images of Manila galleons and pirate vessels danced through his mind. Perhaps the ship of Indian legend had been a trading galleon blown far off course as it plied the Manila-Acapulco route across the Pacific. Or maybe it had been a pirate vessel, full of plunder, making a desperate run north along the West Coast of North America in search of escape through the fabled Northwest Passage, or perhaps merely seeking shelter in a hidden harbor or river mouth.

Jonathan retrieved a couple of the canvas bags he'd brought with him and spread them flat on the ground beside the hole. He began dredging items from the chest and placing them on the bags. After fifteen minutes he'd unloaded the contents except for the ingots. He struggled with those. He estimated each weighed thirty or forty pounds. By the time he'd hoisted those from the chest, sweat saturated his clothes, a strange counterpoint to the coolness of the morning.

He brushed himself off and stood, studying the plunder before him. He focused on the bars. Their color, weight, and the fact they appeared only lightly tarnished suggested, given his minimal knowledge of the subject, they had to be gold. He drew a deep breath and tried to calculate in his mind how much they might be worth. He thought gold currently sold for something on the order of a thousand dollars per ounce, but knew the price jumped around a lot. *So, sixteen ounces to a pound, let's say each bar weighs thirty pounds, that's . . .*

He found himself unable to focus, unable to do the math, but realized he'd probably uncovered a fortune worth . . . what? Hundreds of thousands of dollars? Millions? He couldn't comprehend it.

He knelt and opened one of the leather pouches and emptied its contents onto the spread-out canvas. Several dozen irregularly shaped coins tumbled out. *Silver?* In truth, they appeared more like misshapen pieces of jewelry than real coins. Again his heart fluttered. *Are these the storied pieces of eight? If so, how much would they be worth?* He counted four more bags. *So, thousands of dollars? More? Less?*

He drifted away on an ocean of fantasy, forgetting where he was, what he was doing. Then he blanked totally, confusion reigning, as it seemed to do more and more frequently these days. He remained kneeling as though doing penance at the altar of life.

A soft rumble emanating from deep within Zurry's chest, like the reverberation of a distant diesel engine, snapped Jonathan out of his involuntary reverie. He stood and looked around, expecting to see an elk or bear or bobcat nearby. Nothing caught his eye. He spoke to Zurry.

"Somebody coming, boy?"

He stared back down the dry creek bed. He saw no movement, except for underbrush and wild grass quivering ever so slightly in the breeze. Zurry continued to growl, his nose pointed toward the ocean.

Jonathan surveyed their surroundings, looking for some hint of an invader, animal or human. No threats appeared, but Zurry sensed something. Jonathan placed his hand on Zurry's head and felt the warning vibrations rippling through the dog's massive body. Zurry nudged closer to him, leaned against him, as though in a protective mode.

Then Jonathan got it. *Oh, no. Not now. Please, not now.* He glanced at the treasure that lay at his feet.

Manzanita

SHACK SAT IN a booth near a window at The Big Wave Cafe and watched the sparse morning traffic—cars, SUVs, motorhomes— plodding along Highway 101 underneath a leaden sky. A waitress tossed a menu onto his table, but he ignored it, lost in the wilderness of his thoughts.

He understood Alex's animus toward him now, but remained taken aback by its intensity after so many years. He supposed he deserved it. He'd led her into a rose garden, then left her standing alone in the middle of it, surrounded by thorns, not beauty. He'd never contacted her again, never checked up on her, never asked about her— ignored her, in fact. He'd been uncaring, uncommitted, unconcerned.

She'd raised *their* daughter on her own. She'd been, and still was, a proud, stubborn, intelligent woman, never tracking him down to ask for help or to take responsibility. He'd been an absentee father since the get-go, and would, he now realized, be forever an unwelcome member of his own family.

If only Alex knew that he did care, that he did feel responsibility for his actions. That his expressions of regret were sincere. "I know," he muttered, "a few thousand days late and tens of thousands of dollars short."

He wondered if there were legal recourses to get in touch with his daughter, but then realized she was no longer a minor or a dependent, that he could find her and get in touch with her on his own. Not that he'd be any more welcomed by her than he'd been by Alex.

An empty, hollowed-out sensation wormed its way into his psyche. He buried his head in his hands and leaned forward, his elbows planted on the table. He drifted off into a swamp of black thoughts and assessed what he had become. Middle-aged. Alone. Smoldering bridges behind him. A sorry existence cloaked in a flimsy, tattered garment of good intents woven from lessons learned too late.

"Ready to order?"

He jerked his head up. "What?"

A dark-haired, slender waitress, possibly close to Skylar's age, stood beside his table, tapping a pencil on an order pad. "Are you ready to order? Or would you like to snooze a little bit more?"

"I wasn't snoozing, I was reflecting."

"About what to order?"

"Yeah. How about cheese grits?"

"We've got cheese omelets."

"No grits?"

"What're they?"

Shack grunted. "Any hush puppies?"

"Shoes?" Her tone revealed genuine surprise.

Shack rolled his eyes and opened the menu. "Give me a minute." He scanned the fare quickly. "Seafood omelet." He jabbed his finger at the entry.

"Coffee?"

"Please."

The waitress returned in short order with a pot of coffee and a cup. The cup rattled in its saucer as she placed it on the table. She poured the coffee, but the cup persisted in its jiggling and caused her to miss the mark, the dark liquid splattering onto the table.

"Oh, my," she said, more startled than embarrassed.

Shack glanced toward 101, expecting to see an eighteen-wheeler or log truck lumbering by, but the highway appeared temporarily devoid of traffic.

A sharp jolt rippled through the restaurant, triggering a brittle chorus of clattering dishes and utensils. Several patrons rose from their seats and moved toward the exit. The waitress set the coffee pot on the table and followed them.

Chapter Sixteen

Megaquake

Manzanita
Sunday, July 5

AS ROB SPRINTED toward his beach house, he, ever the scientist, checked his wristwatch. Ten twenty-three a.m. The ensemble of yapping and yowling pets had been his canary in a coal mine. He knew enough about earthquakes to understand what was happening, the sequence of events that had begun to unfold. First to hit would be the seismic "body" waves, called P- and S-waves, that ripple through the Earth's interior.

The leaders, the P- or primary waves, had already arrived. Compressional waves, much like those that zip along a Slinky, they course through rock and water faster than any other seismic waves. Humans may not sense them, but animals do. Because of their speed, they are the first to be detected by seismographs.

A few ticks of the clock behind the P-waves come the S- or secondary waves. They propagate only through solid rock, not water, and thus lag the P-waves slightly, jerking both up and down and sideways.

These harbingers are not the impulses that cause damage, however; they are the warm-up acts, triggering only bumps and rattles. The main event slams in in the form of "surface" waves, seismic ripples that race through the Earth's crust, trailing the "body" waves by only a matter of seconds.

Their names, Love and Rayleigh waves, flashed through Rob's mind as he continued to run, his breathing now deep and labored. Out of shape. But the names Love and Rayleigh would not matter to a population about to be hammered by a megathrust earthquake. They would know and care only that their world seemed to be coming apart beneath them.

His chest heaving, Rob reached the beach house, and paused, head down, hands on knees, gulping air.

"Running from your detractors?" Hector Springer, with what Rob could only describe as a shit-eating grin, stood outside the house. "You invited me to bust your balls if your fantsyquake failed to materialize yesterday, so here I am." A phlegmy chortle escaped from his throat. "But probably what needs to be busted is your crystal ball. Or maybe you could just sell it to help pay your legal bills. The lawsuits are coming, you know." He tugged his pants up and gave Rob a victory smile.

Rob, gasping for breath, pulled himself erect. "Think again, dip shit," he snapped, a childish response, but heartfelt.

The first of the "surface" waves struck, hurling Rob into a picket fence surrounding his house. He righted himself, but a massive undulation, like a huge ocean swell, followed, surging through the ground and knocking him off his feet. The side of his house split with a resounding *CRACK!*

Hector, wide-eyed, tumbled to the pavement beside Rob. "What the fuck?" he blurted. "You said this would happen yesterday."

"I lied."

Screams and yells from other nearby homes and condos filled the morning. Pedestrians, bewildered, knelt in place and watched pines and firs whip back and forth overhead in a frantic ballet. Fissures, like skeletal fingers, opened in the ground, zigzagging through streets and yards. Utility poles snapped and toppled. Brilliant flashes, blue and white explosions of light, arced from severed power lines. Broken electrical cables, like beheaded snakes, writhed on the ground, spitting angry sparks.

The great earthen swells kept coming, tearing the town apart, knocking down flimsier structures, bending and warping others. Many wooden-frame homes managed to remain standing, but jiggled and jumped from their foundations. Some buildings appeared to sink into themselves, slumping into the ground until only their roofs remained visible—shingled mushroom caps marking the location of a collapsed structure. Liquefied soil, Rob knew.

Accompanying the unfolding apocalypse, a death rattle echoed through the city, a deep rumbling as if a hundred freight trains were lumbering by simultaneously. In a discordant counterpoint, the wail and blare of dozens of car alarms filled the air.

A propane tank, sheared of its moorings, tumbled along the street like an errant, fat football. It brushed past a sparking power line and erupted in a mini-fireball.

Hector crawled along the sidewalk, found a fire hydrant and, using it as leverage, pulled himself upright. He took off in a zigzag jog-waddle toward the center of town.

Rob struggled to his feet and, as the ground continued to heave, weaved along the sidewalk leading to his front door, determined to get to Tim and get him out.

Cannon Beach

AT FIRST, NOTHING more than a tiny shake buzzed through the forest. Zurry ceased barking. Jonathan grabbed his backpack and yanked out several more canvas bags. A hard jolt reverberated through the ground, a violent horizontal shake. Almost simultaneously, the floor of the forest heaved upward sending Jonathan sprawling. He glanced up. The trees surrounding him leaned sharply in one direction, then another, whiplashing to and fro. Shotgun-like detonations blasted through the woods as dozens of trees snapped or toppled. The sky darkened with flocks of bewildered, terrified birds soaring above the crown of the forest.

Jonathan reached for Zurry and pulled him close. Together, they curled into a ball, nestling partially in the hole Jonathan had excavated. Jonathan could only hope and pray an eighty-ton Douglas fir wouldn't come crashing down on them, crushing them into the earth along with their newfound treasure. Treasure, Jonathan realized, that teetered on the verge of becoming lost again, maybe this time forever.

The ground continued to rise and fall and shake with such violence Jonathan doubted anything could be left standing. There seemed no end to the ferocity. Another heavy jolt shook loose a great chunk of earth, and Jonathan found himself, Zurry, and their incipient riches sliding down the side of Haystack Hill, a real-life magic carpet ride. Except this ride seemed bent on killing them.

In the wake of the sliding slab, dozens of towering evergreens collapsed as the soil in which they had been rooted for decades disappeared. The din of falling and snapping trees echoed through the forest with the fury of a firefight in the jungles of Vietnam. Jonathan clung to Zurry with a tenacity born of that faraway conflict, a tenacity fueled by both love and fear.

The landslide swept them across South Hemlock Street, the road paralleling the beach. At last, the sliding earth mushed to a halt. Jonathan ventured a cautious peak over the mounds of mud that surrounded them. A great gouge in the earth, littered with fallen trees, marked the path of the slide. Nearby, several homes had been bulldozed from their foundations and now appeared as nothing more than shattered stacks of debris. Elsewhere, nearly every house he could see had sustained some sort of damage ranging from minor to catastrophic. Only a pile of mud stood on the spot where he'd parked his car on South Hemlock.

The shaking of the earth persisted, though it seemed to be relenting, becoming less savage. Jonathan tried to guess how long the peak of the violence had lasted. It seemed an eternity, but, forcing himself to be objective, probably had been less than three minutes, certainly more than one.

Jonathan pushed himself up to his hands and knees. Zurry, looking frightened and confused, rose, too. Jonathan scrambled through the mud and dirt searching for the treasures he'd unearthed, hoping they'd ridden the slide with him and Zurry. To his amazement, probably because the chunk of earth that had swept them down had held together like a slab in an ice floe, he found much of the loot quickly, still intact, wrapped in canvas and coated in mud. His backpack had disappeared, however. He knocked the mud from the canvas bags he'd used as mats and went to work filling them with the treasure.

People, some with go-bags, others with nothing, all dazed, began to appear in the streets. A few seemed to take charge, pointing and urging others to move toward higher ground. Several passed close enough to Jonathan to see him working in the detritus of the slide. "Better come on, buddy," one called out, "a tsunami's coming."

Jonathan acknowledged the alert and said he'd be along shortly. He wondered why the community's warning sirens hadn't sounded, the ones humorously famous by being tested monthly with the sound of mooing cows instead of wailing klaxons. The obvious answer for the lack of sirens: Cannon Beach had lost its electrical power.

Jonathan worked at a furious pace, stuffing three gold ingots into each of the two bags, then piling in as much of the other plunder as he could: silk, the small leather pouches with pieces of silver, chunks of what he presumed to be centuries-old beeswax. He didn't bother with the porcelain. Much of it was already cracked and broken, and what remained intact wouldn't survive being lugged over debris-littered terrain.

Finished, he stood and looked around. Vibrations continued to ripple through the ground. The foot traffic had disappeared. He knew he had to get away from where he was, gain elevation, find safety. Haystack Hill should do it. Maybe he could find a side street leading partway up the hill. He stooped to pick up the canvas bags, planning on toting one in each hand, ferrying them to safety.

"Shit," he said, as he attempted to hoist them. "Damn it all, Zurry, I can't lift these suckers."

In his rush to fill the bags, he'd forgotten each would weigh over a hundred pounds. No longer a young man, when he could have picked them up like grocery sacks, he found himself forced to drag them. He glanced at the ocean. The tide had retreated, leaving Haystack Rock exposed to its base. From all he'd read and heard, he knew he had only a matter of minutes to find sanctuary from the tsunami.

He struggled through the mud and debris, tugging the bags, each leaving a long drag mark like a carcass being pulled by a carnivore. His intent: to find a clear footpath or road leading up the flank of Haystack Hill. He didn't know how far up he'd have to climb, but figured a hundred feet above the beach would do it.

In short order, his leg muscles burned, his shoulders throbbed, his hands cramped. "Can't do this, Zurry," he panted. "Too frigging old." Yet he knew he had to, knew that would be the only way he would ever rise from the economic backwater in which he existed. He drew a deep breath and went back to work. Drag, pause. Drag, pause. He looked again at the ocean. The tide had continued its slide toward the horizon, leaving hundreds of yards of exposed, naked sand. How much time did he have? Five minutes? Ten? Certainly no more than that.

"Please, sir!"

A voice startled him. He released one of the bags and pivoted in place, searching for the source of the words.

"Here. In here. Help." There seemed a desperate edge to the plea.

An elderly man, bent and wizened like a tree that had lived beyond its time, emerged from a partially crushed home. He waved a cane at Jonathan. "My wife. She's in a wheelchair. I need help."

Jonathan let go of the other bag. "I'll call 911," he said.

"No, I tried already. There's no phone service."

Jonathan realized no one would show up anyhow. Debris, landslides, and fallen trees blocked the roads. He glanced at his bags, at the old man, at the ever-retreating ocean. If he ignored the pleas of the old man and fled with the treasure, who would know the difference? The tsunami would claim the couple. How many years could they have left anyhow? He and Zurry would be on Easy Street, and life would go on. Besides, who in the hell had ever given *him* a break? A black man in America.

He reached down for the bags and resumed his slow-motion flight to safety. "I'll send help," he called out.

"No, no. The ocean's coming. Please."

Manzanita

SHACK, MOMENTARILY bewildered, sat rooted to his booth in The Big Wave as the establishment emptied. A huge swell seemed to surge beneath the cafe, cracking walls and shattering windows. Shack bolted from his seat and followed the exodus.

Outside, he struggled to remain standing as the ground rippled and bucked. Trees toppled. Power poles snapped. Buildings slumped.

Several people had sought shelter adjacent to the exterior walls of a nearby lumber company. Shack joined them, though he doubted he would be any safer there than elsewhere. Cracks and fissures spider-webbed over the ground. Portions of the town subsided, as though swallowed by sinkholes. Gasps and soft cries issued from the small group Shack had huddled with. A young girl bawled uncontrollably.

The brutal shaking seemed unending, destined to go on until nothing remained standing. It was as if the only thing humans counted on as solid, firm, and reliable—the Earth—had at last rebelled and decided to rid itself of everything anchored to it. A purge of civilization.

Ever so slowly the convulsions relented, petering out to intermittent shudders . . . nothing left to destroy. Shack stepped into the street and took stock of his surroundings. What he saw reminded him of the war-shattered villages he'd seen in Bosnia and Herzegovina. Except here there were no bomb craters or burn marks, only "benign" destruction. Benign but total. It seemed no building in town had been untouched. While many homes appeared only lightly damaged, sagging or warping, several had pancaked. Others had collapsed into stacks of rubble.

People emerged from where they'd sheltered, many walking deter-minedly up Laneda toward Highway 101, others signaling or calling for help. Several teams of two or three people, volunteer emergency responders Shack guessed, moved toward those who had gestured for help.

He wondered about the people headed toward 101. He turned to one of the people he'd hunkered down with. "What's going on?"

The person, a young man with a muscle shirt and buzz cut, gave Shack a wide-eyed stare. "Tsunami, man. It's coming." He paused. "You didn't know?"

"I'm visiting from Atlanta."

"Okay, listen. Just stay here. Even if it's a big tsunami, we should be safe this far up from the beach. Okay?"

"Okay. How long before it hits? I thought you usually had hours' warning before these things rolled in."

"That's for like earthquakes in Alaska or someplace far away. This one happened just off the coast, I think. We've got maybe ten or twenty minutes before the tsunami hits."

"Jesus," Shack muttered. He wondered if Alex was okay. "Are there designated gathering areas around here?" If there were, he could go in search of her, make certain she'd made it through the quake.

"Assembly areas, you mean?"

Shack shrugged. "I guess."

The man appeared to think for a moment, scratching at a scraggly growth of whiskers on his chin and staring into the distance. "Yeah, there's one about a block north of here, just past the grocery store." He pointed. "Then there's another one on the golf course." He pivoted and gestured south. "It's a little farther."

"Thanks." Shack decided to head to the closer one. That would be the assembly area nearest Alex's house. A quick jog, maybe a minute, brought him to a place called Underhill Plaza, Center for Contemplative Arts. There wouldn't be much contemplation going on today. Several hundred people milled about in the parking lot. They'd formed into small groups, talking loudly, gesticulating, looking apprehensively in the direction of the ocean.

Many, mainly permanent residents Shack deduced, appeared to have what he had learned were their go-bags. He recalled the one in Alex's office. But scores of others, probably visitors, carried nothing. They appeared more confused and stunned, a few even terrified, than did the locals.

He made a quick recon trot through the lot, but didn't spot Alex. He glanced at his watch. It had been just under five minutes since the severe shaking had ended. But just as a reminder, another shockwave, not quite so intense as the earlier ones, rolled through the town. The evacuees fell silent, let it pass, then resumed their conversations. A police officer arrived, gathered the crowd, and began speaking.

Shack didn't stick around. He headed toward the ocean, toward where he remembered Alex's house being. Dead reckoning. At least he wouldn't be arrested, not today, not with the Oregon coast in turmoil. He moved as quickly as he could, scrambling over downed trees, circumnavigating live wires, and jumping over clefts in the road. Destroyed and damaged homes lined both sides of the street. One billowed gray smoke, flames licking through a pile of rubble. The smell of burning wood and rent timber filled the salty air.

The street appeared largely devoid of pedestrian traffic with most residents likely having already evacuated. But a few still hustled toward higher ground, toting their go-bags, or in some cases pulling wheeled duffels, a bit tricky given the condition of the streets.

Shack reached Alex's house, or at least what remained of it. "Jesus, Mary, and Joseph," he said, the words coming in a soft gasp.

The house had caved in. The roof sat where the second story had been; the second story, where the first floor had stood. The foundation of the building had disappeared, swallowed, at least partially, by the ground upon which it had been built. Shack guessed the violent shaking of the earth had caused the rocky, sandy soil to essentially become Jell-O.

He dashed toward the collapsed structure, calling Alex's name. No response. Maybe she got out. He worked his way toward the rear of the damaged home. He found an opening, a former second-story window, now just a bent and broken frame, and stuck his head through it. He called again.

This time there came a barely audible response. "In here. Help."

"Alex?"

"I'm stuck. Hurt. Please." Her voice sounded louder now, but tinged with pain.

"I'm coming." Shack wormed his way through shattered beams and crushed drywall toward the sound of her voice. Water cascaded from a broken pipe. A skunky smell permeated the destruction signaling a propane gas leak . . . as if the impending tsunami weren't enough to worry about.

He slithered on his stomach, like an ungainly snake, down what apparently had been a hallway, a row of rafters brushing the back of his head. Enough daylight filtered in through the broken roof that he could pick his way through the debris without skewering himself on exposed nails or splintered wood.

Once more he called Alex's name.

"Here," she responded.

He changed direction and squirmed to his left, toward a splintered door frame. He forced his upper body through the opening. His heart sank. Alex lay on the canted floor about ten feet ahead of him, her hips and legs pinned beneath a fallen support beam.

"Alex," he said softly.

She turned her head. "Shack," she replied. Her tone seemed a strange amalgam of accusation, exasperation, and hope.

"I'll get you out."

"I can't move." She moaned. "My legs . . . crushed, I think. Hurt like hell."

He wriggled toward her, extended his hand, and stroked her cheek. "You'll be okay." He examined the beam. Heavy, solid. More than he could lift or move, especially in a confined space where he could get no leverage.

He verged on panic. Checked his watch. Ten minutes since the heavy shaking had ended. Which meant what? Ten minutes to get Alex out? How in the hell could he do that? He needed help. He fumbled for his cell phone, yanked it from his pants pocket. NO SERVICE. "Shit." He slammed it onto the floor. The only other option: go back outside, find help.

"I'll be back," he said. "I need to find help."

She shook her head. "There's no help. No time." Her words came out in shaky, pain-riddled gasps.

He already was squirming backward, down the hallway, toward the exit—the shattered window frame. Once out, he sprinted to the front of the home into the deserted street. The distant yowl of sirens, emergency vehicles, filled the morning, but there seemed nothing nearby.

In desperation, he darted toward the beach, then back, looking for someone or something that could help. He spotted a pickup truck, wondered if it might have keys in the ignition. Perhaps he could use it to batter his way through the debris to Alex. Bad idea. With the gas leak, even if he could start the vehicle, a spark from the engine or friction from metal-on-wood could trigger a fire or explosion. Besides, just bulldozing through the wreckage might cause further collapse.

Never in his life had he felt so helpless. As a fighter pilot, he'd always had some control, or maybe just an *illusion* of control, over a bad situation, even if the only option left was pulling the ejection handle and punching out of a doomed aircraft. As the old saying went, he seemed to have run out of airspeed, altitude, and ideas all at the same time.

A mere block or two from the beach, he moved his gaze toward the ocean. He saw only sand, no water. He'd read enough about tsunamis to know what that meant. Every fiber of his being told him to run, get to higher ground, to safety. He couldn't help Alex. No point in them both dying.

He tilted his head toward the sky, as if he might find divine inspiration or intervention. Perhaps he should have spent more time in churches and less in bars. A break in the slate-hued overcast allowed a shaft of sunlight to burst through. A sign?

An eagle, gliding far above the destruction, circled the ray of brightness, working its wings with minimal effort, riding a thermal. For a reason Shack couldn't explain, he watched the great bird for several moments. It seemed to be waiting for something.

Shortly, another eagle joined it. With languid flaps of their expansive wings, they soared away together, leaving the devastation below, and the imminent threat of worse to come, to mortals bound to the Earth.

Indeed, a sign. Shack dropped his gaze from the sky and ran.

Chapter Seventeen

Nine-Point-Three

Manzanita
Sunday, July 5

ROB'S BEACH HOME, a contemporary two-story affair with aged cedar siding, had withstood the earthquake's initial assault and remained largely intact; slumped and cracked, but standing. Rob burst through the front entrance only to find Timothy thundering down the stairs from the second floor.

"Tim, thank God, you're okay." They embraced in an awkward father-son hug.

Tim stared at his father with a wide-eyed what-do-we-do-now look.

"Let's get to the plane," Rob said. He checked his watch again. Ten twenty-seven. Four minutes gone. "Come on, we gotta run." But he knew they wouldn't make it. The airport lay over a mile and a half from the center of town. They hadn't a prayer of reaching it on foot, preflighting the aircraft, and attempting a takeoff before the tsunami flooded in. The airstrip, which stood only twenty feet above sea level at its lowest point, would be one of the first areas to go under water.

Despite the odds, Rob and Tim took off at a sprint.

Hopeless.

They reached the rustic Manzanita News and Espresso on Laneda, a popular coffee shop that should have been packed on a Sunday morning. It now lay partially crushed by a toppled tree.

Amanda Jeffries and her cameraman, Dawson, reached the building at virtually the same instant. She gave Rob a beauty-queen smile and a thumbs-up. "Nice call," she said. "I owe you one. We're gonna scoop every other media outlet in the Northwest. I just talked to the station on my sat phone. USGS pegged the locus of the quake about seventy miles west of Grays Harbor. Preliminary magnitude, nine-point-three."

Rob's stomach knotted, his heart jumped a beat. Bigger than he had feared. Bigger than Alaska in 1964. Biggest since Chile in 1960. The damage and death toll would be immense.

"How long until the tsunami bangs in?" Amanda asked.

"Minutes," Rob panted, still sucking air from his uphill sprint.

"Well, thanks again." She turned to Dawson. "Come on, Daws. Let's get to the beach."

"No," Rob commanded. "Don't go down there. Get back to the truck. You'll be safe there."

She shook her head, dismissing the suggestion. "The incline from the beach to 101 is steep enough it'll slow the wave. We can outrun it when it hits.

"No, you can't. Especially with the roads covered in debris."

"We'll be fine." She beckoned for Dawson to follow her. He turned and looked at Rob as though Rob might have a closing argument that would persuade Amanda. But Rob's thoughts had already returned to saving Tim and himself, not someone who wouldn't listen to reason. Dawson shrugged and trotted after Amanda.

Rob turned to Tim. "We need jet packs, son, or we aren't going to make it to the plane in time."

Tim nudged his father. "There," he said, and pointed. "Not jet packs, but better than jogging."

Several abandoned bicycles, a couple still in a rack, others strewn on the ground, offered hope. Rob and Tim each mounted one and began pedaling at a furious rate. First south on 5th Place, then west on Dorcas Lane, then south on Classic and Garey Streets. Normally an easy ride, but not with the roads cracked and sunken in spots, and in other places, blocked by fallen trees and power lines.

Where the road had subsided, Rob and Tim portaged their bikes over the slumped landscape. Where trees and poles blocked their passage, they steered carefully around them or, in the case of toppled evergreens, scrambled through the boughs. Between obstacles, they sprinted at speeds that would have made them contenders in the Tour de France.

There emerged unanticipated obstacles, too. What looked like a stream of war refugees flowed against them. Rob had forgotten that Nehalem Bay State Park lay adjacent to the airstrip. On a holiday weekend, such as this, the park would be stuffed to almost overflowing with campers, probably a couple thousand.

With only one road in and out of the park, and that route blocked by debris and caved-in pavement, the weekenders had no choice but to hump out on foot. Many carried backpacks. Several seemed to be making good time on mopeds, probably ferried into the park on the rear of motorhomes or RVs. A few visitors had attempted to flee in vehicles, only to become bogged down in a mini-traffic jam of Winnebagos, fifth wheels, and a couple of Airstreams. Now they scurried on foot from the low-lying park, heading toward designated assembly areas at the city recycling center and local golf course.

Overhead, a pall of black smoke from fires in Manzanita streamed beneath the leaden clouds. A continuous wail of sirens from emergency vehicles, apparently going no place, or at least making way only slowly, accompanied the smoke.

Intermittent tremors continued to pulse through the ground. They served as reminders, at least to Rob, of the enormous destructive energy two of the Earth's plates, unzipping after three centuries of moving in lock step, had been able to unleash. And for the coast, additional devastation, massive in scope, lurked only minutes in the future.

At last, the end of the short runway at the airport hove into view. Rob and Tim skidded their bikes to a stop when they reached the tie-down area. Only two other planes, a Mooney M20J and a Cessna 172, sat secured, the owners nowhere in sight.

Again, Rob checked the time. Ten thirty-six. Thirteen minutes elapsed. At a minimum, they had two minutes left. At a lucky maximum, maybe ten. But even that might not be enough. Rob knew, as any pilot does, that an airplane isn't like an automobile. You don't just jump into it, turn a key, and go. There's preparatory work required on the ground before getting airborne. It can't be ignored, even in emergencies. You can hurry through it, but you can't disregard it.

"Release the tie-downs," Rob yelled to Tim. "I'll start the preflight." He removed the gust lock and pitot tube plug, performed a quick manual inspection of the aircraft's moveable surfaces, checked the fuel, then scrambled into the left-hand seat of the cockpit.

His heart thumped at an insane rate. Had he made the right decision? Or should he just forget the Skylane, get himself and Tim to higher ground? He would hate like hell to lose a half-million-dollar aircraft, but at least he had insurance on it.

Saving the plane wasn't the only reason that had driven him here. He wanted to see firsthand, from the air, the damage and destruction levied by a megathrust earthquake and its accompanying Grim Reaper, a mammoth tsunami. Scientific curiosity. He also harbored an ulterior motive. If he hadn't been able to save people with his misinterpreted "vision," perhaps he could salvage a few lives after the fact by directing first responders to where they would most be needed.

Still, Timothy came first. Rob squeezed his eyes shut, tried to calm himself and sort through his options objectively. Like a good scientist. A low ridge sat less than three hundred yards east of the runway. As Rob recalled the evacuation maps, the ridge stood just high enough to be out of the tsunami zone. A short dash across a sandy pine flat could get him and Tim to safety as a last resort.

He flipped open a window and yelled at Tim to get in.

His son clambered into the right-hand seat and fastened his seatbelt. Rob called out, "Clear prop!"—not really needed but proper procedure—and cranked the engine. Now it became a life and death race. *Can we beat the tsunami to the end of the runway?*

Rob attempted a cell phone call to Deborah as he began to taxi. NO SERVICE. It didn't surprise him. There probably weren't many functioning cell towers left.

He surveyed the runway as he maneuvered the aircraft. He didn't like what he saw. Almost directly across from the tie-down area, the runway had fractured and slumped. He could jockey around the damaged asphalt to the south, just barely, but that would leave him—he ran a quick guesstimate in his head—only a little over thirteen hundred feet of runway. The Skylane needed a bit less than eight hundred for a takeoff roll, so they would be okay there. Only one problem: he'd have to take off toward the south, with a tail wind. Normal takeoffs are into the wind, which provides additional boost. A tail wind does just the opposite. A bit dicey.

He stared at the south end of the runway which terminated at the edge of Nehalem Bay, really only a wide spot in the Nehalem River. Except now it appeared as nothing more than a mud flat with a thin trickle of water that used to be the river. The physics of the approaching tsunami had sucked the ocean westward along with the water in the river and bay. When the huge wave surged inland, the river, the bay, the park, and the airstrip would be among the first to become part of the new, albeit temporary, sea floor.

Once more, Rob looked at his watch. Ten forty-three. Twenty minutes since the earthquake had hit. They were living on borrowed time. But maybe just enough that he could taxi to the south end of the runway, turn, and take off into the wind.

"Headsets on," he said. He slipped on his headphones, and Timothy did the same. Each set had an integrated mic to facilitate conversation over the noise of the aircraft. "Okay, here we go. We gotta get out of here."

The aircraft bumped and wobbled over grass and dirt, circumnavigating the caved-in section of the runway. Rob reached the asphalt and began to roll south. Once he got to the end of the runway, he'd execute a 180-degree pivot, point the Cessna into the wind, and take off to the north.

But a glance to the south told him that wouldn't work.

"Oh, shit," he said.

Timothy saw it, too, and looked wide-eyed at his father. "Dad—" He couldn't finish the sentence.

A mound of black water, as tall as the evergreens that populated Manzanita, rolled up the Nehalem, surging toward the end of the runway.

Rob, his chest tightened in terror, stomped the brakes, and the aircraft bobbled to an abrupt stop. His gut churned. He fought to catch his breath. No time to think, to calculate the odds. Too late to run for the ridge. He slammed the throttle to full power and released the brakes. The Cessna lurched forward.

The plane probably had just enough runway to lift off. But maybe not with a tail wind. And maybe not with an airstrip about to be inundated.

"Go, go, go," he urged, as though the plane were a racehorse. Its speed mounted.

He peeked at his son. Timothy sat with his head bowed and eyes closed.

Rob gritted his teeth and grasped the yoke so fiercely his knuckles drained of color. It had boiled down to a pretty simple calculation: fly or die.

He'd never thought much about dying, at least in a philosophical sense, and he didn't now. He focused on staying alive, on getting the Cessna into the air, on fending off the Dark Angel. Action, not thought.

The plane's engine roared at full throat. Rob estimated the Cessna and tsunami, coming at each other on a collision course, were now equidistant from the end of the runway. He needed only to beat the massive swell by a second. If it beat them by that much, they'd die.

Cannon Beach

THE ELDERLY MAN called out to Jonathan once more. "I beg you, sir. Don't leave us."

A Bible verse from Jonathan's Sunday School days in middle Georgia so long ago flashed through his mind. "For the love of money is the root of all evil." Once more he released his grip on the treasure sacks. *Goddammit.*

He scrambled through mud and debris to where the man stood outside his destroyed home. The man, who appeared almost ancient up close, nodded a shaky greeting to Jonathan. "Bless you, my friend," he said. He glanced at Zurry who stood beside Jonathan. "You have a helper."

"Yes, I do."

"My wife is in the entryway. I can't get her out of her wheelchair." He hobbled down a fractured concrete sidewalk toward the remains of his home. Jonathan followed. The front of the house appeared relatively intact. Much of the rear portion seemed to have been swallowed by a massive sinkhole.

While Zurry waited outside, the two men stepped through the front door. "This is my wife, Olive," the man said gesturing at the woman in the wheelchair. "I'm Bill."

"Jonathan," Jonathan said.

Olive, a crippled little feather of a woman, stared up at Jonathan with rheumy eyes, but didn't, or couldn't, speak. Jonathan guessed he'd be able to carry her, but not her and the treasure both. One or the other. He shook his head—disbelief, disgust, disappointment.

He knelt in front of the woman. "Okay, Olive, I'm going to pull you up and drape you over my back and shoulders and carry you out of here, okay?"

Olive gave a slight nod.

"Bill," Jonathan said, "when I get her up, you steady her. I'll squat beside her, drag her left arm across my back, shoot my other arm between her legs, and hoist her up. A fireman's carry."

"You've done this before?"

Jonathan remained silent for a moment, flashing back almost fifty years to the city of Huê in South Vietnam and the Tet Offensive by the North. Fighting in the old, once-beautiful city had been vicious, close quarters, as Jonathan and his fellow Marines picked their way through narrow alleys, mazes of walls, and shelled-out row houses. Flame throwers and bayonets. Yes, he'd done this before, toting young, bleeding Leathernecks on his back to the safety of aid stations.

In response to Bill's question, Jonathan merely nodded and said softly, "Yes." He tugged Olive erect, her husband anchored her, and within seconds Jonathan had her across his back and shoulders. He stood and strode from the house with Bill tottering behind. Wavering sirens rode the wind, a chorus of Valkyries in flight.

Zurry, standing guard where Jonathan had dropped his bags, woofed as the trio approached. "I'll come back for these, boy," Jonathan said. "Right now, we gotta go."

"What's in the sacks?" Bill asked.

"My retirement." Jonathan kept walking. Zurry fell in by his side.

"Your what?"

"Not important. Let's get you and Olive to safety. I'll come back and get my stuff."

"I don't think there'll be time for that." Bill pointed out at the vast expanse of beach—sand and rocky outcroppings—exposed by the retreated ocean. A thin strip of silver, a lustrous, shimmering wave front, had materialized on the horizon. The tsunami, Jonathan presumed. A shiny ribbon of death.

He halted and watched it for several seconds, transfixed as it seemed to both slow in forward speed and grow in height, still several miles off. He guessed—and that's all it was, a guess—they had perhaps four or five minutes to escape. He adjusted Olive's position on his back and resumed his walk.

"Wait," Bill said.

Jonathan halted. Bill caught up with him. He pointed at Zurry. "What's his name?"

Why the hell are you asking me this now? "Zurry, short for Zurich."

"He's a Bernese mountain dog, right, from the Swiss Alps?"

"Come on, man. We're wasting time."

"Zurry can help you."

Jonathan stared. "How?"

"I know a little bit about these dogs, sir. My wife and I used to show Newfies, Newfoundlands, in AKC competitions. We made friends with a lot folks who had working breeds, big dogs. Berners were originally farm dogs. Among other things they pulled carts."

"You're not thinking he could pull those bags, are you? No way. They're over a hundred pounds apiece."

"Berners, believe it or not, can pull up to a thousand pounds."

"Yeah, probably on smooth terrain and with a wheeled cart. We don't have a cart and we sure as shit don't have smooth terrain."

"If what's in those sacks is important to you, I'm sure Zurry could drag a couple of hundred pounds."

Jonathan, his shoulders beginning to throb, shifted Olive's position again. He studied the old man, then shifted his gaze to Zurry.

"If you've got some rope," Bill said, "I could rig a harness for him. It wouldn't take long."

Jonathan glanced once more toward the ocean. The wave had morphed into a massive swell, rolling toward the coast. He extrapolated and guesstimated. Four minutes, tops. "You'd better be able to do it in about a minute."

"Where's the rope?"

In my backpack, which is gone. "Forget it. It's lost. Let's go."

Bill studied the bags that lay like gray boulders in the mud. "I can cobble something together and sling 'em over Zurry's back like saddlebags."

"He can't carry them. They're too damn heavy." Jonathan found it bizarre to be arguing against himself. He wanted to salvage the treasure, probably worth millions, but he didn't want to harm Zurry, his greatest friend.

Bill solved Jonathan's dilemma for him. He dropped to his knees, tugged the bags together, unfastened their necks, and tied them together in a professional-looking secure knot. His hands flew at a speed belying his advanced years. "I used to be merchant marine," he explained. He stripped off his outer shirt and wrapped it around the knot, fashioning a soft, smooth strap. "There." He struggled to his feet and stepped back from his work. "If Zurry can't handle the load, we'll cut it loose." He called the dog. Zurry hesitated.

"It's okay, boy," Jonathan said.

Zurry trotted to Bill who ruffled the fur on the animal's head. "You can do this, Zurry," he said softly, his mouth close to the dog's ear. He motioned for Jonathan. "We'll lift the bags together and drape the strap across Zurry's back. Can you manage with one hand?"

Jonathan's left hand, the one he'd extended between Olive's legs, grasped her left hand, keeping the woman firmly in place across his shoulders. "You bet." *For a million bucks I can.*

They hoisted the bags together, the old man wrestling his sack up with both arms. Zurry's back sagged under the load, but his muscular legs held ramrod straight. The odd quartet set off once again, Jonathan with Olive, Bill limping beside Zurry who plodded determinedly in Jonathan's wake.

Jonathan picked his way through the wrecked landscape as quickly and as carefully as he could. Across mudflows and rock slides, around fallen power poles and broken pavement. The main exodus of residents seemed to have reached safety already with only one or two laggards remaining visible. Jonathan knew he had only a matter of two or three minutes to find refuge.

The tsunami swept up the beach, logs and even small boats erupting out of the top of the surge like volcanic effluent. The mountainous swell charged toward the upper reaches of the sand, preparing to breech the final berm that fronted the beachside homes. Jonathan chanced a glance at Haystack Rock. Over two hundred and thirty feet tall, black-green water had already submerged the lower third of the towering sea stack.

They needed to find elevation in the next sixty seconds or they would die. The roar of the tsunami filled his ears. His focus narrowed to the singular task of survival: finding a way up Haystack Hill. A road, a trail, a footpath. Anything.

Chapter Eighteen

Tsunami

Manzanita
Sunday, July 5

SHACK SPRINTED toward the rear of Alex's destroyed house, but broke off his dash when he heard voices from in front of the home. He pivoted and ran back to the street. Two people appeared, a young woman carrying a microphone, and a somewhat older man toting a television camera.

"I need help," Shack yelled.

The couple, hurrying in the direction of the beach, halted.

"There's a lady trapped in the house." Shack pointed. "I can't get her out alone." His voice, constricted by anguish and fear, must have sounded anything but commanding and heroic.

"The tsunami's coming," the young woman said. Her gaze flicked from Shack to the cameraman to the ocean and back again.

No shit. "I know, I know. If I could just borrow your camera guy for a minute, I think we could free the lady. Okay?"

"One minute," the reporter said. "Daws, go help him. Shoot some video, too. But sixty seconds and you're outta there." She glanced again at the ocean. Her eyes widened.

Shack saw what she did, a big roller several miles out, slowing but growing; a great black swell churning across the naked littoral. The realization that the life expectancy of everyone near the beach could be measured in mere minutes slammed into him like a heavyweight's haymaker.

"This way," Shack yelled, and once more darted toward the back of the house, this time with help in trail. They reached the mangled, shattered window frame.

"No way I can get through that with my camera," the man named Daws muttered. He stripped off the camera and set it on the ground.

"What the hell are you doing?" snapped the reporter, who had followed them. "We need that video. Great stuff."

"Amanda, damn it, this isn't a story. It's real life." Daws didn't wait for a response, he wriggled into the wreckage, following Shack.

"Dawson, take your fucking camera!" Amanda screamed.

He didn't. Ignoring Amanda, he scrabbled through the ruined house behind Shack. "Hey, man, I smell gas."

"That's probably the least of our worries," Shack said, continuing to squirm through the debris.

They reached Alex who lay still, her unblinking gaze locked on Shack. "You shouldn't have come back," she said, her words soft, barely audible.

"There're a lot of things I shouldn't have done in my life," Shack said. He patted her hand. "I brought help."

"No," she whispered, "it's too late. Too heavy."

Shack assumed she meant the debris that imprisoned her.

Daws slithered up beside Shack. "That's a support beam on top of her. There's no way we can move that." He kept his voice low, likely meaning his words for just Shack, not Alex.

A wave of nausea surged through Shack. He knew Daws was right. He'd been fantasizing, thinking they could rescue Alex. Even two men, given the confined space in the collapsed house, had no chance of shifting the beam, let alone lifting it.

"I know, I know," Shack said, his voice tight with emotion, with defeat. "Get out of here. And thanks for trying." The two men, on their stomachs and resting on their elbows, shook hands.

"Aren't you coming?" Daws asked as he began to back out.

Shack shook his head. No.

"She's your wife?"

Shack hesitated, then answered, "Yes." *She should have been.*

"What are your names?" Daws continued to worm his way toward the exit.

"I'm Shack, Shawn. McCready. She's Alexis . . . Williamson."

Daws disappeared from view. "God be with you," he said.

Probably too late for that. Shack grasped Alex's hand and wiggled closer to her. Their faces remained inches apart.

"You need to go," she murmured. She seemed beyond pain now, perhaps in a state of psychic Valhalla, or on a stairway to the stars, halfway to heaven.

"No, I need to be here." He squeezed Alex's hand tighter.

A faint smile, like a thin ripple on a still pond, spread over her lips. A gossamer ray of sunlight sliced through the wreckage and illuminated Alex's face with a trace of gold.

"My dark-haired, golden girl," he whispered, and kissed her on the lips.

With his free hand, he slipped off his belt. He released Alex's hand so he could work with both of his. He cinched one end of the belt around his left wrist, then coiled the loose end around a shattered wall stud and tied it off.

Alex watched with a questioning gaze.

"Just to make sure I stay with you," he said, "so I don't get washed away." A half-truth. The real reason for the tether he didn't wish to explain to her. Drowning, he knew, is excruciating. A human being, no matter how noble or heroic his intentions might be, will instinctively fight or flee to remain alive, will struggle reflexively for that last, life-sustaining sip of air, and damn the cost.

Shack wouldn't allow his body to betray him. He would remain with Alex until the ocean claimed them. He supposed an outsider might judge it as his cross to bear, a way to whitewash his sins, to atone for his failures. But it was more than that. It was what he *wanted*.

He nestled next to her, once again gripping her hand, knowing it would be the last human touch either of them would feel.

The thunder of the tsunami had become faintly audible now, the wave flooding the beach, storming toward the protective berms and seawalls and all that lay behind them. Relentless in its assault.

A remnant of a smile clung to Alex's lips. "You should have left."

"I've done enough of that." He squeezed her hand ever more tightly.

Her mouth moved but no sound came. Shack thought he read her lips, a silent *Thank you.*

"Tell me about our daughter," he said, his voice pinched with emotion. His eyes misted over, but not because of fear.

Cannon Beach

THE TSUNAMI surged over the last of the dunes separating the beach from the higher ground beyond. It boiled into the streets and the weathered gray and brown shake-sided homes that sat above the sand. It seemed to Jonathan less like a wall of water and more like a rogue wave from a violent winter storm. Except this wave didn't just

139

burst over the protective berms and then slide back into a churning sea. No, this swell didn't retreat. It kept coming, pushed by a massive dome of water behind it, flattening, drowning, and engulfing everything in its path. A flash flood from the ocean.

The surge charged toward Jonathan, Zurry, and the elderly couple. Ahead of them, Jonathan spotted a road running partway up Haystack Hill. "There," he shouted, and, still lugging Olive on his shoulders, turned into the street as the initial rush of water swirled around his ankles.

Bill and Zurry lagged behind. Zurry's back, burdened by the hundreds of pounds it had been tasked to bear, slumped into a concave curve. The dog's gait became unsteady, wobbly.

"Come on, Zurry," Jonathan yelled, "we're almost there." He broke into a trot, gaining elevation as the leading edge of the tsunami swept uphill to his rear in unceasing pursuit.

The sea, where it never should have been, had morphed into a seething, black witch's brew of trees, mud, utility poles, and outbuildings. Massive chunks of driftwood and even a couple of automobiles danced and spun on top of the torrent.

Bill, up to his waist in water, struggled toward Jonathan. Zurry's body disappeared beneath the churning floodwaters leaving only his head visible.

As the road steepened, Jonathan's breath came in great, gasping gulps. He had no idea how much elevation he had to gain to find safety from the tsunami, but knew he had a decision to make, and had to make it now. He'd distanced himself from the frontal assault of the flood, so had gained an advantage, but still the water came. Despite that, he calculated he had a smidgen of time. He placed Olive on the ground, her back propped against a mailbox post.

"Hang on, Olive," he said, "I'm going after Bill."

He darted back down the hill into the seething water and grasped Bill's hand, yanking him none too gently toward Olive.

He dragged him to Olive's side. "Take care of her, I'll be right back."

Once more he waded into the flood, this time searching for Zurry. But it seemed too late. His best friend had disappeared. The realization hit Jonathan in the chest like a vicious knife wound. He doubled over and howled in anguish—plaintive, atavistic.

Manzanita

THE SKYLANE'S acceleration felt almost leisurely, too slow. Rob glanced at the airspeed indicator. The Cessna needed eighty miles per hour to get airborne. The needle passed sixty. The leading edge of the tsunami washed over the tidal flats beyond the end of the runway.

Seventy.

Timothy lifted his head and opened his eyes. He stared through the windscreen. "Dad!" Terror threaded his voice.

The seawater surge swirled over the terminus of the runway, rolling over the big, white-painted number "33" that indicated the runway's heading.

"Damn it all, damn it," Rob yelled. The plane and tsunami were seconds apart. They weren't going to make it. He glanced at Tim. Their gazes locked. Father and son.

"Sorry," Rob said. "I love you, Tim."

The plane lifted, wobbled, slowed a bit as the fixed landing gear knifed through the surface of the rising mountain of water.

"Oh, Jesus, thank you!" Rob shouted. Somehow they'd made it. Just enough airspeed to stagger aloft as the enormous surge beneath them grabbed at the tires of the Cessna. Now they skimmed over the surface of the rising ocean, the climb rate of the aircraft keeping them barely out of harm's way.

"Wow, Dad. There's something to tell my kids about."

Rob stared at his son. "What kids?"

Tim turned beet red. "I mean when I have some."

"Don't rush it."

Rob dialed in the radio frequency of the Seattle Air Route Traffic Control Center. Contacting the center was not required for VFR flights, but he hoped the center might have some intelligence regarding the extent of the earthquake damage, at least around Puget Sound.

"Seattle Center, Seattle Center, this is Skylane seven-three Delta Echo departing Nehalem Bay State Airport. Over." He waited for a response. None came. He tried again. Still dead air.

"Not good," he said to Tim.

"The tsunami?"

"No. The tsunami will be confined to the coast. More likely the earthquake knocked out power, but air traffic comms will have backups. I'll try again in a few minutes."

Rob kept the Skylane headed south, flying over the little beach towns that dotted Highway 101. Except . . . there were no little beach towns, and no Highway 101. In spots, the ocean had thundered as far as a mile inland. The villages had been leveled, the highway, washed out or submerged.

The funky little communities of Nedonna Beach, Manhattan Beach, and Rockaway Beach had ceased to exist. That had become ocean bottom, swept bare by the force of the tsunami.

The water, black and swirling, churned with the dreck of what minutes prior had been people's homes, businesses, vehicles. In an instant they'd become part of a tragic amalgam of floating roofs, store shelving, SUVs, beach umbrellas, dog houses, propane tanks, and on and on.

Rob's chest tightened as he spotted his first body—a figure, face down in the water, spinning in place like a four-armed starfish. He continued to scan the surface, only then realizing there were many more bodies. *Many* more. Some appeared, at first glance, to be just driftwood or large fish. The dark ocean, filled with tons of debris, made it difficult to discriminate. But if he watched long enough, he found he could identify features that made the flotsam human: arms, legs, torsos.

"Dad," Tim said over the intercom, alarm ringing in his voice, "there are dead people down there."

"I know. There'll be a lot more. I'm sorry, son."

Out the left side of the aircraft, Rob caught glimpses of large clusters of people who had made it to higher ground ahead of the tsunami. They waved frantically at the Cessna. Rob waggled the plane's wings, not that he could do anything for them. Whatever had happened here had happened in scores of other locations up and down the coast for hundreds of miles. Help would come. But it might take days, not hours.

"I don't get it, Dad, why didn't more people run? Didn't they know the tsunami was coming?"

Rob banked the Cessna slightly and set a course for Tillamook Bay.

"They knew, they just didn't believe."

"How come?"

Rob pondered the query before answering. "Well, my theory is that as humans evolved, they learned to be afraid of imminent, tangible threats. You know, things like lions and tigers and bears . Start talking megaquakes and tsunamis, events that come along only every few centuries, and it's hard to get people's attention. The risks, however real they might be, seem hypothetical, academic, distant."

"Pie-in-the-sky stuff, right?"

"Right. They're not exactly threats that ignite a flight-or-fight response. Give me a good ole woolly mammoth attack any day."

Tim leaned his head against the window and stared at the devastation below. "I think you got one, Dad," he said, his voice monotone. "I think you got one."

Chapter Nineteen

Destruction

Airborne Over the Oregon Coast
Sunday, July 5

ROB GUIDED THE Skylane over the northern end of Tillamook Bay and the tiny town of Garibaldi. The town's dock and marina, including the Coast Guard's facilities, sat submerged beneath the Pacific. Much of the residential area of the community, situated on a hillside, had escaped the tsunami, but not the earthquake. Landslides, fires, and toppled power poles defined the town's fate.

Highway 101, which runs through Garibaldi and hugs the bay's shoreline, had largely ceased to exist. Either the tsunami's surge or quake-induced landslides, sometimes both, had rendered the road useless.

Rob held the plane at five hundred feet as he flew down the bay, or at least what used to be the bay. Only the uprooted and severed remains of evergreens, trees that until moments ago had populated a sandy spit separating the bay from the ocean, now suggested where the western boundary of the sprawling estuary had been. The spit had been washed away. For all practical purposes, the Pacific Ocean, at least until its water receded, had expanded its domain into the foothills of the coastal mountains. The water beneath Rob, not unlike the flooded areas he'd already seen, had become foul, churning with the tragic manifestations of disaster: houses, boats, vehicles.

A few survivors clung to wreckage in the bay-cum-ocean and gestured frantically at the Skylane. Rob knew there was nothing he could do for them, but again he waggled the aircraft's wings in acknowledgement, letting the victims below know they'd been spotted.

"Dad, look." Tim spoke through the interphone and pointed out to the left and ahead of the Cessna.

"Our favorite spot," Rob acknowledged, dismayed, his voice flat.

The Tillamook Cheese Factory, famous not only for its cheese, but for its ice cream, fudge, and gift shops, stood in shallow ocean water in a meadow near the Wilson River. The surge had not reached much beyond the buildings comprising the plant. Cracks and fractures scarred the exteriors of the structures, but the facility appeared largely intact. Hundreds of cars and SUVs jammed the surrounding parking lots, not unusual for a holiday weekend, but most of the vehicles, fender deep in water, had become metallic islands for groups of refugees who sat on their roofs and waved as Rob flew over.

Rob had never quite reconciled the fact that despite Oregon's plethora of natural wonders—Crater Lake, Mount Hood, Multnomah Falls, the Oregon Dunes—the cheese factory drew more visitors per year than any other attraction. That's not to say he and his family hadn't themselves been significant contributors. Virtually every jaunt to the coast had eventually brought them to the place where such delicacies as Tillamook Mudslide ice cream—the name suddenly seemed eerily prescient—Marionberry Pie fudge, or Tillamook Cheesesteak sandwiches beckoned. Now such innocent pleasures seemed suddenly and disastrously part of a distant past, a once-upon-a-time Camelot that might never be reclaimed.

Rob continued southward toward the city of Tillamook. He noted that the 101 bridge over the Wilson River had been badly damaged and rendered unusable. A short distance on, two more bridges, over sloughs, had been washed out.

Tillamook itself, except for the western end of town, had been largely spared by the tsunami. But, similar to the previous destruction he and Tim had witnessed, fires and devastated infrastructure gave mute testimony to the epic earthquake. Rob dropped to a lower altitude and buzzed the city.

"Look at that," he said to Tim, and pointed.

Below them, an entire block of buildings burned with impunity. Black smoke billowed skyward, blending into the low, gray overcast that draped like a death shroud over the devastated landscape. Rob could see no emergency crews battling the flames. He guessed the streets had been rendered impassible, or perhaps shattered water lines had made firefighting impossible. How do you plan for contingencies such as that?

Rob rolled the plane to the right, made a U-turn, gained some altitude, and headed back toward Manzanita, Cannon Beach, and Seaside.

"Try Mom on the cell again," he said to Tim.

Tim removed his headset and punched in Deb's number on his phone.

Rob tried Seattle Center once more, but to no avail.

Tim turned toward his dad and, cell phone to his ear, yelled, "It just rings busy."

Rob motioned for him to put the headset back on.

"What's going on?" Tim asked. "Why can't I get through?"

"You're lucky to even get a connection. Most cell towers are down or have been knocked out of alignment. Fiber optic cables have been snapped. Even if you manage to establish a link, like you just did, the circuits are totally overwhelmed, and probably will be for weeks."

"This is really bad isn't it, Dad?" Deepening concern registered in his voice.

"Yeah, I'm afraid so."

As the plane purred northward, Rob tried to recall the statistics he'd seen relative to the number of people likely to be affected when Cascadia ruptured. They were mind numbing, and prepared in anticipation of a nine-point-zero quake, not a nine-point-three.

The combined metro population of Vancouver, Seattle, and Portland is close to eight million. Roughly another three million live in smaller towns and cities west of the Cascades. That's a total of eleven million, give or take—the population of Ohio, someone had once pointed out—most of whom will be without electricity, gas, and communications for weeks. That's assuming they still have homes. Thousands won't.

And what about emergency services, water, and food? How, for instance, do you get to grocery stores if the roads are wrecked? More to the point, how do you get supplies to the grocery stores themselves?

Tim continued to study the sprawl of destruction below. He looked over at his dad. "So is this like Hurricane Sandy?"

"No. Much worse. Just think about the area involved. Here, it's the entire Pacific Coast from Vancouver Island to northern California. That's six hundred miles. Sandy clobbered mainly Long Island and New Jersey, a stretch of what, maybe a hundred miles? And most of the damage there was confined to the immediate coasts. Here, quake damage will extend far inland. I'm sure the Willamette Valley and Puget Sound took a violent hit. We'll check it out later."

Tim, clearly stunned by the enormity of the disaster, merely nodded.

"Grab a notepad out of the map pocket," Rob said. "We'll make a record of what we see as we head back up the coast. Sooner or later we'll be able to talk to someone."

Tim retrieved the notepad, then swiveled his head, searching the sky around the aircraft. "Funny we haven't seen any other airplanes."

"Nobody along the coast is going to be taking off now. And earlier, it wasn't the kind of bright, sunny morning that would have enticed a lot of private pilots."

"How about helicopters?"

"I think the Coast Guard in Astoria has some Jayhawks, but I doubt their facility fared well."

"News choppers?"

"The problem there is getting crews to the choppers. Sundays, especially holiday Sundays, can be pretty slow news days, so a lot of folks have the day off. And barring that, there's the challenge of negotiating streets littered with debris, intersections without traffic signals, and pancaked overpasses."

"That TV chick in Manzanita probably got some great footage."

"Yeah, if it didn't cost her her life."

They flew back over Nehalem Bay and Manzanita. The initial tsunami surge appeared to have taken out most of Manzanita except the northern residential area. The assembly areas seemed to have been spared, though the one on the golf course stood as an island, surrounded by water. The rush of the ocean had fallen short of 101, which ran along higher ground above the town, but at least one slide on Neahkahnie Mountain had severed the highway.

Rob circled back over the village and dropped to a lower altitude. He passed above the KGW-TV satellite truck which obviously had survived, but appeared abandoned. He didn't spot Amanda or her cameraman. Not a good sign. If they hadn't heeded his warning, and had gone to the beach to record the tsunami's arrival, they had been killed.

Rob turned north again and climbed, following 101 around the western edge of Neahkahnie Mountain where the topography consisted of steep cliffs plunging to the ocean. A short distance north of Manzanita, in Oswald West State Park, the highway bridge over Necarney Creek sat crumpled in the stream below. A few minutes later, just south of the tiny village of Arch Cape, he discovered a quarter-mile-long highway tunnel had collapsed.

"How are they ever gonna get help in here?" Tim asked.

"Helicopters, but it'll take several days to marshal an organized response. Heavier supplies will probably have to be airlifted in by planes like C-130s. They only need a couple of thousand feet to land and take off."

"C-130s?"

"Four-engined turboprop planes. You remember when we saw the Blue Angels, they had a plane called 'Fat Albert' that carried all their stuff?"

"Yeah."

"That was a C-130."

"Any around here?"

"I don't think so. I seem to recall the Air Guard has some in Idaho or California, but I don't know exactly where. Anyhow, it's going to take a while to get relief plans cranked up, so large-scale assistance isn't going to be arriving here any time soon."

He lowered the Skylane's nose and slowed the aircraft as they approached Cannon Beach.

Manzanita

"OUR DAUGHTER is beautiful," Alex whispered. "Tall, smart, funny . . ." Her voice trailed off. Shock? Pain? A foot already in heaven?

Shack clung to her hand with vise-grip tenacity, listening to her fading words, but hearing more the thunderous forte of their last moments on Earth. *Don't leave, don't leave, don't leave,* he repeated over and over to himself. He cursed himself for his lack of bravery. As a fighter pilot on a strafing or bombing run, he'd never feared for his life, always knew he could fight back or find a way out.

Now he had become a silent-movie damsel in distress, tied to the tracks as a locomotive hurtled down the rails. He didn't want to die. Didn't want to run. Wanted to believe in miracles.

A cascade of water smashed into the house, and he knew there were no miracles.

The ocean, cold, numbing, powerful, rose with lightning swiftness to entomb him and Alex in a watery sarcophagus.

In a final gesture of love, or more likely desperation, they pressed their lips together as though they might find a few more precious seconds of life in each other's lungs. But the ocean's onslaught forced them apart, and they released their souls.

For Shack, the blackness and pain came swiftly, almost mercifully—a quick passage from one world to whatever lay beyond.

Peace, it seemed, a strange incongruity. He found himself in a still meadow, golden in daffodils and sunlight, filled with the melodies of songbirds. He held hands with Alex and Skylar as they strolled through the field, lush with flowers and soft, green grass, an Arcadia of opportunities missed.

The quiet laughter of the two women joined with the pianissimo twittering of the birds, filling the air with an intimacy and tranquility Shack had never known. Alex kissed him on the cheek. Skylar leaned her head against his shoulder and murmured, *Daddy*.

Paradise found, but only for a gossamer moment. In a fleeting instant it vanished, crushed in darkness and drowned in a tsunami of his own tears. Shack knew what lay beyond. The eternal void of a life squandered.

Cannon Beach

JONATHAN FOUGHT through his emotional agony, righted himself, and frantically searched the swirling waters for Zurry. The glut of wreckage and dreck that spun and eddied on the surface of the surge made spotting the dog, his huge size notwithstanding, virtually impossible.

Guilt, like a twelve-ton weight, descended upon Jonathan with crushing force. The loss of his long-time companion could be laid directly at his feet. He'd asked too much of Zurry, burdening him with a load he had no hope of bearing. He should have just let the damn treasure go, chalked it up to another defeat in life, and played out his time on Earth in the company of his great, furry friend. They wouldn't have been rich in a monetary sense, but their cups would have overflowed with love.

Jonathan blinked back tears. But then, in the water, he spotted something. He squinted, trying to get a clearer view. Yes, he was certain: Zurry's great snout, snorkeling through the surge like a parti-colored seal. He seemed caught in a swift current about fifty yards away where the tsunami swarmed over the lower slopes of Haystack Hill.

In a blur of motion, Jonathan stripped off his boots, jacket, and pants. He patted his hip to make sure his hunting knife remained in its sheath, then plunged into the flood. The icy water stunned him, but he forced himself to overcome the almost paralyzing shock by flailing his arms and kicking his legs fiercely, propelling himself toward Zurry.

Driven by adrenaline, he closed the gap between himself and his friend. But a renewed rush of water caught Zurry and bore him away. Once more, his head disappeared beneath the turbulent surface.

Jonathan, terrified the burst of adrenaline would wear off and leave him as nothing more than human driftwood, redoubled his efforts to overtake Zurry. He torpedoed deep into the frigid surge and, using dead reckoning, knifed through the debris-laden water in pursuit of his dog. He lost track of time underwater, but his lungs, on the verge of exploding, told him the moment to surface had come.

He burst into the air like a breaching whale, his mouth wide, gasping for oxygen. The flotsam and jetsam of what had once been Cannon Beach swirled around him as if he were imprisoned in a filthy snow globe.

"Zurry," he screamed, before ingesting a mouthful of salt water. He spat it out, then spun in place, searching for any sign of the dog. Nothing. He plunged deep once more, determined to find his friend. Or die trying.

Again he surfaced, no longer certain if he were even heading in the right direction. Had he moved closer to or farther away from where he'd last spotted Zurry?

"Damn it to hell," he sputtered in frustration.

He made a quick 360-degree turn, thought he saw something about ten yards behind him, and stroked toward it.

Zurry, his eyes wide with fear, turned to stare at his master. Just as Jonathan reached him, the dog snapped his mouth shut and sank out of sight.

Jonathan yanked his knife from its sheath and dove after him. The visibility in the black water hovered near zero, but Jonathan caught just a glimpse of one of the canvas bags tied to Zurry and grabbed it. Between the weight of the treasure and Zurry, and his own bulk, they rocketed toward the bottom of the sea, wherever that might be now, like an iron anchor.

Jonathan, using touch more than sight as a guide, swiped his knife at the ropes securing the canvas sacks to Zurry. But it would take more than blind swipes to unfetter his friend, he realized, and grasped the ropes with his free hand. As they continued their plunge through the depths, he sawed desperately at the bindings with his knife.

At last the bags released. The treasure—his retirement, the object of a decade-long search, the stuff of legends—disappeared into the murky waters to become a legend once more. Jonathan gave Zurry a mighty upward shove and together they broke the surface.

They found themselves only a short distance from the terminus of the tsunami's run and paddled, both near exhaustion, toward a hillside thick with evergreens and huckleberries.

Zurry beside him, Jonathan crawled on all fours away from the water's edge. The tsunami likely had reached its maximum run-up and would retreat, but from what Jonathan understood, additional surges would follow.

Finally, they sat, side by side, soaking wet, in a small clearing on the hill, and surveyed the forever-altered coast of northern Oregon, a once and future kingdom of natural beauty.

Jonathan draped his arm over Zurry's shoulders. "Just a boy and his dog," he said softly. "Well, old man and his dog," he corrected.

Zurry licked Jonathan's cheek, plopped onto his stomach, closed his eyes, and within a matter of seconds settled into a rhythmic snoring.

Chapter Twenty

Airborne

Airborne Over Cannon Beach
Sunday, July 5

ROB DROPPED THE Skylane to a few hundred feet above the surface over Cannon Beach and skimmed over what used to be the seashore, now submerged. The town itself had largely ceased to exist. It appeared as if a second large wave had just thundered through the community.

The Pacific Ocean had claimed most of the inhabited areas of the town and covered Highway 101 in several spots. Only Haystack Hill had escaped the flood and now sat like a forested Noah's Ark as seawater sloshed around its base on three sides.

Perhaps the term "Atlantis" could have been used to describe Cannon Beach, at least what was left of it, but that seemed far too benign a portrait. What sat beneath Rob could be better labeled a garbage slough. Building tops poking from the water stood as shattered sentinels in a churning sludge composed of every sort of detritus imaginable: vehicles, bodies, oil, gasoline, roofs, houses, bathtubs, lumber, trees, signs, boxes, furniture, small boats, beach umbrellas, surfboards, and even a horse, still saddled, swimming mightily through the viscous mire.

Rob, feeling slightly ill, turned his head away and looked westward, over the ocean. The Pacific. The name means peaceful. He shook his head at the irony. Goaded by a geologic clash far below its surface, the "peaceful" ocean had attacked along a six-hundred-mile front. The assault would relegate Hurricane Katrina and its appalling New Orleans's death toll to a footnote in the history of U. S. natural disasters. The death toll along the Oregon and Washington coasts would be fearsome.

A holiday weekend. Jam-packed seaside communities. Thousands of tourists unfamiliar with evacuation procedures and gathering points. He wondered, callously he knew, if there were even enough body bags in the state to handle the dead. A rush of bile from his churning stomach surged into his throat, but he choked it back, trying to swallow with it the rising tide of his emotions.

He glanced at Tim who sat silently in the Skylane's passenger seat, staring at his feet.

"Better make some notes, son," Rob said over the interphone.

Tim looked up. Tears filled his eyes.

"That's okay," Rob said. "Never mind. I think we'll remember this."

Tim nodded and turned away.

The tsunami inundation would eventually recede, of course. Dry land would re-emerge. The Pacific would, for the most part, become bucolic again. But the North Coast of Oregon would be forever altered, both its landscape and its people.

Feeling as if a dagger had been driven deep into his soul, Rob continued to fly northward, toward Seaside and Astoria. He feared what he would find.

Seaside

A FEW MINUTES' flying time brought the Skylane to Seaside and the conjoined town of Gearhart. Seaside, long a favorite destination of vacationing Oregonians, had been the site of saltworks for the Lewis and Clark Expedition over two centuries ago. Rob recalled visiting the city as a boy in the 1980s: a fun place for kids, its streets lined with arcades, t-shirt shops, and salt-water taffy vendors. Now there were no streets or buildings visible, only the ocean.

The scenes here were no different from what Tim and he had seen in Cannon Beach—utter devastation. It seemed what the earthquake hadn't claimed, the tsunami had. Even 101 sat underwater, though the ocean flood had begun to ebb.

Rob climbed and circled the two towns. People at the assembly points, where the truncated coastal plain abutted the foothills of the Coast Range, waved as he flew over. Searing acid again surged into his esophagus as he realized there seemed to be almost as many bodies floating in the water as there were standing in the assembly areas.

He recalled that Gearhart had designated some optional high ground within the city as last-resort evacuation destinations. These were to be used as safe havens for those unable to make it outside the tsunami-inundation zone, mainly because of physical limitations, before the first wave hit. These optional sites were spots expected to remain dry in all but the worst-case scenarios.

This had been a worst-case scenario. Maybe it had even exceeded that.

Rob guided the plane over the now-submerged banks of the Necanicum River. He dipped the wing and looked down.

"I've heard that an Indian tribe lived here hundreds of years ago," Rob said. "I wonder if they were here when the tsunami in 1700 hit."

Tim shook his head, in sadness it seemed, as he gazed at the ruined landscape. "It was so beautiful here, father," he said softly.

Rob could barely make out the words through his headset.

Astoria

THEY REACHED ASTORIA at the mouth of the Columbia River a few minutes later. The regional airport sits on a low spit of land west of the city. The spit, separating the ocean from the river, had disappeared beneath the tsunami's onslaught. It had become an archipelago of elongated islands. The floating carcasses of private aircraft and Jayhawk helicopters marked the location of the now-submerged airport.

Rob pointed at the helicopters. "There won't be any help from Coast Guard choppers today."

Tim didn't respond, his gaze fixed forward, on the four-mile-wide mouth of the river.

Rob followed his son's stare. "Jesus," he said, the exclamation catching in his throat.

The Columbia River Bar, where the river meets the ocean, is known as the Graveyard of the Pacific. The tag is well deserved, for many a vessel had met its demise in the turbulent seas, heavy winds, and powerful currents that stalk the bar. Today, however, the graveyard had shifted into the mouth of the river. A horrific panorama of wrecked and capsized cabin cruisers, commercial fishing boats, tugs, barges, freighters, and even a small oil tanker littered the water's surface as far as Rob could see. Wreckage appeared to cover every square yard of the churning, swirling tsunami-flooded river.

"It looks like a gigantic cesspool," Tim said.

Rob couldn't disagree. On a more positive note, he spotted two large Coast Guard search and rescue vessels, presumably out of Cape Disappointment on the Washington side of river, plowing through the dreck.

Semper Paratus.

He banked the plane toward the city and dropped lower so he could get a good look at the Astoria-Megler Bridge connecting Oregon and Washington. The approaches to the steel cantilever-span portion of the bridge near Astoria had collapsed. The span itself, high enough for ships to pass under, appeared to have survived, though Rob wondered about the integrity of its concrete piers. Closer to the Washington side where the river is non-navigable, the bridge sits low to the water. So low, in fact, that the span had disappeared beneath the surge of ocean water into the river's mouth.

"Won't be using the 101 bridge for a long time," Rob noted. The next bridge was almost fifty miles upriver at Longview, Washington.

Astoria's residential areas, located primarily on the steep slopes of a ridge line, had largely escaped the tsunami, but not the quake. Slides and fissures crisscrossed the landscape. Many homes sat in shambles or buried in mud near the bottom of the slopes. Others, twisted off their foundations, clung like wounded birds to their precarious perches.

Much like in Tillamook, black smoke from numerous fires billowed skyward, flattening against the low-slung, slate-gray cloud deck. Rob spotted only one or two crews battling what looked to be more than two dozen blazes.

"It looks like the end of the world, Dad," Tim said, his voice broken and subdued.

"For a lot of people, it might be."

"Can we go home now?" Weariness, the emotional kind, permeated Tim's request.

"Sure. We'll fly along the river back to Portland. That way we can stay VFR. Won't have to get into the clouds over the mountains."

"Do you think Portland is okay?" Even over the interphone, Rob sensed the apprehension permeating his son's voice.

He paused before answering, wondering whether to be honest or not. No point in skirting the truth, he decided. Tim would know soon enough.

"There'll be a lot of damage," he answered. "You know, there was always a lot of concern that Portland was much less prepared for a big quake than Seattle."

"What about the airport?"

Rob shrugged. "I don't know about PDX, but we should be able to land at Hillsboro safely. Even if the runway there is screwed up, we don't need a lot."

He called Seattle Center again, this time getting a response.

"Skylane seven-three Delta Echo, go ahead."

"Skylane seven-three Delta Echo is VFR at twelve hundred feet over Astoria, departed Nehalem Bay, heading for Portland. We've been surveying the earthquake and tsunami damage."

An extended period of silence ensued.

Then, "Roger that, seven-three Delta Echo. You may be one of very few aircraft up anywhere west of the Cascades. Both Sea-Tac and Portland International have been closed to all commercial and private traffic." Another pause. "How's it look where you are?"

"Like the Apocalypse."

"Here, too. We're on aux power. Reports are that the control towers are down, collapsed, at both Sea-Tac and King County. Don't know about Portland."

"We're headed for Hillsboro."

"Tower or no, you should be okay as a light aircraft. Anything else I can do for you, Delta Echo?"

"Maybe. Out of your bailiwick, I know, but I'm a geologist. I'm curious about how the Puget Sound fared in the quake. What have you heard?"

"Nothing good. All second hand, of course. There's no air traffic, and not much on the ground. Lots of bridges and overpasses on I-5 bit the dust. The Alaskan Way Viaduct pancaked. The western approaches to the Floating Bridge are toast. Hundreds of brick and concrete structures in the older sections of the city, you know, like around Pioneer Square, are reportedly nothing but rubble. Fires all over the place. And rumor has it three or four high-rises in the city toppled. Oh, and the Space Needle, too."

"Space Needle?" Rob couldn't hide his surprise. "That wasn't supposed to happen."

"That's what I'd heard, too, Delta Echo."

"Okay, thank you, Seattle Center. Best of luck. Skylane seven-three Delta Echo, out."

"Godspeed, Delta Echo."

Rob changed the radio frequency to monitor the emergency channel at 121.5 MHz. He didn't expect to hear anything this soon after the quake and tsunami, but it seemed a good idea, a just-in-case move.

He picked up a call almost immediately after changing frequencies.

"Aircraft recently departed Nehalem Bay State Airport, this is Nehalem Bay Fire and Rescue. If you read, your urgent assistance is requested. I say again, this is Nehalem Bay Fire and Rescue calling aircraft recently departed Nehalem Bay State Airport. Do you copy?"

Chapter Twenty-One

The Request
Airborne Over Astoria
Sunday, July 5

ROB AND TIM exchanged glances as the call came in over the guard channel, a VHF wavelength normally reserved for aircraft in distress. Rob, surprised at having his plane specifically identified—obviously someone had noted his takeoff—responded immediately.

"This is Skylane seven-three Delta Echo. We departed Nehalem Bay about forty-five minutes ago. I assume you're looking for us."

"Roger that, Skylane seven-three Delta Echo. Thank God you're still in the area. We need your help."

"Not sure what I can do, but go ahead with your request."

"We've got a severely injured female here, probably with a shattered pelvis and internal bleeding. A local physician examined her and determined she needs to get to a trauma center stat. We've triaged the casualties here, and this one is by far the most severe of those who might make it, but not without level-one trauma intervention."

"Understand, Nehalem Bay. Not sure where I come in, though." Rob put the plane in a gentle turn, back toward Manzanita. He didn't know what the fire and rescue guys expected him to do, but they certainly had piqued his curiosity.

"Delta Echo, the nearest level-one trauma facilities are in Portland. We were kind of hoping you might be able to land somewhere around here. Then we could load the patient into your aircraft and let you get her to Portland."

"Sorry, Nehalem Bay. Besides not being equipped for medevac, I don't know where in the hell I could land. The airstrip is underwater and the beach is history."

"We were thinking 101. There's an ex-Air Force pilot here who thinks it could be done."

"With all due respect, Nehalem Bay, I'm a weekend VFR flyer, not a former Air Force jockey. What you're asking is way above my skill level."

A period of dead air followed, with Rob hearing nothing from Nehalem Bay Fire and Rescue. After a minute or so, a different voice transmitted.

"Skylane seven-three Delta Echo, this is Shawn McCready. I go by Shack. I'm a retired Air Force pilot, and I think there's a short stretch of undamaged highway on 101 where you can get down. Look, you don't need to be a shit-hot zoomie to do it. Steady nerves and a steady hand will hack it."

"Sorry, I'm not your guy. I've already had one narrow escape this morning, and with my son onboard, I'm not about to test my limits again."

"Delta Echo, I understand your reluctance, I really do. But—" The guy's voice broke, and Rob realized whoever he was talking with— *Shack, was that his name?*—probably had a personal stake in saving the life of the patient.

The man on the ground resumed speaking.

"I know about narrow escapes, sir, believe me, I really do. I had one myself about an hour ago. Quite frankly, I should be dead. So should the lady. But we've been given a second chance and I don't want to blow it. I want her to live. I know it's asking a lot of you, but I wouldn't make the request unless I thought it was doable. I guess, sir, I'm begging."

Rob's heart rate ticked up several notches. He swallowed hard. He stared up at the gunmetal overcast, now just a couple of hundred feet above him, deliberately keeping his gaze off the devastation below.

How do you tell someone who's begging, No? How do you take a pass on saving someone's life? If you don't take a pass, how much jeopardy do you put yourself in to do it? Hell, how much risk do you put your child at to do it?

He looked over at Tim and keyed the interphone. He knew Tim had been listening to the transmissions on the guard channel. "So, what do you think, Tim? You think your old man's a superhero?" He kept his tone light, not wanting to let on how much the thought of attempting a landing on a narrow highway walled by trees, and possibly riddled with fractures from the quake, terrified him.

Tim obviously didn't buy in to his father's whistling-past-the-graveyard shtick. He fixed his gaze on Rob. "What if it were Mom or Maria down there?" He let his response go at that.

"The trouble is, it's not Mom or Maria down there. For whoever it is, I'd be risking not only my life, but yours, too. Is it worth it?" *Why am I asking a sixteen-year-old this?*

"I dunno, Dad. How do you measure the worth of a human life? Is yours worth more than someone else's. Is mine? Look, you're a good pilot. You can get this plane down in one piece. I know you can. I'm in if you're in."

Shit. The undying faith of kids in their fathers. The bulletproof belief of teenagers in their own immortality. Rob wished he bore the same confidence in his flying skills that Tim did.

Rob went back on the emergency frequency. "Delta Echo to Nehalem. The wingspan on this plane is thirty-six feet. I know damn well 101 isn't thirty-six feet wide."

"Include the shoulders and it's close."

"Close! What the hell is that supposed to mean? I can't land with 'close.' I've either got clearance or I don't. And it sounds to me like I don't."

"We've got guys out there with chainsaws already, clearing away overhanging branches and bushes, and removing trees that fell on the highway."

Rob slowed the Cessna, wanting to buy time to make a decision. Or more truthfully, wanting to buy time to figure out a way of gracefully refusing the request. There's no way he wanted to attempt squeezing his plane into a narrow canyon of evergreens while barreling down a highway—for that's what it was, not a *runway*—at sixty-five knots. One little ill-timed nudge on the yoke this way or that, one little puff of crosswind, and there'd be two more Cascadia fatalities.

He remained silent, not responding immediately to Shack, unclear even if the guy was part of Nehalem Bay Fire and Rescue. On one level, he wanted to help. On another, he knew if he tried, he'd be on a fool's errand, attempting to carry out a *Mission Impossible*. On the silver screen, of course, Tom Cruise would come through. There'd be a spectacular landing, the aircraft would be saved, and the medevac accomplished.

All Rob could envision, however, was a smoking hole in an Oregon forest.

"I can't do this, Nehalem Bay," he replied. "I'm sorry. I just don't have the expertise."

"Delta Echo, listen," the guy named Shack responded. "You've got the expertise. That's not the issue. What you need is a little extra courage and a resolve to make the landing.

"Look, it'll be no different than any other landing; same set of skills involved. And I know you've got the courage. You've already proven that. I'm told you're Dr. Elwood, the guy who spoke out about the possibility of this disaster in the face of loads of ridicule. That took courage. If you commit to this, you can do it. I saw guys accomplish similar things over and over when I was in the Air Force. It's a routine landing in a different setting, that's all."

Yeah, a routine landing with absolutely zero tolerance for error.

Rob keyed his mic. "I'll think about it."

"Give us half an hour, Delta Echo. We'll have 101 looking like a runway at Portland International."

That makes me feel a hell of a lot better. Portland International could be in the Columbia River now.

Rob throttled back the aircraft even more and continued south along the coast. He remained appalled by the sights below. The Oregon coast had become a graveyard of people, homes, and dreams. How many dead? He couldn't guess. He knew only that he'd seen dozens of bodies floating in the tsunami waters, the toll magnified by the influx of visitors for the holiday. How many bodies had he not seen? He could only imagine. Hundreds? A thousand? He swallowed hard and gagged at the thought.

"You okay, Dad?" Tim on the interphone.

Rob nodded. "So what do we do, Tim? This is a no-bullshit serious decision. Think about it really hard. There're no Hollywood special-effects or happy-ending fantasies here. Fears and all, lay out your thoughts."

Tim stared out the windscreen into the gray morning and took his time before responding. He drew a deep breath before he replied.

"I'm scared. But I think everybody is. You, the folks on the ground, the lady who might be dying. I read someplace that heroes are just ordinary people forced by extraordinary circumstances to do extraordinary things. Or something like that.

"So here we are. A couple of ordinary dudes in an unbelievable situation. Like the guy in Manzanita said, it's a routine landing. You can do that. You're a cool pilot. Mr. Smooth. Forget the stupid trees. Just land the plane, Dad."

Rob pinched his lips together. *Sure, that's all there is to it.*

"Delta Echo to Nehalem Bay. Reluctant doesn't begin to describe how I feel, but I'll give it a shot. I'll make a couple of flyovers before I attempt a landing. Just let me know when you're ready."

"Roger that, Delta Echo. Thank you. You'll do fine."

"Where's the stretch of road you've picked out?"

A different voice responded, probably one of the EMTs. "Delta Echo, it's just north of town. There's a straight stretch of highway about a half-mile long just before the big bend. You know it?"

"Driven it many times." *Never considered landing a plane there.*

"We'll position some guys at the north end of the stretch to turn you around after you land. The Air Force guy says you'll have to land in that direction since it's uphill."

Rob knew to try landing in the opposite direction would be foolhardy. The highway drops sharply in elevation as it approaches Manzanita. A landing attempt in that direction would require at least twice as much distance as a normal touchdown.

The EMT kept talking. "We'll bring the patient up to you in a truck, get her loaded on your plane, turn you around, then off you go."

Just like that. A piece of conceptual cake.

"Put the pilot back on, if you don't mind," Rob said.

After a short delay, the response came. "Shack here, Delta Echo. How can I help?"

"It's bad enough I'm going to be landing in what's basically a New York City alley," Rob said, "but it'll be uphill, too. Fairly steep. I've never done that before. Seems like I could hammer in pretty hard."

Rob steered the Cessna around the western flanks of Neahkahnie Mountain and approached Manzanita. Below, on 101, at least two dozen men, maybe women, too, labored on the highway, clearing impediments, making it safe—*joke*—to land an airplane.

"Delta Echo, what's your normal landing rollout?" Shack asked.

"About six hundred feet."

"Great. So here's what I'll do. Because an inexperienced pilot will likely perceive he's coming in too high on an approach to an uphill landing, I'll spray paint some big orange Xs on the highway marking a target. Just aim for that. Forget about what you perceive."

"Roger that, Shack. Thanks. Any other tips?" Nothing like on-the-job training, especially when your life depends on it.

"Keep plenty of back pressure on the yoke. You might need a short blast of power just before touchdown to cushion the landing. Don't worry if you bounce when you come in. Many first-timers will on an uphill attempt. Remember, you don't get points for style, just for getting it down."

Preferably right side up.

"Okay," Rob responded, forcing confidence he didn't feel into his voice, "while I'm waiting for you guys to finish your chain-gang work, I'll fly some practice approaches."

Rob flew back over Manzanita. Much of it remained submerged. Homes, vehicles, and tons of what would now be considered trash bobbed in the wake water of the tsunami. He spotted relatively few bodies. Perhaps the fact the city's topography inclined more steeply from the beach to elevations out of the tsunami's reach than in towns such as Cannon Beach and Seaside had given residents a chance to reach safety. That and the fact that tsunami escape procedures had been drilled into the populace.

Rob made two rehearsal runs to the jury-rigged runway before the call came.

"Delta Echo, this is Nehalem Bay Fire and Rescue. We're ready if you are."

"Roger that, Nehalem Bay. On my way." *Not ready, though.* Rob's fingers tightened around the yoke with such fierceness he would have strangled it had it been a person.

"Shack, here, Delta Echo. Plant your gear on those orange Xs. Focus on the center line. Don't worry about what's on either side of you. Easy sleazy."

Bullshit.

Rob looked over at Tim. Tim nodded.

"Harness tight, son. If it looks like we're going into the trees, head down, crash position, right?"

Tim nodded again.

Rob made a straight-in approach. Ten degrees of flaps. Eighty knots. Eyes on the center line.

What the fuck am I doing?

Twenty degrees of flaps. Slow to seventy knots.

Where're the damn Xs?

The drone of the Cessna's engine filled his ears.

There!

Adjust power. Sixty-five knots. Steady back pressure on yoke.

Get the gear down on those orange marks.

A green blur of evergreens and alders filled Rob's peripheral vision. The right wing tip clicked against something. Still, he focused on the center line, concentrated on hitting the Xs. The runway, the road, seemed to be coming up too fast. He goosed the power to soften the touchdown.

Too late. The landing gear slammed into the pavement with a resounding "thunk."

"Deer!" Tim screamed.

A huge elk, head held high, trotted directly in front of the Cessna.

Chapter Twenty-Two

Life Flight

Manzanita
Sunday, July 5

SHACK SAT HOLDING Alex's hand, festooned with IV leads, in the back of a Nehalem Bay Fire and Rescue EMS truck. Alex, immobilized and sedated, rested on a gurney secured to a sidewall of the vehicle. The paramedics, along with a vacationing doctor, had described her situation as dire. With a probable crushed pelvis and internal bleeding, the only hope she had of surviving would be to get her to a level-one trauma center. And, with roads and highways impassable after the earthquake, there existed only one transport option: airlift. In this case, that option rested with a fair-weather, weekend flyer whom Shack had never met.

Shack knew better than to lament the situation. It's a wonder he had an option at all. In truth, he should be dead. So should Alex. Though he didn't count himself a religious man and had never believed in miracles, he had to admit what had happened to him and Alex had been, if not a miracle, certainly miraculous.

When the tsunami thundered in and the two of them gasped what had seemed their final breaths and surrendered their lives to whatever lay beyond, the surging water tore the fallen support beams from Alex's body. Together, he and Alex, water suffusing their lungs, shot to the surface, the last few molecules of life-giving air sequestered deep within their lungs.

They rode the maelstrom of swirling ocean into the upper reaches of Manzanita. Rescuers found them, Alex wailing in pain, about ten feet up in the branches of a canted Douglas fir. Yes, to some it would be labeled a miracle. But Shack knew it for what it was: the laws of chance, physics, and hydrodynamics at work in a random universe.

EMTs managed to stabilize Alex and pump her full of morphine, but acknowledged she teetered on the edge of death. It had been bad enough that massive timbers had crashed down on her in her own home, but then to be flung about like a chunk of storm-tossed driftwood as the tsunami swept her inland had only exacerbated her already grave situation.

"I'll be back in a second, Alex," Shack whispered in her ear, and released her hand.

He stepped down from the truck, wincing as the ribs he'd injured—probably broken—when the tsunami hit, reacted. He turned to watch the pilot of the Cessna Skylane make his approach to 101.

"More power, more power," he muttered to himself as the plane neared the highway at too steep an angle. Easy to do when the highway sloped up. The pilot realized it, too, and reacted, gunning the engine in an attempt to soften the landing.

Then the elk.

"Shit!" Shack yelled.

A dozen other people watching the action screamed, too.

The aircraft, with the pilot unable to make a complete correction to cushion the touchdown, hit the highway hard. And bounced. Over the elk. The Cessna's left wing strut brushed the animal's antlers as the plane leapfrogged the elk. The startled animal, with probably enough drama this day to last a lifetime, galloped into the woods.

The Cessna touched down again, this time for good, the pilot riding the brakes. Somehow he'd held the center line. Other than the big bounce, which probably had saved his life, as well as the elk's, he'd made a perfect landing.

Shack sprinted up 101 toward the plane as it rolled to a stop. He reached the craft just as the pilot stepped from the cockpit.

"Hey, man, that was super," Shack said, panting, out of breath from his dash. "You can fly right seat for me anytime."

The pilot, his tanned face as pale as a winter's frost, held up his hand—stay back. He dashed for the shoulder of the road and vomited.

ROB SPIT THE LAST of the acidic effluent from his mouth, wiped his lips with the back of his hand, drew a deep breath, and walked back, rather wobbly, to his welcoming committee.

"Sorry," he mumbled. "Not used to landing uphill on a hiking trail with an elk on it."

"Couldn't have done better myself," Shack said. "That was terrific.

By the way, I'm Shack, the guy you were talking to on guard." He extended his hand.

Rob eyed it, shook his head. "Better wait 'til I disinfect myself."

Shack laughed. "I understand. Don't know that I ever upchucked after a landing, but I think I had to change my underwear once or twice."

Rob noted Shack's voice bore a raspy timbre, something he hadn't caught over the radio. The guy looked badly beat up, too, with a large cut on his head, and his arms crisscrossed with scratches and bruises.

Shack caught Rob's appraisal. "Swallowed a lot of salt water when the tsunami hit," he explained. "In fact, I thought I'd drowned. Got the stuffing pummeled out of me by all the crap in the surge."

Tim joined the two men. Rob introduced him to Shack.

"Were you scared, son?" Shack asked.

"Yes, sir."

Shack smiled. "Then your dad hasn't raised a fool."

Red lights flashing, the EMS truck came up the road. Shack turned to track it.

"Somebody I care about is in there," he said

"Wife? Daughter?" Rob asked.

"Let's just say a good friend. I can't say how much I appreciate your help, Dr. Elwood."

"Call me Rob."

Shack nodded. "Anyhow, I know you've gone above and beyond. If we can get her to Portland quickly, she might have a chance."

"What happened?"

Shack gave a quick overview. Alex trapped in her house, crushed by fallen support beams. He remaining with her as the tsunami thundered in. Both stepping over a threshold to whatever came next.

"Guess it wasn't quite time for us to find out what that was," Shack concluded.

"You stayed with her?" Tim asked, his eyes wide.

"I owed her that," Shack said.

"What's her name?" Rob asked.

"Alexis Williamson."

"The lawyer?"

Shack nodded.

"You knew her previously?"

"A long time ago." He paused. "It's a three-beer story."

"You'll have to tell me sometime."

"Some tales are better left untold."

Rob decided that was all he was going to get out of Shack, and let it go.

Six or seven men pivoted the Cessna so it faced downhill, ready for takeoff. Overhead, a sortie of crows orbited, scolding loudly, likely upset at the unprecedented turmoil that had disrupted their world.

A pall of smoke remained over Manzanita. The smell of burning wood and plastic mingled with the scents of crushed evergreens, mud flows, and marine life ripped from its oceanic home. A break in the overcast allowed a shaft of sunlight to briefly brighten the shattered countryside: the fallen trees, the sunken slopes, the fissured earth.

Four EMTs transported Alex, strapped on a backboard, to the plane. A fifth EMT walked beside her, carrying three IVs, each contained in heavy mesh netting. Clear plastic tubing ran from the bags into Alex's right arm.

The technicians studied the Cessna for a moment, then one of them called out, "Hey, the back seat is too narrow for us to squeeze her in on a backboard."

"Damn it," Shack muttered. With a stricken look on his face, he turned to Rob.

"Get me a wrench," Rob called out.

An EMT darted back to the truck and returned with several crescent wrenches.

Rob selected one, clambered into the plane, and went to work on the rear seats. Within five minutes he had the seat backs lowered to almost a full reclining position.

"Try it now," he said to the technicians.

With skill born of experience and ingenuity, they maneuvered Alex into the plane, then locked the backboard in place using tape, cords, and pillows.

One of the EMTs approached Rob. "Unfortunately, we've had to handle Ms. Williamson pretty roughly. That's not the usual protocol for someone with a broken pelvis. But once we got her out of the tree and realized the extent of her injuries, we immobilized her as quickly as possible. We secured her on the backboard, got her into some MAST trousers, and inflated them."

"MAST trousers?" Rob said.

"Redundant, I know. MAST stands for Medical Anti-Shock Trousers. They should help slow any internal bleeding. We piggybacked some IV bags together. They're designed to work sequentially to keep

168

her blood pressure up. We suspended them from an air vent, but keep an eye on them. You might end up having to hold them yourself."

"I appreciate all you guys have done," Shack said.

"I wish we could guarantee her survival, but you know, given the circumstances . . ." The EMT's voice trailed off. "Just get her to Portland as quickly as you can."

Shack nodded, apparently unable to speak.

Rob turned to Tim. "Sorry, son, you'll have to sit this one out. Shack needs to ride in the passenger seat."

"I get it, Dad."

"Go into town and find Lewis. He'll take care of you."

"Will you be okay?"

"After what I've been through already, I don't think it can get any worse."

Tim, surprising Rob, gave him a quick hug. Something teenaged sons absolutely don't do with their fathers. "Take care, Dad."

"So far, so good," Rob responded. Overcome by a mini-surge of emotion, he strained to get the words out.

He turned to a nearby EMT, a guy who looked like he might be in charge. "What have you got set up in Portland?"

"We've contacted Legacy Emanuel Medical Center. They've got a level-one trauma facility. They're located about four or five miles from Portland International, and said they'd try to get an ambulance or EMS vehicle over there to transport the patient. That might be a challenge, though, given the state of the roads. But they think they can do it."

"What about a medevac chopper?"

"As you can imagine, there's nothing available."

"Is PDX aware we're coming?"

"We've notified them. They said there's minor runway damage, but I gather you don't need a lot of distance for landing."

"Fifteen hundred feet should do it. The longest runway at PDX is over two miles long. We'll be fine."

"Can you give me an ETA?" the med technician asked. "I'll relay it to Portland."

Rob ran through a quick mental calculation. "Probably about forty, forty-five minutes."

Shack, his face knotted in concern, leaned into the conversation. "I didn't think Portland was that far."

"I'm not instrument qualified," Rob said. "I'll have to fly to Astoria, then up the Columbia River to stay below the cloud deck."

"Screw that," Shack responded. "I can fly instruments. We can go direct over the mountains. They aren't that high. I'll let you handle the takeoff and landing. We gotta get Alex to the trauma center as fast as possible. Okay?"

Rob decided Shack had a point. The guy undoubtedly had logged hundreds of hours of IFR flight time, and there certainly wouldn't be any other traffic in the air to worry about at the moment. Rob addressed the EMT: "Make it a little over twenty minutes."

"Got it. I'll let Portland know, and we'll stay in touch with you on the emergency channel."

With Rob flying and Shack in the passenger seat, the departure went smoothly, Rob again holding a laser-like focus on the center line of the highway as he took off. They raced through the tree-lined corridor of U. S. 101 and got airborne quickly on the downhill run.

"I'm getting good at this," Rob said.

"Do I detect a ring of sarcasm in your voice?" Shack asked.

"You do." His throat still burned from his post-landing barf.

Rob called Seattle Center and let them know they were bound for Portland IFR.

"You got the controls," Rob said to Shack.

The Cessna entered the overcast at eighteen hundred feet and popped out on top at thirty-five hundred into bright sunshine.

"Nice day up here," Shack noted.

"In the summer, almost always," Rob said. "By the time we reach Portland, the cloud deck should be pretty much gone."

Shack and Rob turned their heads frequently to check on Alex who remained motionless and pale on the backboard in the rear seat. The jury-rigged IV bags appeared to be holding their own, though Alex's breathing seemed to have become rapid and shallow; fighting off shock despite the IV infusions. Rob guessed she didn't have a lot of time left.

They began their descent over the western reaches of the Portland metropolitan area. True to Rob's prediction, the clouds scattered out allowing bright sunshine to bathe a scene of massive destruction: sunken and cracked roads, landslides, fractured farmland, fallen trees and power lines, crumpled bridges and overpasses, and areas of badly damaged—in some cases toppled—buildings. Not surprisingly, pillars of smoke dotted the landscape.

"Jesus, what a mess," Shack said. He transferred control of the Cessna back to Rob. "Take us home, partner."

Rob set a course for Portland International, over the West Hills, over the city center, over the Willamette River, to PDX adjacent to the Columbia.

A short while ago he'd made a comment to Tim he didn't think things could get any worse. In an instant, he witnessed the violent assassination of that Pollyannaish sentiment. The ground below him blurred in ripples and rolls. Trees swayed as if caught in a hurricane. Additional fissures zig-zagged across the Earth.

"What the fuck?" Shack exclaimed.

Rob's gut tightened. "An aftershock, a big one."

Chapter Twenty-Three

The Impossible

Airborne Over Portland
Sunday, July 5

ROB IMMEDIATELY attempted to contact the tower at Portland International, but received no response. He tried approach control. Nothing. He went back to the guard channel and called Nehalem Bay Fire and Rescue. He got an answer.

"Delta Echo, good to hear from you. We just had another big shake here. What the hell is happening?"

"Aftershock. A huge one, I'm guessing."

"Damn right. Things have gone from worse to appalling. This wasn't expected was it?"

"It probably wasn't factored into disaster response plans, but big aftershocks aren't unprecedented. I'm afraid the Northwest is in uncharted territory now as far as catastrophes go."

"Not a pretty place to be." A pause, then: "Hey, doc?"

"Yes?"

"Is there another tsunami coming?"

Rob didn't know, but understood it wouldn't be impossible. "I have no way of knowing, Nehalem Bay, but keep everyone in the assembly areas. Don't let them back into the evacuation zones for at least another half hour. No, make that an hour, just to be sure. Keep your first responders out of there, too."

"Roger that, Delta Echo."

Cannon Beach

JONATHAN, ZURRY next to him issuing great sonorous snores, had watched the waters of the tsunami retreat and counterattack three times. None of the subsequent surges, however, exceeded the high-water marks of the initial flood. He, Zurry, Bill, and Olive remained safe on a gravelly road among a sheltering copse of evergreens and huckleberry bushes on the slopes of Haystack Hill.

Finally, the ocean seemed to tire of its assault and fell back from the beaches and harbors of the coast one last time. Jonathan stood and walked a little way up the road to check on Bill and Olive. Olive still rested against the mailbox post where he'd left her. Bill sat on the ground beside her holding her hand. He managed a weak smile as Jonathan approached.

"We survived," he said, "thanks to you."

Jonathan knelt in front of the couple. He could see they'd been crying.

"I'm sorry about your house."

"We lost everything," Bill said, and leaned his head against Olive's. "Except each other." He reached out and touched Jonathan's arm. "Hey, I'm glad you found your friend." He nodded at Zurry.

"Thank you. And thanks for trying to help me save my . . . stuff." He let slide the fact they'd almost killed Zurry in the process.

Jonathan shivered slightly as a gust of wind swirled down the road, working its way through his soaked clothing. He stood and looked out at the ocean. Between him and a beach now littered with debris and wreckage, stood a wasteland of mud, rocks, sand, splintered homes, shattered trees, crushed vehicles, crumpled pavement, and drowned wildlife. Already a stench of death and decay had crept into the air.

He gazed, disconsolate, at what no longer could be called an ocean-side paradise of beach homes and cottages; at a place where residences had once nestled among salal and seagrass and wild blackberries, and found asylum from winter storms behind wind-flagged pines and spruce and fir. But no longer. The landscape had morphed into a post-apocalyptic movie set, an urban dump that likely extended for hundreds of miles north and south, a countryside with a salty sheen devoid of life and hope.

Yet he spotted life, people beginning to creep back into the no-man's land from wherever they'd sheltered. And he knew where there was life, there was hope.

"Come on, Zurry, old buddy. Wake up. Let's go take a look."

Zurry snapped his huge head up, struggled to his feet, shook himself, water flying in all directions, and walked slowly to Jonathan, limping a little.

He stopped as the ground shook and trembled again, heaving and yawing. Olive uttered a tiny, pitiful scream. Bill said, "Oh, no." Jonathan sank to his knees and reached for Zurry.

The shaking, sharp and violent, lasted less than thirty seconds, then relented. Jonathan scrambled up and squinted at the western horizon. Once again, the ocean seemed to be sliding away from the coast, perhaps gathering its forces for yet another charge toward the Pacific beaches.

"Well, maybe we got a few minutes, Zurry." Jonathan chose a landmark, an empty refrigerator sans its door, that he thought defined the directional bearing he'd followed to rescue Zurry.

"Let's look in that direction, boy. Maybe the bags were heavy enough they sank instead of being carried away by the tsunami."

He waded, gloppy step by gloppy step, through viscous mud and sand toward where he thought he'd found Zurry. The aftershock appeared to have opened fresh cracks in the re-formed terrain, crevices that might have unearthed something previously buried.

Keeping one eye on the ocean, the other on the uneven ground, he moved slowly. And slowly lost hope. *The black man's lot.*

He realized that exhaustion had overtaken him and that he'd be unable to continue his search, at least today. He turned to struggle back up the hill.

Zurry barked, his nose jammed against a muddy mound of sand.

Really? Jonathan kicked at it. The coating of mud and sand fell away. He knelt and tugged at something that looked like the edge of a piece of canvas. He tugged again. And smiled. He knew the mud-encrusted material held significance, but suddenly couldn't remember why. He blinked. Perhaps a burial shroud for a fellow black from centuries ago? Or maybe for a brother Marine from mere decades past? He remained confused, but knew, given time, clarity would return. It always did, though he begrudged the increasing frequency with which such blank spells seemed to recur.

He tilted his head toward the slate-gray sky and waited.

Airborne Over Portland

ROB THROTTLED back the Cessna as he approached the West Hills of Portland, a range of low hills, generally less than a thousand feet, separating the Willamette River from the western suburbs of the city. He continued his conversation with Nehalem Bay Fire and Rescue.

"We're over Portland now. Have you heard anything from PDX or Legacy Emanuel since the second quake?"

"Negative, Delta Echo. We thought we had everything set up, then the comms went dark. Bad shit. Hold your position and I'll try to find out what the situation is now."

"I can't believe this," Shack said over the interphone.

Rob glanced at him. His face registered both anger and resignation.

"We'll do something," Rob said. *I just don't know what yet.* "Don't worry."

He looked down at the West Hills and realized the area had taken a horrific hit, probably exacerbated by the presence of the Portland Hills Fault. Numerous landslides scarred the slopes of the range. The crumpled skeletons of dozens of homes littered the paths of the slides, as though razed from their foundations by giant bulldozers. The main highway over the hills, U. S. 26, had been severed in several spots by slides and cave-ins. The tunnel at the base of the hills, where the highway intersects the Interstate system, had collapsed.

Downtown Portland sat battered and smoking. The newer skyscrapers seemed to have survived, but now lacked much in the way of glass in their windows. The glass, like fields of diamonds, sparkled in millions of tiny shards on the debris-laden ground. Many older buildings had been reduced to piles of rubble. Fires and shattered water mains shot a strange mixture of smoke and water into the air.

"Jesus," Shack said, "it looks like Sarajevo in '95—the Bosnian War."

"Thankfully it's Sunday," Rob noted, "so at least most offices and stores were probably empty."

He banked the Cessna to fly north along the Willamette, the river bisecting Portland. The main span of the Marquam Bridge, I-5, rested on the bottom of the river. He pointed out the wreckage to Shack. "There's what was supposed to be the safest bridge in Portland."

He continued north. The new Tilikum Crossing, opened in 2015, seemed to have withstood the dual earthquake assault. But the bridge had been designed only for light rail, busses, bicycles, and pedestrians, not private vehicles.

The Hawthorne Bridge appeared heavily damaged. Impassable. The Morrison and Burnside Bridges appeared intact, but closer inspections at some point in the future might well uncover significant structural deficiencies.

The old Steel Bridge, a multimodal passage—autos, light rail, and Amtrak—now sat like a bony dinosaur on the river bottom

The approaches to the Fremont Bridge, I-405, had crashed onto the banks of the Willamette, pulverizing whatever had existed beneath them.

At the northern end of the stretch of a dozen bridges spanning the Willamette, Rob reached the BNSF rail bridge and the St. Johns Bridge, both of which had ceased to exist as viable river crossings.

He spoke to Shack on the interphone. "Well, it looks like Portland's going to be a divided city for weeks, probably months, to come."

Shack seemed less interested in that than their more immediate problem. "Call the fire and rescue guys again. See if they've heard anything yet. We gotta get Alex down."

Rob made the call. The response came quickly. "Still working on it, Delta Echo. We're in touch with the trauma center, but they don't think they'll be able to get a vehicle to the airport. Not after the second quake. The streets and roads are shot to hell. We also heard the runways at PDX are too badly damaged to be used, even by light aircraft. The place is closed. There's another problem, too."

How many frigging more can there be? "What's that?"

"Bonneville Dam. Apparently it's sustained some significant cracks. They don't think it will fail, but just in case, well, that's another reason the airport is shut down. It's right on the river, and if the dam lets go . . ." The EMT didn't finish the sentence.

"Where's Bonneville Dam?" Shack asked over the interphone.

"It spans the Columbia about forty miles upstream from Portland," Rob answered. "It was built back in the 1930s, long before we worried about big quakes. If it gives way, then—"

"Then you've got a tsunami coming *down* the Columbia."

"Essentially, yes."

"What about the real one, the one that wrecked the coast?"

"Probably wasn't a big deal here. Maybe a little water rise, but not a huge one."

Shack leaned back in his seat. "And I thought this place was supposed to be a Shangri-La."

"So did a lot of people," Rob said.

He went back to the emergency channel. "Nehalem Bay, Delta Echo here. I understand all the issues. I know they're not your fault, and not even your problem. I get it. But we've got a dying patient onboard here. We need a solution."

"Roger that, Delta Echo. The trauma center guy says they have an idea. I don't know what it is, but they said they'd get back to me in five minutes after they make some coordination calls. Hang tight."

"Nothing else to do," Rob said.

Shack rolled his eyes, turned his body gingerly while clutching his ribs, and checked on Alex. He reached back, grunting in pain, and stroked her forehead.

Rob continued north over the river, noticing it began looking more and more like an open sewer with huge gasoline and oil spills eddying in brown and green swirls on its surface. Tugs and barges that had torn from their moorings drifted in the fouled water as did a flotilla of houseboats, several on the verge of sinking. People trapped on them waved frantically as Rob flew over.

Rob looked on helplessly. *Can't help you.*

"Where'd all that greasy shit come from?" Shack asked.

Rob pointed to his left. "There. It's called a critical energy infrastructure hub." A stark industrial complex of tank farms, pipelines, marine terminals, and high-voltage electrical substations stretched for several miles along the west bank of the Willamette, just short of its confluence with the Columbia.

"What all is in there?" Shack asked.

Rob banked the Cessna slightly so they both could look down.

"Pipelines, storage facilities, electrical transmission lines, marine tanker terminals; basically, Oregon's lifeblood."

"Looks like the state may bleed to death," Shack said, a touch of bitterness in his words.

The complex had been reduced to crumpled wreckage, including bent and toppled transmission towers. Oil and gasoline flowed unabated from damaged and destroyed tanks and pipelines, streaming into the Willamette, fouling the waters in a soupy blackness that would soon reach the Columbia and head downstream toward Astoria.

In one location, an area thick with storage tanks, dense, tarry smoke billowed from flames leaping unchallenged toward the sky.

"Pretty soon, the damn river will be on fire," Shack said.

Rob brought the airplane back to level flight. "Another thing, that hub supplies virtually all of the fuel to the airport. PDX is going to be crippled for a long time."

Shack didn't say anything, just shook his head in what seemed sad resignation.

Rob continued to stare, almost blankly, at the scene below. He hadn't yet been able to come to grips, either intellectually or emotionally, with the enormity of what had happened, with what he'd witnessed over the past two or three hours. Perhaps it didn't qualify as the death of a region, but it came damn close.

The Pacific Northwest, particularly areas west of the Cascades, had been dealt a devastating blow. Not one of Katrina or Sandy proportions, no. Not even close. Something much, much larger. A mega-disaster. New Orleans after Katrina, and the New Jersey and Long Island shores in the wake of Sandy, had presented overwhelming recovery and rehab challenges, but this, what had happened here, could prove insurmountable.

No, don't think like that.

The region *would* recover. Like *Boston Strong: Northwest Resilience*. It might take years, or even decades, but the Pacific Northwest would return, more vibrant and beautiful than ever.

A radio call interrupted Rob's reverie.

"Delta Echo, this is Nehalem Bay Fire and Rescue. Do you read?"

"Loud and clear," Rob answered. He turned the plane back toward the city center.

"Delta Echo, we've coordinated a plan with Legacy Emanuel . . . if you're game."

If I'm game? Why wouldn't I be game? "This isn't going to involve landing on a highway again, is it?"

"Uh, no, Delta Echo."

"Let's hear it then. Short of airdropping our patient, which we can't do, I gotta get her down somehow."

"Understood. But this could be really dicey."

An unease crept over Rob. The guy on the other end of the transmission seemed reluctant to plunge into the details of whatever had been planned.

"Okay, Nehalem Bay, but I thought I'd done 'dicey' already."

"You have, but . . . uh . . ."

Rob's unease intensified. Though he'd never faced cancer, he guessed he might be feeling something akin to a patient awaiting to find out if a malignant tumor is inoperable or not. He glanced at Shack who'd been listening to the exchange. Shack scowled, puzzled, concerned. He obviously didn't like the hesitancy he was hearing, either.

"Come on, Nehalem Bay, lay it on me," Rob snapped, not meaning to sound quite that harsh.

"Roger that, Delta Echo. You're familiar with the location of Legacy Emanuel, right?"

"Vaguely. On the east side of town, a little north of the Coliseum?"

"Right. They're about a half mile east of the river, near the I-5/I-405 interchange."

"Got it. So what's the deal?"

"The hospital has coordinated with the Multnomah County Sheriff's Office to facilitate a pickup of the patient, but it won't be routine."

"Well, I kind of understand that. Nothing about today has been routine."

"Maybe you'd better talk directly with Legacy Emanuel, Delta Echo."

"Look, I appreciate the effort everyone has put into this, Nehalem Bay, but how about dropping the mushroom treatment and telling me what the hell the plan is. Is that an unreasonable request?"

"No, sir." The speaker paused.

"Well?"

"Well, it involves the Sheriff's River Patrol Unit."

"Say again, Nehalem Bay." Rob thought he'd misheard.

"It involves the River Patrol Unit."

Rob allowed the words to sink in. *River Patrol?* It didn't take him long to divine the "plan." He felt as if his life were being squeezed out of him by a python. Of all the flying tasks he'd been called upon to carry out the past few hours, he knew with great certainty this would be the one he couldn't. No way, no how. His aviation skills had been maxed out, depleted, exhausted, terminated.

"Oh, *hell* no," he exclaimed, a bit too loudly.

Chapter Twenty-Four

The River

Airborne Over Portland
Sunday, July 5

"WHAT WAS THAT, Delta Echo? Didn't understand."

"The plan is to have me land in the river, right?" Rob responded, not wanting to repeat his immediate gut reaction.

"I'm afraid there aren't any other options, Delta Echo. Airports are closed. Roads impassable. The River Patrol Unit thinks they can fish you out of the water before the aircraft sinks."

"Thinks?" he exclaimed.

"Well . . . uh, they haven't done this before."

"Haven't done it before?!"

"I'm sorry, Delta Echo. It's the best we could do."

Rob yanked the plane none too gently into another turn, reversing his course, but continuing to orbit over the river. His anger at being called upon, again, to perform a seemingly impossible task had temporarily overridden his fear of considering how he might actually attempt it.

Shack laid a steadying hand on Rob's arm.

"This is just unfuckingbelievable," Rob snapped over the interphone, "just unfuckingbelievable."

"I know, I know," Shack said, his hand still resting on Rob's arm, "but like the Nehalem Bay guy said, what other choices do we have?"

"I'm going to Hillsboro airport," Rob said. "I know I can get us down there, even if the runway is shit."

"Where's Hillsboro?"

"A little over ten miles west."

"Trauma center?"

"There are a couple of hospitals."

"But no trauma centers?"

"None that I know of."

Shack turned to look at Alex. "She's on her second IV bag already. She's not going to make it much longer without trauma care."

"We don't know that."

"We do know it. That's why the EMTs in Manzanita put her on the plane. Look, I hate to play this card, but what if that were your wife or daughter in the backseat? Would you be dicking around trying to find an alternative to a trauma center?"

"I'd be 'dicking around,' as you put it, trying to keep them, and us, alive."

"Sorry, didn't mean to sound insensitive." Shack removed his hand from Rob. "I know you're stressed. We both are. I—"

A call from Nehalem Bay interrupted. "Delta Echo, you still there?"

"Roger that, Nehalem Bay. Give me a moment."

Rob went back on the interphone. "So what do we do? What would *you* do? You're the Air Force commander."

The Cessna flew through a layer of smoke drifting over the river. Below, the conflagration in the tank farm appeared to have spread. One of the tanks erupted in a red-orange fireball. Arcs of flaming fuel jetted skyward in all directions. Rob rolled the Cessna out of harm's way.

"In the military," Shack said, "the mission comes first. Our mission is to save Alex's life."

"I'm not in the military."

"Neither am I, but it's my legacy. I think there might be something in the Bible that addresses the situation, too."

"I'm sure there is. But what about us? We could just as well lose three lives as save *one* if I dump us in the drink." *Not to mention deep-sixing a half-million-dollar airplane.*

"In this case, *you're* the aircraft commander. You make the decision."

"No. How about *you* taking over? I've never ditched an airplane before."

"Neither have I."

"But you've got a hell of a lot more flyboy experience than I do."

"Not in a Cessna. You've got the touch to land this thing. Besides, I'm hurting." He pointed at his ribs.

Rob's heart rate accelerated, thudding away with a disco beat. "I can't do it, Shack. I just can't."

Shack inclined his head toward Alex. "She might appreciate it if you'd try."

Rob drew a deep breath, squeezed his eyes shut for a brief moment, then called Nehalem Bay.

"Okay, brief me on the plan."

"Roger, Delta Echo. Legacy Emanuel Med Center is about a half mile from the river. They think they'll be able to get a vehicle through the debris to the river where the River Patrol guys can hand off the patient."

"I think you left out all the 'ifs,' Nehalem Bay."

"Yeah, I know, but we're trying to sound positive."

I guess somebody has to. "Go on."

"We're told there's an open stretch of water on the Willamette just north of the Fremont Bridge. If you're able to land just short of the bridge, that'll put you close to the med center."

"Everybody understands, I assume, this won't be a landing. It'll be a crash. I'm not flying a plane with pontoons. And, oh, by the way, the river is filled with all kinds of crap, things adrift—pleasure craft, tugs, barges, houseboats."

"Roger that, Delta Echo. Maybe you'd better talk directly to the River Patrol."

"Can I reach them on guard?"

"Negative. They don't have that capability."

Rob and Shack exchanged glances. Shack pinched his lips together and shook his head. Over the interphone he said, "How the hell did they think we could do this if we can't even communicate with the rescuers?"

Rob flashed a forced smile, his first of the day. "Because maybe they know I'm like a Boy Scout, always prepared." *Except for ditching in rivers.* He reached into the center console, fished out a hand-held radio, and gave it to Shack. Then he called Nehalem Bay again.

"I assume we can reach the rescue boat on channel 16?"

"Roger that, Delta Echo."

"Okay, thank you, Nehalem Bay. We'll get in touch with them."

He spoke to Shack. "Since I fly near the ocean a lot, I bought a portable VHF marine radio. You know, just in case. The emergency channel is 16. Dial it in and call the River Patrol Unit."

"Better dig out the pilot's operating handbook, too," Shack said. "We'll need to go over the ditching procedures."

"Right," Rob said with a total lack of enthusiasm. He reached into a pocket on the door beside him and fumbled for the manual.

Shack removed his headset and, using the hand-held unit, made the radio call to the rescue boat.

"This is aircraft Skylane seven-three Delta Echo calling the Multnomah County Sheriff's Office River Patrol Unit. We're preparing to ditch in the Willamette. Do you read? Over."

"We read you, seven-three Delta Echo. This is the Sheriff's River Patrol—five Mary twenty-seven. We're standing by to help. We need to coordinate details. Over."

"Five Mary twenty-seven, thank you," Shack responded. "As I understand it, we're expected to touch down just north of the, uh—" He glanced at Rob.

"Fremont Bridge," Rob yelled over the engine noise.

"Fremont Bridge," Shack said. "Is that your understanding?"

"Roger that. You got an ETA?"

Shack slipped on the headset to communicate with Rob. "We got an ETA for ditching?"

Rob shrugged. He really didn't want to think about it, but said, "Let's say fifteen minutes. That should give us enough time to review the procedures."

Shack responded to the River Patrol. "Be ready in fifteen."

"We'll be there. Got three deputies on board. Been doin' grab-and-goes all day, so we're pumped. If the plane stays afloat for a couple of minutes, we can help. If it goes underwater right away, it's going to be . . . well, a challenge."

"It's our intent to make like a floatplane."

"I'm sure it is. Okay, here's the deal. As soon as you stop moving, get the doors open. Don't wait. If you wait, and the craft is sinking, you won't be able to open the doors against the water pressure. Do you have life preservers on board?"

Rob, who'd removed his headset, too, had been listening. He spoke to Shack. "No. Never figured I'd need any."

"Negative," Shack said over the radio.

"Okay, then be sure to remove your shoes and heavy clothing before you ditch. We'll toss you a rope or life preserver once you're in the river. We'll have a swimmer in the water who will get your patient out of the plane and onto a sled. We'll get her into the rescue boat and then to shore where an EMT vehicle will pick her up. Sound like a plan?"

"Roger, rescue. We'll let you know when we're coming in."

Rob opened the pilot's operating handbook. He and Shack went over the ditching procedures together, step by step.

"You can do this," Shack said after about ten minutes. "It's paint-by-numbers. I'll call off the checklist to you. All you have to do is execute. You're a good pilot. You proved that in Manzanita."

"Right," Rob said, his tone flat.

"I'm serious."

"Look, I'm worried about the damned landing gear. It's not re-tractable. I can see it hitting the water first and flipping us over. We'll turn turtle and sink upside down. Drown like—"

"Shut up, Rob. The gear won't flip us. If you touch down at almost stall speed, by the book, the gear will dig into the water and decelerate the plane. Maybe rapidly, but we'll still be shiny side up. Let's do this. I've got your back."

"The mission, right?" He glanced back at Alex.

Shack nodded. "The mission."

"Okay. I'm ready. As my mom used to say, 'Everybody's got an expiration date.'"

Shack responded with quiet resolve. "Ours isn't today, brother. Ours isn't today."

Rob wished he could be as certain. But for some reason, he at least felt emboldened. Scared shitless, but emboldened. "Call the rescue boat. I'm gonna make one last pass along the river, scope it out, then ditch."

Rob took the Cessna back north, passing near the burning tank farm. A red-and-white Portland fireboat had arrived on scene, but its attack on the streams of blazing fuel snaking toward the river appeared ineffectual. In the river itself, two small orange-hulled Coast Guard vessels pulled people off drifting houseboats. Several unattended barges spun lazily in the current as they headed downstream toward the confluence with the Columbia.

"Okay, recon run," Rob said to Shack.

He turned south, descended to eight hundred feet, dropped his speed to ninety knots.

"Keep your eyes open for power lines crossing the river," he said to Shack.

The Cessna passed back over the St. Johns Bridge and the BNSF rail bridge, both of which had missing spans. To his left, the University of Portland campus sat on a bluff overlooking the river. It appeared several buildings had ridden landslides to the bottom of the bluff.

Just south of the campus, the Swan Island shipyard facility sported a number of toppled cranes. They sprawled like giant steel skeletons adjacent to the ships they'd been offloading.

As he reached the end of the shipyard, Rob put the Skylane into a slight right-hand turn.

"Here's where we make our final approach."

The Fremont Bridge stood about a mile ahead of them. He spotted what looked like a rescue boat waiting near the eastern end of the bridge, at least what remained of the bridge. The main span, a steel arch supporting a double-decked highway, remained intact, but the elevated approaches to the bridge from I-5 had been reduced to piles of concrete and warped steel.

"The river looks clear," Shack said. "Just little chunks of debris here and there. Should be okay by the time we make our go-around."

"Better be."

Rob waggled the wings of the Cessna as he approached the rescue boat. Someone waved in response.

"I hope they know what they're doing," Shack said.

"Are you shitting me? You'd better hope *I* know what I'm doing."

He pulled the plane up, turned, and flew back downriver. He and Shack removed their shoes and outer shirts. They reached the fire-ravaged tank farm where Rob turned again and pointed the plane back in the direction of the Fremont Bridge.

"Okay, I guess this is it. Call River Patrol."

Shack made the call, then leaned toward Rob and extended his hand. "However this comes out, and I think it will end okay, I want to thank you for your friendship and courage. I think Alex would, too. You're a good man, Rob Elwood."

They shook, but Rob let the compliment pass. The task at hand consumed him. He'd read about the so-called "pucker factor" that pilots in harrowing situations experience, but had never encountered it himself. Now he did. His anus fastened itself to his seat like the sucker on the tentacle of an octopus.

"Here we go," he said, his voice full of false bravado. In truth, he wanted to be anyplace but in an airplane trying to land in the Willamette River.

Shack held the operating handbook open on his lap.

Rob descended to three hundred feet, flew abeam of Swan Island, and set the plane on its final glide path. About a minute to landing.

"Okay, call off the steps."

"Aim for 55 knots at touchdown. Close to stall speed. Set the flaps at twenty degrees." Shack's voice sounded strong and commanding.

"Got it," Rob said, unable to get any other words out. He adjusted the flaps.

"Fifteen hundred RPM," Shack said.

The Cessna slowed and Rob watched the water surface flashing beneath him, coming up, it seemed, way too fast. His knuckles turned white as he held the yoke in a death grip.

Forty-five seconds to go.

"Slow it a bit," Shack said, "you're a little hot."

Sweat beaded on Rob's forehead and dripped into this eyes, blurring his vision. Despite that, he spotted the rescue boat, SHERIFF emblazoned on its cabin, pulling into the center of the river, getting out of the way of the plane's path.

Thirty seconds.

"Good descent," Shack called out. "Back off on the power just a tad. Twelve degrees' nose-high." More than that and the tail would hit first, forcing the nose down and into the water. Less, and the nose would drill directly into the river like a torpedo.

The Cessna flew just over a hundred feet above the Willamette now. At least the surface appeared flat, no wakes or waves. *Maybe I can do this.*

"Holy shit!" Shack screamed.

The marine radio squawked at the same time. "Abort, abort!"

Rob saw why. Directly in front of him, a huge boathouse and attached dock, a fugitive from somewhere upstream, emerged from underneath the bridge. It took up half the width of the river, riding the current, plowing through the water like a polar icebreaker.

"Pull up," Shack yelled.

Rob gave the Cessna full throttle, but knew time had run out. They'd clear the derelict boathouse, but not the bridge. "Goddamnit," he screamed in frustration and rage.

"Under the bridge, go *under* the bridge," Shack bellowed.

Their only option. The plane skimmed beneath the lower deck of the bridge, clearing it by mere feet. Once past the Fremont, Rob pulled up just in time to roar over the semi-submerged wreckage of the next bridge upstream, the Broadway.

His arms and hands shook palpably as he gained altitude and turned the Skylane northward once more, positioning the plane for another attempt at ditching.

"Jesus, Shack, I don't know if I can do this again," he said, his voice trembling.

"Sure you can. You're a veteran now. You nailed that first approach, and you reacted like a pro when you had to abort. Take a few deep breaths and we'll try it again."

Shack called the rescue boat and told them to stand by for another try.

Rob flew a lazy circle for a few minutes and managed to steady himself. Then, with Shack calling out the steps, he began the ditching procedure for a second time.

They passed the thirty-second mark with no problems.

"River's clear," Shack said.

Rob bobbed his head in acknowledgement as he focused on the spot in the river where he wanted to touch down.

"Mixture control to idle," Shack commanded. "Fuel shutoff valve closed. Magnetos and master switch off." Fire prevention measures.

The engine stopped as designed and the cabin went silent except for the rush of the wind.

Fifteen seconds.

"Keep the wings level," Shack barked. "Unlatch your door."

Rob cracked the door open. Air whistled through the opening.

"Nose too high!" Shack yelled.

"Shit." Rob pushed the yoke forward.

But time had run out. Shack threw his arms in front of his face. Rob tucked his chin into his chest. The undercarriage beneath the tail smacked into the water with a thudding splash. The plane decelerated with frightening force, hurling Rob against the seat harness, the harness biting into his chest like barbed wire.

The plane rocked forward. The tail lifted. The nose buried itself in the river. Green-gray water washed over the windscreen.

Chapter Twenty-Five

Aftermath

Portland
Sunday, July 5

"GET OUT, GET OUT!" Shack yelled.

The nose of the Cessna bobbed up, bursting from the river like a surfacing submarine. Rob unfastened his harness, popped open the door. Water poured into the cabin.

The coolness of the river ignited Rob's senses. At least it didn't approach the numbing chill of the Pacific. He dog-paddled away from the plane, a quick, splashy retreat. A flotation device, a square cushion tethered to a rope, plopped into the water beside him. He grabbed it.

A rescue swimmer already was at the door of the now-sinking plane, working frantically to free the backboard and Alex.

The Sheriff's boat sat in the water near the rear of the aircraft. Its twin outboards burbled noisily as its operator struggled to hold it in a static position relative to the Skylane as both rode a strong current. Rob guessed the massive amount of wreckage and debris in the river had funneled it into mini-rapids and swifter-than-usual channels.

The boat looked to be a thirty- or thirty-five-footer with a long, flat deck in front and a cabin toward the rear. A drop-down door in the bow, like a military landing craft, sat open, waiting for the swimmer and Alex.

On the opposite side of the plane, Shack, also grasping a flotation cushion, plowed through the water like a body boarder as a deputy on the deck of the boat tugged him in.

The swimmer, wearing a dry suit, gloves, and helmet seemed to be having difficulty getting Alex out of the plane. Rob paddled back to him.

The swimmer gave Rob a quick once-over. "You okay?"

"I'm fine, just bruised. Let me help." He let go of the flotation cushion.

"Grab the right-hand handle of the backboard," the swimmer said. "Let's see if we can keep it level and pull the patient out together."

The swimmer had already disconnected the IV bags, but the backboard seemed hung up on something inside the aircraft.

"I think it's snagged on a seatbelt," Rob yelled.

The swimmer didn't hesitate. He scrambled into the plane, into water already two feet deep and rising fast, and fumbled underneath the backboard. "Got it!" He slid her out.

Alex issued a long, low moan.

"Okay, pull together," the swimmer commanded.

He and Rob tugged the backboard from the plane and wrestled it onto a yellow Life Sled that bobbed in the water next to the submerging Cessna.

"Get away from the plane, quick," the swimmer said. "It's going down."

Rob grabbed the flotation square again and hung on. He watched, virtually drained of emotion, as the Cessna nosed over, the dripping tail rising from the river like a sounding whale, and plunged to the bottom of the Willamette.

The rescue swimmer, ignoring the drama, had the sled and Alex in the patrol boat within seconds. The same deputy that had pulled Shack aboard got Rob into the vessel and slammed the bow door shut. He flashed a signal to the boat's operator who gave full throttle to two big Mercury outboards for the short run to shore. The boat seemed to move almost as fast as the Cessna had on landing.

Seconds later, the operator slowed the vessel and nosed it onto a rocky beach. The deputy on the deck dropped the bow door. Together, he and the rescue swimmer, now out of his dry suit, ferried Alex through a narrow stand of trees to an EMS vehicle waiting on an access road. Rob and Shack, shivering, followed.

The med techs in the truck got Alex settled and quickly reattached IVs to her.

Rob stood outside near the rear of the vehicle. He spoke to the deputy who'd worked the deck.

"I can't thank you guys enough. I gotta say, you know your stuff. I'm Rob, by the way." He extended his hand.

"Travis," the deputy answered, shaking Rob's hand. "The rescue swimmer is Kevin, the operator, Todd. I'm just glad we were in position to help out."

"Well, thanks to all of you for pulling us out of the drink."

"It's what we train for. Sorry about your plane though."

Rob shrugged. The realization hit him that his loss would be minor compared to everything else that had transpired today. Lives, homes, and businesses had been destroyed across tens of thousands of square miles.

And he wondered, now that he'd had a chance to decompress from the tension of the last couple of hours, whether his own house still stood. He thought about trying to call Deb, but knew with communications out all over the Northwest, that would be futile. He patted his pockets. No matter anyhow. He didn't have his phone. It likely rested on the bottom of the Willamette with the Cessna.

Hey, I hope your lady friend will be okay," Travis said.

"I guess it's up to the trauma docs now."

"It is. Anyhow, gotta get going. We got dozens of more calls queued up."

Rob noted the absence of the muffled roar and rumble of traffic that normally filled Portland on a busy summer Sunday. In its stead, only the wail of sirens and alarms rode a smoke-tinged breeze.

"Good luck," Rob called after Travis. But the deputy had already disappeared behind the trees, headed back to the rescue boat.

Rob clambered into the EMS truck. Someone threw a blanket over his shoulders. Shack, already wrapped in one, sat next to Alex while a pair of EMTs worked on her. Rob sat opposite them.

"Hey," Shack said, "hell of a landing, partner. Nobody could have done it better."

"Almost ended up like a torpedo."

"*Almost* doesn't count against you. You know the old saying, any landing you can walk away from, or in this case, swim away from, is a good one. Ya done good. In my book, you're a hero."

"Yeah, some hero. I got a pissed-off wife and a plane-turned-river reef."

"Why pissed-off wife?"

"Because I went public with my vision about the quake and tsunami."

"But you were right."

"Not entirely. I got the day wrong."

"Jesus. BFD. I can't help but think the *event* is what should have mattered, not the fact you missed the timing by a few hours."

"I don't know if I saved any lives though."

"Not up to you. You did your part."

"Hang on, guys," one of the EMTs said.

The truck took off. The driver didn't bother with its siren—not much traffic to warn—he merely turned on the emergency flashers. The vehicle wound its way through a maze of debris, cracked roads, fallen power lines, and at least one structure fire, as yet, un-fought.

"Apocalypse," Shack said. "It's like the damn Apocalypse."

"I guarantee you, it's the same in every city from British Columbia to northern California."

Shack shook his head, slowly, sadly. "But worse where we came from, on the coast?"

"The tsunami flattened everything near the water. And I still don't know if they got hit by a second one." He paused and looked down at the steel-plated floor of the EMS vehicle. "I guess it doesn't make much difference. There probably wasn't much left to wreck."

Alex mumbled something and Shack reached for her hand, leaned his head close to her mouth.

The EMTs stepped back. "Should be about five more minutes and we'll be at the med center," one of them said.

ALEX TURNED HER head toward Shack. She glanced at Rob and the EMTs. "Who are these people? Where am I?" The words came out with surprising clarity and strength. Maybe something in the IVs had rejuvenated her, at least temporarily.

"You're in an ambulance," Shack said. "You're going to a trauma center in Portland."

"Portland?"

"You were flown here from Manzanita."

She fell silent, perhaps trying to process the information.

"Yes," she said, her voice slightly lower in volume. "I remember. I was trapped in my house. Something fell on me. Then the water came." Her eyes seemed to soften as she stared at Shack, gripping his hand. "You stayed." Her voice fell to a whisper. "You stayed with me. You didn't leave."

Shack didn't respond, merely nodded, struggling to keep his emotions in check.

Alex stopped speaking but kept her gaze locked on him. After a few moments she said, almost inaudibly, "Did you love me?"

Did I? Maybe I did and was too fucking stupid, immature, and self-absorbed to realize it.

"I always loved *you*," she whispered. "But I always hated you, too."

He choked back a lump the size of a lemon in his throat.

"Yes," he said softly. "I always loved you."

She managed a weak, fleeting smile, then closed her eyes and seemed to fade into unconsciousness.

The truck jolted to a stop at the emergency entrance of Legacy Emanuel. A latticed steel tower, perhaps one that had supported a satellite or microwave relay, lay crumpled on the roof of the entrance's portico.

Attendants from the medical center sprinted to the truck and within thirty seconds had Alex on a gurney rolling toward the ER. Rob and Shack, looking like half-drowned refugees, draped as they were in heavy blankets and without shoes, trotted behind.

A male nurse waylaid them at the entrance to the ER. He directed them to a waiting room where they sat with throngs of others, many of whom appeared injured and were likely waiting to be seen, or at least processed.

ROB WANDERED OFF in search of coffee. When he returned, without his quarry, he joined a small crowd gathered around a TV, obviously satellite fed and running on the hospital's auxiliary power. He watched as dire report after dire report came in from CNN. Videos of the unfolding disaster remained unavailable, but the network reported they had crews en route despite the challenges of actually making it into the Pacific Northwest.

The grim news seemed endless. All major airports west of the Cascades were closed. I-5 was reported impassable, except for short stretches, from the California-Oregon border to British Columbia. I-90 east out of Seattle was shut down, the Interstate severed by numerous land- and rockslides. I-84, a near-sea-level route through the Columbia River Gorge, was closed to traffic until the integrity of Bonneville Dam could be assessed.

At least for the near future, and no one knew whether that meant days or weeks, the Northwest, west of the Cascades would remain cut off from the remainder of the nation. The government, for once, didn't drag its feet. The region already had been declared a federal disaster area.

National Guard troops and resources from all fifty states were being mobilized. Utility companies from coast to coast and Canada were in the process of dispatching teams. Search and rescue crews, not only from the U. S., but from such diverse and earthquake-experienced nations as Japan, China, Chile, New Zealand, and even Iran were reported as ready to go.

Rob had no idea, and he doubted anyone else did either, how all of the assistance that was prepared to move into the region would actually be able to. And if and when they got here, where they would find staging facilities.

As a start, an unsubstantiated report indicated active duty military personnel were already at work attempting to repair the runway and expand emergency communications at Joint Base Lewis-McChord near Tacoma, Washington. The sprawling base housed an airlift wing and an Army corps.

More credible information, CNN reported, indicated rescue and recovery equipment and forces, including civilian first responders and reserve-component military personnel, were being marshaled east of the Cascades at undamaged bases in Washington state. Sites included Fairchild Air Force Base near Spokane, and Grant County Airport, a former Air Force Base, near Moses Lake.

The headlines continued. From across the globe, pledges of financial assistance already were flooding in, from Germany, France, Great Britain, Australia, South Africa, Saudi Arabia, and on and on. Rob remembered one report he'd read on the loss estimates for a magnitude-nine strike on the region: thirty-two billion dollars for Oregon, forty-nine billion in Washington.

But this had been a nine-point-three followed by an eight-something.

Rob, tiring of the dirge for his homeland, began a search for Shack. He found him curled into a chair in a corner of the waiting room, still wrapped in his blanket, seemingly alone with his thoughts and fears . . . or maybe his prayers.

"Nothing from the ER yet?" Rob asked.

Shack shook his head. His gaze appeared lost and hollow, focused on nothing.

Rob sat beside him. "Let's go see if we can find some food."

Shack shook his head again, declining. "She didn't deserve this," he mumbled.

"Nobody did," Rob answered, keeping his voice low, attempting to add a modicum of comfort to Shack's obvious misery.

"True. A lot of folks are suffering today." Shack looked around the waiting room. He extended his arms between his knees, clasped his hands together, and hung his head, staring at the floor. "It's a shitty world we live in."

Rob thought the assessment harsh, but didn't counter it. He supposed he might feel the same if it were Deb or Tim or Maria in the ER. Everyone has a different frame of reference, one often twisted and cracked and sometimes broken by life's events.

A young doctor dressed in blue ER scrubs, a surgical cap patterned with fir trees and raindrops, and a surgical mask dangling beneath his chin, entered the waiting room.

THE SURGEON SPOTTED Shack and Rob and walked toward them. Shack arose and shed his blanket. He studied the face of the approaching physician and his soul imploded.

He'd seen that expression before, on the faces of surgeons in the Air Force. After a young captain, "Wild Bill" McIntosh, had crashed his A-10 Warthog on the runway at Bagram Airfield; after Lieutenant Art Rolloff had bailed out of his crippled F-22 Raptor at too low an altitude near Langley AFB; after Wiley Overton, the young son of his ops officer at Langley, had been hauled from a grinding motorcycle crash.

Shack stood on wobbly legs as the surgeon stopped in front of him and Rob.

"I'm Doctor Danny Wolcott," he said. "I wish I had better news." He dropped his gaze to the floor.

Shack, unable to remain standing, sank to the ground on his knees. Rob and the surgeon pulled him erect and helped him to a chair. His eyes misted over, blurring the people and room around him into an impressionist's painting. Pain from his cracked ribs jabbed at him like a prize fighter's punch.

Rob said something to him, soothing words, but he didn't understand them. The surgeon took a seat on one side of him, Rob on the other.

"I'm sorry," the surgeon said, "my fault. I should have chosen my words more carefully. I didn't mean to come across as the Grim Reaper. Ms. Williamson is alive."

Shack jerked his head up and stared at the doctor. "Yes?" Hope, like an antidote to the physical and emotional pain that overwhelmed him, surged through his being.

The doctor rested a hand on Shack's arm. "There is a 'but,' however."

Shack waited, knowing "buts" seldom brought good news.

"I'm afraid there was just too much damage to her spinal cord. It's unlikely she'll be able to walk again." He kept his voice low and controlled, professionalism tinged with compassion.

Shack, on an intellectual level, recognized the report as devastating. But it didn't dampen the elation he felt that Alex had lived.

"I heard what you gentlemen went through to get Ms. Williamson here," the doctor continued. "I know *you* did everything you could to save her. I just wish *we* could have done more."

Shack nodded, trapping an incipient sob in his throat.

"She had massive hemorrhaging from the iliac artery in the pelvic region," Doctor Wolcott said. "That was our primary focus, to repair the rupture and stanch the bleeding. To save her life. I wish we could have addressed her spinal cord injuries, but—"

"I know you did the best you could, doctor," Shack interjected, his voice burdened with stress.

"Maybe we need to take a look at you, too, sir. You've winced a couple of times. Ribs?"

"Nothing I can't live with. I think you've got more serious issues on your plate."

Doctor Wolcott stood. "Sadly, that's true." He paused. "Ms. Williamson will be in ICU for quite some time while her vascular damage heals. She'll also be heavily sedated. So it may be several weeks before you're able to visit her."

"And after the ICU?" Shack asked.

"She'll be transferred to a spinal injury rehab center. Probably initially here in Portland. There's an excellent one, RIO."

Shack shot the surgeon a questioning look.

"Oh. Rehabilitation Institute of Oregon. It's located at the Good Samaritan Medical Center. I'm assuming it survived the quake. It's on the northwest side of town." He shook his head, a signal he still couldn't quite accept what had happened to the city . . . to the region. "Then, after things get back to normal"—he sighed heavily and looked around, perhaps wondering if things would ever get back to normal—"she may need to be moved to a regional facility. There's one in Eugene, and a great one in Seattle, but that may have to wait until the transportation infrastructure is cobbled back together. Anyhow, Ms. Williamson has a long, hard road ahead of her. Let me say this though, if she's got more friends like you two, I think she'll do just fine."

Shack stood and shook the surgeon's hand. "Thank you for all you did, doc. I know this is a trying day for everyone."

"Yes. It's one we'd trained for, but also one we hoped would never come."

"You did good," Rob said, standing beside Shack.

Dr. Wolcott nodded and retreated into the ER.

Shack drew a deep breath and leaned against Rob. A blizzard of emotions swirled through his soul.

ROB RESTED A HAND on Shack's shoulder and allowed him to deal with whatever thoughts and feelings had flooded into his psyche.

Shack remained silent for a long period, and Rob allowed him his space. He watched the dozens of others crammed into the waiting room and tried to imagine how many times and in how many places a scene similar to what he and Shack had just gone through would be played out today. How would you describe it? Gut-wrenching? Heart-rending? Excruciating? Tragic? No. No words could handle it.

Finally, Shack sighed heavily, sadly, and spoke. "All I wanted to do when I came here, to Oregon, was apologize to her."

"To whom?"

"Alex."

"Why?"

"Like I said, a long story." He let it go at that.

"Maybe we should go in search of something to eat," Rob suggested. "I heard the Red Cross has something set up in the parking lot."

Shack didn't acknowledge the recommendation. Instead he said, "Do you suppose the innocent are punished for the sins of the guilty?"

"I don't think that's doctrine in any religion I know of."

"Perhaps it should be." He seemed to reconsider for a moment, then said, his words subdued, "Or maybe it's just that the sins of our youth inevitably come back to haunt us. I mean, here's Alex, full of fire and vitality in one moment, then facing life confined to a wheelchair in the next."

"Shack, the Northwest just got clocked by probably the worst natural disaster in the nation's history. It's something that's happened in the past, and something we knew would happen again. No one was targeted. Not the innocent. Not the evil. It wasn't God's wrath directed at anyone. It's something that's been going on for millions of years and probably will continue for millions to come. The restless Earth.

"It's just that when we get caught up in a cataclysmic event, we, as humans, tend to take it personally and try to read something into it that isn't there. In the end, we were just in the wrong place at the wrong time."

"Dust in the wind."

Rob wanted to believe they were more than that, but maybe not. Maybe all of us, he thought, are mere specks of dirt riding the unpredictable currents of life, and ultimately death, in a vast, dark universe.

Both men didn't speak again for a time until Shack broke the silence. "All that," he said, his voice low and hoarse, "all that."

Rob stared at him. "All what?"

"What Alex went through. What we went through. Crashing. Losing the plane. Then Alex ending up so badly injured. It's not right. Just not right." His voice faded.

"Nothing is, not today."

"She's a beautiful lady, Rob. She didn't deserve . . ." Shack's voice faltered again. He brushed his forearm across his eyes, and stood. "I guess I am hungry. Let's go find the Red Cross."

As they waited in line for a tuna fish sandwich and a Coke, Rob asked Shack what his plans were.

"Since there probably isn't much I can do here for a while, I'm going in search of my daughter . . . *our* daughter, Alex's and mine. She is, was, attending a university in Salem."

"A daughter?" Rob failed to hide his surprise. "You never mentioned that before."

"Part of the three-beer story," he said.

"Yeah? When do I get to hear it?"

"After I get my life sorted out. What about you? Where do you go now?"

"I'll probably throw some blankets on the floor and bed down in the hospital tonight, then try to make my way home on foot tomorrow, if I can find some shoes."

"Where's home?"

"Lake Oswego, a suburb about seven or eight miles south of here. I should be able to make it in a day."

A rumble and rattle rippled through the parking lot. Most people standing in line knelt in place. A few screamed. Nobody panicked. Veterans now, or maybe just too exhausted, both mentally and physically, to give a damn anymore.

"Another aftershock," Rob said. "They could go on for days."

They reached the Red Cross food service truck and received their handout.

Shack examined the sandwich. "At least it's not an MRE."

"MRE?"

"Meals Ready to Eat in military lingo. Or more popularly, Meals Rejected by Everyone. It's the armed forces' answer to a weight-loss program."

For the first time that day, Rob laughed.

They seated themselves on a toppled light pole in the parking lot and gobbled their sandwiches along with a bag of chips and a peanut butter cookie.

As they ate, Shack said, "When everything settles down, how do I get in touch with you?"

Rob reached into his pants pocket, found his wallet, and dug out a soggy business card.

"My email and cell phone are on there," he said. He handed the card to Shack. "It may be several weeks before you can get through, though."

Shack studied the card. "Yeah, I know. But I'll be in the area for a long time. Alex isn't going on this journey by herself, although she doesn't know it yet." He flashed Rob an inscrutable grin, and Rob wondered if three beers would be enough to handle the story he hoped to hear someday.

"Look," Rob said, "if you need a place to stay, get in touch with me or make your way to Lake Oswego. Well, that's on the assumption my place survived, I guess."

Sirens continued to warble through the damaged streets. Overhead, streamers of black smoke mingled with puffy, white cumulus. In the parking lot, more and more people, many looking like shell-shocked combat troops, wandered into the medical center.

Shack finished his meal and dumped the wrappers into a trash bin. "Well, I suspect I've got some details to take care of inside."

He spread his arms and approached Rob. "Man hug," he said, his voice still raspy. "But not too hard. Ribs, remember?"

They embraced briefly and stepped apart. To Rob's surprise, it hadn't felt awkward.

"Thanks for all you did, brother," Shack said. "Sorry about your airplane."

"Battle damage, isn't that what you guys call it?"

"Yeah."

"You thinking about going back to Atlanta anytime soon? Didn't you say that's where you're from?"

Shack seemed to stare into the middle distance, perhaps searching for an avatar of himself, and didn't answer immediately. Finally, he said, "I'm an Oregonian now."

Chapter Twenty-Six

Rio

Portland, Oregon
Wednesday, August 19

SHACK FOLLOWED his daughter, Skylar, into Alex's room at RIO, the Rehabilitation Institute of Oregon located in the Good Samaritan Medical Center. After tracking Skylar down, a process that had taken several weeks, Shack and she had returned to Portland where they learned Alex had been moved to RIO. With phone service at last partially restored, they'd been able to call Good Sam's and make arrangements for a visit.

Skylar, sobbing—a reflection of relief more than anything, Shack judged—darted to her mother's bed and fell into her arms. The two embraced for a long time, whispering to one another. He stood by silently, watching mother and daughter, marveling at how much Skylar looked like her mother: tall, shapely, exquisite features, but with blond, not dark, hair. Apparently her hair color had been the only thing she'd inherited from him. Probably a good thing.

Alex appeared pale and drawn. Small wonder. At the same time, she seemed more beautiful than ever, at least to Shack.

The starkness of the room with only a bed, dresser, beside table, and parking space for a wheelchair, struck him as depressing. Perhaps that was the least of the concerns of those who spent time here, however.

Skylar at last broke the hug with her mother, backed away, and turned toward Shack. "Your turn," she said, dabbing at her red eyes with a Kleenex.

Shack stepped to Alex, bent over her, and kissed her on the lips. "You look great."

"Bullshit," she whispered.

"You won't ever agree with me, will you?"

She smiled. "Maybe I need to change my ways."

"You think? Anyhow, it's wonderful to see you," he said, a tiny catch in his throat.

"I'm a cripple now, you know."

"You could have been just a memory."

She closed her eyes. "Yes. It might have been better if I—"

"Cut it out," Shack snapped. "Don't go all 'woe is me' on me now. You've . . . well, we've . . . come through too much."

She opened her eyes, reached out, and grasped his hand. "Yes, I know. You and your pilot friend. What was his name?"

"Rob."

"Yeah. I heard about your adventures. Mine, too, I guess. How you got me out of Manzanita, flew me to Portland, crashed in the river."

"Which leads me to something I want to tell you. Do you recall the old saying that if you save someone's life, you're forever responsible for it?"

"Who said that?" She released his hand.

"It might be an old Chinese proverb, or maybe Polish. I don't know."

She closed her eyes again and tipped her head back in her pillow. "Don't tell me you're going to use that as an excuse to stay with me." A tinge of hardness coated her words.

"I don't need an excuse," he said softly.

She turned her head and stared at him. "Maybe you should rethink that. Look, if you're feeling guilty because you believe your actions might somehow have dictated my exodus to Oregon where I ended up as a victim of a megaquake, get over it. I made my own decision, executed it, and lived with it. I couldn't have been happier here. So don't go falling on your emotional sword for me."

He leaned in close to her. "I wouldn't think of it."

A nurse entered the room and shooed Shack and Skylar out temporarily while she checked Alex's vital signs and took care of the bedpan.

After she'd finished, Shack and Skylar returned.

Alex sat propped up in bed. "So," she said, "tell me how your first meeting went."

Skylar looked at Shack, Shack at her.

"Go ahead," Skylar said.

"Well, it took quite some time, given the circumstances, for me to find her. But I finally located her in one of those camps . . . what are we supposed to call them?"

"Full-Service Temporary Lodging Villages," Skylar said, "courtesy of the U. S. government."

"Yeah, right. She was stuck in a ratty house trailer in a refugee camp." He shifted his gaze to Alex. "She didn't know what had happened to you."

"And I sure as hell didn't believe him when he got around to telling me he was my father," Skylar added.

"*That* took some convincing," Shack said. "I had to answer a lot of, well, personal questions about our relationship. Then even after she accepted I might really be her dad, she decided I was a bastard for never contacting her, even though I told her I never even knew she existed before I went to Manzanita." He paused. "But I guess I was still a bastard."

Neither Skylar nor Alex disagreed, he noted, but he understood where their attitudes came from.

"So after that?" Alex asked.

"We signed up for one of those civilian volunteer teams that were springing up all over the place," Skylar said. "We requested Manzanita and got bussed there after about a week or so. It gave us a chance to see what we could salvage from your house and office."

"Then we helped with general cleanup and salvage work," Shack said. "Tiring but rewarding."

"Where did you live?"

"In a camp the Army set up," Shack said. "Tents, but they were warm and dry and comfortable. It gave us a chance to"—he looked at Skylar—"bond, I guess is the right word."

Skylar smiled. "A work in progress."

"Isn't everything," Alex said, her voice barely above a whisper.

"We'll make it." Shack said.

"So what's next?" Alex looked from Shack to Skylar.

"Back to Manzanita," Shack said, "to continue to help with the cleanup. And . . . should I tell her, Sky?"

Skylar nodded.

"We're going to build a house."

"*We?*" Alex said.

"Skylar and me," Shack answered. "We've already sketched out a design for a home that will accommodate your . . . limitations, for as long as you have them."

"I plan on living there, Mom," Skylar said. "I can help you and maybe even assist in getting your law practice up and running again; at least as soon as I pass the bar."

"How about you?" Alex said, fixing her gaze on Shack.

He stared out the room's window into the intense blue sky of a hot August afternoon. "That'll be up to you," he said.

"I see."

The nurse reappeared. "Well, I need the patient for a little while. She's got a session scheduled with our Zero-G Gait and Balance System."

"So you expect her to be able to walk again?" Shack said.

"She wouldn't be the first."

He moved closer to the nurse. "Honestly, what are her odds?" He kept his voice low.

"Fifty-fifty." She smiled. "Either she will or she won't. Truthfully, we don't know. But I do know it's often not the medical aspects that are the most important factors. It's the psychological ones. A positive attitude, determination, and the will to work your butt off."

"She'll do well then," Shack said.

Shack, Alex, and Skylar said their goodbyes and established a time for their next visit. Shack and Skylar stepped into the hallway, but Shack halted and said, "Hold it a minute." He returned to the doorway and stuck his head back into Alex's room.

"I just remembered something," he said. "Part of the old Chinese or Polish proverb, or whatever the hell it is."

"Yes?"

"My responsibility to you, the part about being forever responsible for your life, is fulfilled if you save *my* life."

"Then I'm afraid you're stuck with me forever."

"No, I'm not."

"I can't save your life."

"That's where you're wrong. You already have." He shut the door, took his daughter's hand, and headed toward the lobby. Skylar leaned her head against his shoulder.

Chapter Twenty-Seven

Home

Lake Oswego
Monday, November 9

RAIN HAMMERED against the windows of Rob's house in wind-driven fury as the first powerful Pacific storm of the autumn slammed into the Pacific Northwest. He hoped the blue tarpaulin draped over his roof would hold. So far, so good. He guessed that if he could see a view of his neighborhood from a drone, it would look more like an azure tent city than an affluent suburb. Perhaps by spring the overloaded roofing contractors would be caught up on their work.

In truth, *he'd* been lucky. His house had weathered the megaquake, suffering only minor damage, "minor" being a relative term. The house had shifted slightly on its foundation, but remained standing, albeit in a fashion that made it appear in the early stages of osteoporosis. Still, it remained habitable. When it might be repaired, he had no idea. In the meantime, he and his family would continue to live in the "Listing House by the Lake."

"Easy to deliver dinners," Rob had told Deb. "Just set the plates on the kitchen counter and they'll slide toward the dining room."

"And no need to worry about privacy here," she'd added. "Most of the doors are wedged open."

Although Rob and she had found humor in that, Tim and Maria hadn't. Teenagers don't appreciate being trapped in a home where they can't sequester themselves in their bedroom burrows. And they certainly would remain trapped through the autumn, since virtually all of the schools west of the Cascades had shuttered their damaged facilities until after the first of the year.

Prior to returning home, Timothy had had his own adventure. He'd remained in Manzanita for almost a month with Lewis after Rob had taken off with Shack and Alex on their "life flight." Although

Lewis's home had been destroyed by the tsunami, he'd taken Tim under his wing. They'd found shelter in the basement of a local church, and kept themselves busy helping with cleanup and recovery operations. They'd often put in sixteen-hour days.

Tim had finally hitched a ride back to Portland after Highway 26 over the Coast Range had been repaired and reopened. It had been an agonizingly slow trip with only one lane open in long stretches.

With both of his children home safe, Rob tolerated their nearly constant whining and bellyaching about their "incarceration." Even that had diminished after he explained to them what the alternative could have been: being squeezed into a FEMA trailer or government yurt—yurts only in Oregon, he imagined—in a so-called temporary settlement. Temporary, he explained, could mean years for some people, if the experiences in the wake of Hurricane Katrina in New Orleans offered any guide.

Rain continued to machine-gun against the window in Rob's study. He guessed the big Honda portable generator he'd purchased long before the quake would come in handy again. Even after power had been restored post-quake to Lake Oswego, after over two weeks without, brownouts had established themselves as a way of life. Now, the gale-force winds howling outside would only exacerbate the problem.

As he tapped on his computer keyboard, his cell phone rang.

"This is Rob," he said, answering it.

"Hey, buddy, how're they hangin'?"

Because of its unique cadence, Rob instantly recognized Shack's voice.

"Shack! What the hell? I thought you'd dropped off the face of the Earth. After we parted ways in Portland, nothing."

"I'm sorry, partner. Things were kind of stressful for a long time."

"I know. For all of us. So where are you?"

"Manzanita."

"Really?"

"Yeah, it seems almost like home to me. Like I told you at the medical center, I'm an Oregonian now."

Rob pushed away from his desk and leaned back in his chair. "Guess you'd better bring me up to date."

Shack did, telling him about tracking down Skylar, their reunion with Alex at RIO, their plans to build a home in Manzanita.

Rob stood and walked to the rain-splattered window and looked out. Firs and spruce whipped back and forth in the wind. Soggy brown and gold leaves, ripped from deciduous trees, tumbled through the air in short flights to landings on puddled streets and saturated lawns.

"So how's Alex doing?" Rob asked.

"She's still in rehab, but she's been moved up to Seattle to the University of Washington Medical Center. I think it's called the Northwest Regional Spinal Cord Injury System. It's considered one of the tops in the country."

"Is she making progress?" The question came with a modicum of trepidation.

"Actually, yes. I just learned a few days ago that she took a couple of steps," Shack's voice cracked with emotion, "on her own while wearing a harness."

"That's great, Shack. Give her my best next time you talk to her."

"I will."

The lights in the study flickered. "Hold on," Rob said to Shack, and called for Tim to make sure the generator was ready to go, if needed.

"Stormy there, too, I guess?" Shack said.

"Welcome to winter in Oregon."

"So I've heard. Anyhow, I want you and your family to come visit when we get the house finished and Alex moved in."

"Love it. So you're going to be staying with them, too?"

A brief silence ensued, except for the steady beat of the rain.

"That's still a TBD, I guess," Shack answered. He fell silent, then changed the subject. "So, your plane. What's up with it?"

"Still on the bottom of the Willamette. Kind of low priority to be dredged up."

"Insurance?"

"Sure. But you know insurance companies. Always glad to take your money. Always eager to keep it."

"What's the hang up?"

"Not an accident, they say. I *deliberately* crashed it into the river."

"Are you shitting me?" Shack's voice rose an octave. "They didn't even consider the circumstances. Give me their fucking phone number. I'll call and set them straight myself."

"My lawyers got it, Shack. Relax. Things will work out."

"They damn well better. After all you did."

Rob decided to vector the conversation to a new tack, attempting to tamp down Shack's obvious anger. "Tell me, how are things going there with the cleanup?"

"Okay. Slow. But hey, not without excitement."

"Tell me." Rob paced back to his desk and sat.

"Well, a few days ago we had some visitors. Skylar and I were working with a small crew of volunteers. There were maybe half a dozen of us clearing debris off a beach north of town, when these three kids, kind of ratty looking, in their twenties I guess, came out of the forest above the beach and walked down to us. We thought they'd come to help."

"But they hadn't?"

"No. One of them brandished a hunting rifle, the other two stalked around trying to look tough."

"What did they want?"

"Cash, credit cards, watches, rings, cell phones. Anything."

"Nice. Tell me you didn't do anything stupid."

"Me? No. My combat days are behind me."

The lights in the study blinked off and on once more, then faded away completely.

"Hold on again," Rob said. He stood and walked to the hall. "Tim, crank up the generator," he called. He returned to his desk. "Power failure," he said into the phone. "Go on."

"So these kids are standing there in their macho, gang-banger mode, when one of them says, 'What's that? I heard something,' and looks back into the woods. Another one of the goons says, 'Put a sock in it, you moron. It's probably just a rabbit or 'coon or something.'"

"But it wasn't?"

Shack laughed. "Not by a long shot. This huge dog, big as a mobile home, comes tear-assing out of the trees, charges right at the guy with the gun. The kid fires a wild shot into the air, and the dog is on him. Bowls him over like he was a duckpin. The other two pricks take off like scalded cats down the beach. One of them cuts loose with this ripping fart you could probably hear all the way to Astoria. I'm guessing he had to burn his underwear." Shack chuckled again.

"And the guy with the gun?"

"The dog stood guard over him until this old black dude showed up, his owner."

"I know him. He's the guy they call Neahkahnie Johnny."

"Right. And that's another story. Anyhow, we, with help from Johnny's Shetland-pony-sized dog kept the guy face down in the sand until the cops showed up and hauled him off to the pokey."

Outside, the generator chugged to life, and the lights in the house, a bit dimmer than before, blinked on.

Rob tilted his chair back and put his feet up on his desk "Tell me the other story," he said, "the one about Johnny."

"Well, as I've heard it, this guy's been looking for some sort of buried treasure around here for years."

"Yeah, Johnny was a fixture on Neahkahnie Mountain."

"So the speculation is that he found the loot, although nobody remembers seeing him on the mountain since last spring."

"Then why the speculation?"

"People say before the quake the guy didn't have a pot to piss in. Now he's in the process of building a house in Manzanita, out of the tsunami zone by the way, that folks say is going to run in the million-dollar range. The thinking is the earthquake and tsunami may have had something to do with unearthing the buried booty."

"Maybe, maybe not. What's Johnny say?"

"Not much. Smiles and says he invested wisely."

"Perhaps he did."

"I've seen the plot of land where the house is going up. Spectacular view from a hillside on the outskirts of Manzanita. There's a sign on the lot that says THUNDERBIRD AND WHALE. Curious name."

"Not really," Rob said.

"Why?"

"Thunderbird and Whale refers to a Native American legend that surrounded a great quake and tsunami that occurred there in 1700. I think Johnny's trying to tell us, without really telling us, that he found the treasure, at least some it, and it had something to do with either the 1700 disaster, or the most recent one."

"So the mystery continues."

"What's life without mysteries?"

They talked for another half hour before hanging up. Rob invited Shack and Skylar to spend Thanksgiving with them. "If you can stand crooked houses, jammed doors, and leaky roofs," he added.

"Moot points if you've got a six pack," Shack said. "Three beers apiece, enough to cover my 'rest of the story' tale."

"You're on."

"One more thing," Shack added, "if I haven't said it before, I want to say it now. Because of what you did for Alex and me—going so far outside your comfort zone, putting your life on the line, losing your plane—you'll always have the admiration and friendship of this broken-down old fighter jock. Maybe a lot of people dismissed you as a prophet, but I sure as shit will never dismiss you as a hero."

"Thank you, Shack." Rob fought to get the words out without his voice failing him.

After they said their goodbyes, Rob sat at his desk listening to the rain rake the side of the house with what sounded like bursts of automatic weapons fire. Deborah slipped silently into the room and walked to his desk. They'd made their peace months ago, Deborah asking for forgiveness for her outburst and abandonment, Rob apologizing for his insensitivity to her fears. A tsunami, he thought, allows everyone to start with a clean slate.

Enticing kitchen aromas trailed Deborah. Baking salmon, simmering pumpkin soup, fresh-cut green beans.

"And squash?" he said, sniffing the air and wrinkling his nose.

"You'll eat it and you'll love it," she said, giving him a playful pinch.

"You're the boss, buttercup."

She didn't respond, and he waited, knowing she hadn't come upstairs to make small talk.

"You got another request for an interview," she said after a moment. "A TV station in Seattle called, wants to talk to you about earthquake predictions, mysticism, and dreams."

"I hope you told them where to go."

"As politely as possible."

He had no intention of promoting the popular sobriquet he'd been tagged with: The Oregon Oracle. He was a geologist, and from here on out would discuss only hard science and seismology. He'd already turned down dozens of requests for interviews from media outlets ranging from local radio stations to CNN, the *New York Times*, *USA Today*, and *Time* magazine. He no longer wanted any part of being a seer.

Which brought the mysterious woman Cassie to mind and something he'd been meaning to do for a long time, but had never gotten around to. His intentions had been, as they say, OBE—overtaken by events. The aftermath of the quake and tsunami had overwhelmed him.

He called up Troy University's website on his computer and searched under Faculty for someone named Cassie. He never had gotten her last name.

Deb looked over his shoulder. "What are you doing?"

"Remember the woman named Cassie I ran into several times before the quake? I told you about her. Tim and I first met her in the Ghost Forest in March. Then she appeared at my news conference. And finally, we crossed paths in Manzanita just a few minutes before the quake."

"Yes. As I recall, you said she was in some sort of communications program, or doing research with Indians?"

"Strategic Communication was what she labeled her field. But she said she'd become more of a cultural anthropologist and was studying the history of Native American tribes in the Northwest. She also seemed very interested in prophecy."

"Prophecy?"

"The topic came up every time we met. It's almost like she knew the subject was, or would become, relevant to me."

"Was she pretty?" Deb pulled up a chair and sat beside him.

"Why do wives always ask that?"

She shrugged.

"It's curious you ask that question, because I never figured out the answer. Sometimes, in the right light, she appeared beautiful. At other times, she looked almost ancient." He paused and thought about it. "No, maybe not ancient. Ageless might be a better word." He tapped in another entry on his keyboard.

"I wasn't really worried," Deb said. She stared at the computer screen. "Did you find her?"

"No. And I don't think I expected to."

Deb tossed him a questioning look. "Was she lying about her background?"

"I don't believe so. Thinking back, she said she was from Troy. Just plain Troy. I *assumed* the university part."

"There are lots of towns named Troy in the U.S."

"True. Anyhow, since she repeatedly brought up the topics of prophets and prophecies whenever we met, I began to think there might be . . . well . . . an alternative explanation regarding who she was."

Something, a broken tree branch perhaps, slammed against the roof with a hearty thud.

"Are we going to flutter off into Far-Fetched Land again?" Deborah's tone indicated she meant it lightly.

"Here's the thing. While the vast majority of us are rational human beings, it doesn't mean the things that happen to us or around us are rational."

"Like dreams or visions of earthquakes and tsunamis?"

"Exactly. There are events that occur in our lives we absolutely can't explain, that don't make sense, at least to us. But that doesn't mean they didn't happen or that we made them up, or that we're tripping off into Far-Fetched Land, as you described it."

"Sorry." She massaged the back of his neck. "You know I didn't mean it seriously."

"I know." He pecked her on her cheek. "Anyhow, just because things happen that are well beyond our comprehension doesn't make those events any less real or any less valid than those we can explain. The things that don't seem rational, for which we have no explanation, are just as much a part of our being as tripping over a rug—"

"—or crashing an airplane into a river," Deb said, finishing his thought.

"The bottom line is, we'd like to think that we, as humans, are at the pinnacle of intelligence and understanding." He looked directly at Deb. "But we aren't."

She offered an almost imperceptible nod. "So what does all this have to do with Cassie?"

"Cassie is short for Cassandra." He let his response hang in the air, waiting to see if Deb would pick up on it.

She cocked her head at him.

"Remember your Greek mythology?" he asked.

"Not much."

"Cassandra was the daughter of the king and queen of Troy. According to legend, she was both beautiful and insane."

"Insane?"

"Yes, but her perceived insanity was the result of being cursed by the god Apollo, perhaps for refusing him sex. The most common version of the legend is that Apollo gave Cassandra the gift of prophecy in hopes it would encourage her to accept him as her lover. It didn't work. She spurned him."

"Always comes back to sex, right?"

Rob smiled. "Maybe. Anyhow, Apollo, angered at his rejection, spat into her mouth, cursing her prophecies to never be believed. As it turned out, that included her warning about the destruction of Troy by the Greeks."

"So you think Cassie is, was, the mythical Cassandra?" The tone of Deborah's voice betrayed deep skepticism.

He gave Deb a pat on her shoulder, stood, walked to the window and stared out.

"No, of course not," he said. "That would be impossible, wouldn't it, in this day and age where everything has a practical, common-sense, scientific explanation?"

Deb moved to stand beside him. "I agree, it would be impossible." She slipped her arm around his waist. "Kind of like a scientist having a vision of an impending catastrophe."

He nodded. "Yes, kind of like that."

He continued to stare out the window. Scudding clouds, like a gray army, swept overhead in a rain-drenched blitzkrieg. A stand of evergreens, in deference to the gale, leaned over hard like tall sailboats in heavy weather. A chimney flue rattled, a pine cone tumbled along the driveway, a seagull, fighting the wind, hovered in place.

Rob watched the seagull for a long time.

The End

Recommended Emergency Supplies in Megaquake Territory

1. Water for seven to ten days (one gallon per person per day)

2. Food for seven to ten days (non-perishable—you may need a manually operated can opener, too); and don't forget pet food

3. First aid kit

4. Adequate supply of prescription and over-the-counter medications

5. Moist towelettes, trash sacks, and plastic ties for sanitation purposes

6. Flashlights

7. Adequate supply of batteries

8. Radios (battery-powered or hand-cranked), including NOAA Weather Radio for emergency information. Note: broadcast towers may be down for days or weeks in the wake of a major earthquake

9. Shelter supplies (tent, tarps, ropes, blankets, duct tape)

10. Sturdy shoes, boots, and gloves

11. Dust masks to filter contaminated air (cotton t-shirts work, too)

12. Wrench to turn off utilities such as natural gas or water

13 Multipurpose (A-B-C) fire extinguisher

14. Cash (ATMs may not be working or inaccessible)

Nice to Have, Though Not Necessarily Affordable For Most

1. Portable generator

2. Satellite telephone (land lines and cell phones may be useless for days or weeks after a major quake)

Author's Note

I grew up in western Oregon. It seemed, at least in terms of natural threats, a bucolic place in which to spend my youth. For instance, severe thunderstorms and tornadoes there were about as common as the Northern Lights in Georgia. Hurricanes were nonexistent. Such storms are born over warm oceans. If you've ever dipped a toe into the Pacific along the Oregon coast, you know it's water in which Polar Bear Plungers could train even in August.

There were the occasional big winter storms, of course. But they certainly didn't bear the DNA common to the meteorological monsters that inhabit other parts of the nation. I did, incidentally, experience the Northwest's "Big Blow" in 1962 that hurled winds over 100 mph into Portland. Scary, but hardly Cat-5 stuff.

We'd get decent snowstorms once in a while, too. But true blizzard conditions were rare (see Northern Lights comment above).

Earthquakes? I recall a decent little shake in the late '40s, but Northwesterners didn't dwell on such things. After all, we didn't live on the San Andreas Fault. Like I said, western Oregon seemed to me Nature's Camelot.

No, we didn't live on the San Andreas Fault. It turned out, I discovered only a few years ago, something much more threatening lurked beneath us: the Cascadia Subduction Zone.

After I graduated from the University of Washington, life's events sent me away from the great Northwest. I ended up, not by design, spending my adult years on the East Coast in areas ranging from New England to the Southeast. Still, I frequently journeyed back to the Motherland.

On one of my return trips to the Oregon coast, maybe about ten years ago, I noticed some signs similar to those you see along the Atlantic and Gulf coasts that proclaim HURRICANE EVACUATION ROUTE. The signs in the Beaver State, however, said TSUNAMI EVACUA-

TION ROUTE. Really? My interest was piqued. Not quite to the extent I thought about doing a novel, but I certainly was curious and began asking questions.

Then, a little over two years ago, my brother Rick, who lives part time in Manzanita, put me in touch with a digital news article headlined "Massive Earthquake Threatens Pacific Northwest." I read and reread the article, stunned by its dire implications.

The material I'd studied about Ebola, in doing research for my novel *Plague*, was scary. But this stuff about the Cascadia Subduction Zone was even more frightening because it involved something that *will* happen, not something that *might* happen, or something that happens only in the mind of a novelist. At any rate, Cascadia (the fault) ignited my imagination.

I did a flood of research before I began writing. It is story and characters that drive a novel, of course, but I wanted to make certain the threats depicted in *Cascadia* (the novel) were scientifically accurate.

My sources included books, DVDs, articles, research papers, and geologists and seismologists. Some of the more prominent books included:

Cascadia's Fault—The Coming Earthquake and Tsunami That Could Devastate North America by Jerry Thompson

Full Rip 9.0 by Sandi Doughton

The Next Tsunami—Living on a Restless Coast by Bonnie Henderson

A key DVD was:

Shockwave: Surviving North America's Biggest Disaster, Filmwest Associates

One of the more useful studies I employed (not exactly light reading) was:

"Earthquake Risk Study for Oregon's Critical Energy Infrastructure Hub" by Yumei Wang, Steven F. Bartlett, and Scott B. Miles

Also very helpful were the evacuation brochures and maps provided by the State of Oregon Department of Geology and Mineral Industries.

Among the experts who kept me on track, or at least tried (if there are faults in my technical descriptions, they are mine, not those of the people who advised me), were John Vidale, director of the Pacific Northwest Seismic Network and a professor at the University of Washington; Jody Bourgeois, a University of Washington geology professor; and Patrick Corcoran, Oregon Sea Grant Hazards Outreach Specialist and an associate professor at Oregon State University.

Patrick, by the way, while very helpful, even to the extent of allowing Rob, my protagonist, to steal some of his thoughts, didn't care for my approach of employing a "worst-case scenario" in *Cascadia*. He believed I should have focused on a more probable eventuality involving only a *partial* rupture of Cascadia and a somewhat smaller (but still huge) earthquake and tsunami. I acknowledged his suggestion, but explained that novelists are enamored by worst-case scenarios.

The scenes in the novel that involved flying, crash landings, and rescues, also required expert oversight. Help with flying and tricky landings came from two gentlemen, Harold Schild, a local pilot from Tillamook who's had plenty of experience in western Oregon; and Tom Young, a private pilot and retired Air National Guard flight engineer. Tom is also a fellow novelist who's written several outstanding military thrillers. I highly recommend you check him out at: tomyoungbooks.com.

Another "brother" writer who assisted me was John House, a medical doctor with a multitude of urgent care experience, who vetted my emergency care and hospital scenes. John has authored several novels, including *Trail of Deceit*, a great adventure set on the Appalachian Trail. That book certainly has my stamp of approval.

Allow me to say here that all of the characters in *Cascadia* are products of my imagination. Their words, actions, and physical descriptions are *not* drawn, even in part, from people I know. I did employ several "real-life" first names in the river rescue incident, however: Travis, Kevin, and Todd. Travis is Lieutenant Travis Gullberg of the Multnomah County Sheriff's Office River Patrol Unit. Kevin and Todd work with Travis on the boat depicted in the rescue scene. Travis was a tremendous help in making sure I correctly (I hope) described the equipment and procedures employed.

Curiously, one of the most difficult topics I had to tackle was the genesis of my protagonist's nightmares (visions). Here I turned to religious authorities to help me out. The results surprised me, in that there turned out to be a modicum of scientific or philosophical theories actually supporting what Rob experienced.

Specifically, two men, probably on opposite ends of the religious ideological spectrum, guided my efforts: The Reverend Lewis Keizer and the Reverend Doctor Warren Lathem. Warren, however, told me, "As my grandfather used to say, 'I don't care what they call me as long as they call me for supper.'"

Both Lewis and Warren are friends of mine; Lewis from many, many years ago—grade school, in fact—and Warren from more recent times when I joined the Methodist church he formerly headed. You may note the reverend in the novel assumed both of their names, Lewis Warren.

A couple of long-time Oregon residents, my brother Rick, and Douglas Dick, made certain my descriptions of the coast, Manzanita in particular, stayed on target. Rick splits his time between Portland and Manzanita. Doug is Manzanita's Building Official.

I got some wonderful help from weather buff Mary Shafer regarding the metal detection tools and procedures used by Neahkahnie Johnny.

My editor at Bell Bridge Books, Deborah Smith, did her usual masterful job of making my prose even more readable than I could have on my own.

Finally, and perhaps most important, are those who helped me craft *Cascadia* into a tale that, I trust, kept you turning the pages. There were my "beta" or first readers: my wife Christina, my brother Rick, Doug Dick, my agent Jeanie Loiacono, and Gary Schwartz, a voracious reader and master literary critic. There was also my Barnes & Noble critique group that includes regulars such as John Sheffield, Terry Segal, John Tabellione, Richard Buhler, John Madrid, Victoria Barkan, Susan McBreairty, and Jim Seltzer.

I can't thank enough all those who helped me. Hopefully, their assistance contributed to *Cascadia* becoming not only an exciting read, but a scientifically factual one.

About the Author

H. W. "Buzz" Bernard, a native Oregonian born in Eugene and raised in Portland, is a best-selling, award-winning novelist.

His debut novel, *Eyewall*, which one reviewer called a "perfect summer beach read," was released in May 2011 and went on to become a number-one best seller in Amazon's Kindle Store.

Buzz's second novel, *Plague* ("One of the best thrillers of 2012"— novelist Al Leverone), came out in September 2012 and later won the 2014 EPIC eBook Award in the suspense/thriller category.

His third novel, *Supercell* ("Races along with the speed of a twister"— novelist Michael Wallace) became a Kindle best seller and winner of the 2015 EPIC eBook Award in the suspense/thriller category.

His fourth novel and the third in his "weather trilogy," *Blizzard* ("A terrific book"—novelist Deborah Smith) was released in 2015.

Before becoming a novelist, Buzz worked at The Weather Channel in Atlanta, Georgia, as a senior meteorologist for thirteen years. Prior to that, he served as a weather officer in the U.S. Air Force for over three decades. He attained the rank of colonel and received, among other awards, the Legion of Merit.

His "airborne" experiences include a mission with the Air Force Reserve Hurricane Hunters, air drops over the Arctic Ocean and Turkey, and a stint as a weather officer aboard a Tactical Air Command airborne command post (C-135).

In the past, he's provided field support to forest fire fighting operations in the Pacific Northwest, spent a summer working on Alaska's arctic slope, and served two tours in Vietnam. Various other jobs, both civilian and military, have taken him to Germany, Saudi Arabia, and Panama.

He attended the University of Washington in Seattle where he earned a bachelor's degree in atmospheric science and studied creative writing.

Buzz currently is president of the Southeastern Writers Association. He's a member of International Thriller Writers, the Atlanta Writers Club, and Willamette Writers.

He and his wife Christina live in Roswell, Georgia, along with their fuzzy and sometimes over-active Shih-Tzu, Stormy. Buzz is represented by Jeanie Loiacono of the Loiacono Literary Agency.

Made in the USA
San Bernardino, CA
26 September 2016